Reality Check

Reality Check

Eric Pete

www.urbanbooks.net

Urban Books, LLC
78 East Industry Court
Deer Park, NY 11729

ISBN 13: 978-1-60162-333-1
ISBN 10: 1-60162-333-X

First Mass Market Printing January 2012
First Trade Paperback Printing August 2009
Printed in the United States of America

10 9 8 7 6 5 4 3 2 1

Distributed by Kensington Publishing Corp.
Submit Wholesale Orders to:
Kensington Publishing Corp.
C/O Penguin Group (USA) Inc.
Attention: Order Processing
405 Murray Hill Parkway
East Rutherford, NJ 07073-2316
Phone: 1-800-526-0275
Fax: 1-800-227-9604

To Marsha,

The person who pushed me off that ledge nine years ago because she believed a man could fly. For I am not me without you. To come full circle with this one is a joy. To be able to share it with the world is a blessing. Eight novels later, I thank you.

Can't stop. Won't stop. Believe that.

—Eric

1

Glover

Beeeeep!Beeeeeep!Beeeeeeeeep! Beeeeeeeeep!
Its red lights taunted me from out of the fading darkness.

Shit. Why does my alarm always go off right when I'm about to get my freak on? I guess my mystery lover would have to catch me on the next dream go-round. One day I would catch a glimpse of his face.

Lawd, I hate Mondays. Everybody does. Well, except for beauticians because it's their day off. Of course, I never felt like going to work. It was simply something I did while trying to figure out what I really wanted to do. Damn trust fund babies and celebrities in this town. They'll ruin a sister's good work ethic in a heartbeat.

Lionel mentioned it again last night. Always the seductive proposition coming from those sexy lips of his. That was just before I made him go home. Some women out here would jump at the chance to have someone like Lionel take care of them, but, hey . . . I guess I'm one of the independent ones. Did I forget to tell you that I'm also vivacious, witty, intelligent, and can work it *like no other*?

Lionel is my boyfriend. I say that because we aren't officially engaged. We met by chance more than two years ago, when I was going through a rough dry spell. I was at Mariana's having a chicken caesar salad after work while he was downtown meeting with a client. I sat there feeding my face and saw this rather debonair brother at a nearby table.

Tall and dark-skinned, he wore a suit that reeked of the finest quality. Almost as impressive as his build and his perfect teeth. He was having a business meeting with a middle-aged white man, who appeared to be interested in more than "bid'ness," as was evident by the way he eyed the subject of my imagination. I hoped to myself, *Please don't be gay*, realizing I was craving the well-built bit of chocolate too.

Their business was concluded with several quick signatures to paperwork. The client left first and passed right by my table. I resumed eating as if I hadn't been eavesdropping. Lionel was passing next when he slowed and mumbled under his breath.

"Thought that was funny, huh?" He didn't even break his smile.

"Excuse me?" I answered, almost choking on a crouton. I quickly grabbed a napkin and covered my mouth.

"I saw you watching my predicament with Mr. Brewster. Did that amuse you?"

"Huh? Oh. That. Well, I wasn't . . ." I fumbled in vain.

"And the answer is no. I'm straight."

Whew.

He sat down and officially introduced himself to me. A few months after Mariana's, the beginnings of what you would call this relationship of ours, we were dating exclusively.

Lionel is a securities broker and financial planner for Barnes & Greenwood, with more than his share of success through both good times and bad. I'd be lying if I said that success didn't sometimes go to his head, but he was so charming that I ignored it. He'd asked me countless times to move in with him, but I had my reservations, in spite of the occasional sleepover. Call me stubborn or just plain old fashioned, but I had an issue without having a wedding date selected and all. I was pretty sure I loved him, but wanted to be certain the weekend jaunts to Las Vegas or New York weren't swaying me instead. I was young at the time, but remembered talk of how a silver tongue had driven a wedge between my mom and her family back in Virginia so many years ago.

Our long talk was coming soon, but first I needed to get my ass out of bed before Mona arrived. Heaven knows she was gonna get me evicted with her loud honking.

2

Max

The raucous bass from the rapper A.K.'s "Realer Than Ya Know" bellowed through the ceiling above me. Smitty's normal routine. Don't get me wrong; I liked the song, and A.K. was a fellow Louisianan, but it was way too early for it. I tried ignoring the raspy command to "drop back or get knocked the fuck back" while cracking my blinds. The morning light coming from beyond Venice Boulevard flooded my tiny single-bedroom apartment, invigorating me.

My momma, Orelia, always used to joke that I'd wake before the roosters. A country joke, but a real disposition, courtesy of my pops, of whom I was the spitting image. He died in a chemical plant explosion back in Louisiana when I was in the third grade. Momma still clung to her memories. One of the main reasons for wanting her "baby" to stay close to home, I guess.

Discarding thoughts of returning home, I inserted my earbuds and turned up my modest iPod Shuffle. A strange mix to hear Alicia Keys' melodies lay atop the chorus from beyond my walls. Sure, the tenants complained about him, but Smitty's silly ass was the closest thing to a best friend I had since moving to the City of Angels.

I'd graduated from McNeese State University with a BS in business administration more than two years ago. After getting that paper, I went to work on collecting the other kind of paper as a slot attendant at one of the casinos, saving a nest egg before coming out west in the last six months. I'd considered moving to Houston, but decided more distance was needed to avoid being pulled back to Lake Charles and the prospects of either no money or the easy street money that sent too many fools to either their graves or prison. Y'see, I didn't entirely sleep through class. My college professors had taught me that mobility was the key to a higher standard of living, and that all paths to success led away.

Of course my momma didn't want to hear that noise. Lake Charles was good enough for her and my pops, so it had to be good enough for me. The only solace she took in my move was that her brother and his family resided in nearby Carson, so I would have some family to look out for me.

Familial bonds ran deep in terms of how I was raised to view the world.

I removed one of my earbuds when I saw my vibrating cell dancing on the table. I was about to dine on a light, cheap breakfast of Frosted Flakes and orange juice, but decided to answer.

"Hello?"

"What up, Maxwell?" It was Smitty. I hated the way he called me by my full name. I should never have told him.

"Smitty, I know you da man and all, but you need to turn that shit down this early in the A.M.!"

"Why you gotta fuckin' yell?" I hadn't realized it, but his music was off. Made me feel stupid. "You know me," he continued. "I need something to help me get up after busting guts all night."

Smitty was a smallish jokester who talked way more game than he really possessed.

"You ready to go on this job search, man? Or are you gonna just sit around and continue to talk shit?"

"Naw, I'm ready. Tired of being broke too. I started to come downstairs earlier and knock on your door, but decided to watch Mrs. Griggs doing her morning laps in the pool."

"Aww." I moaned over missing out on the spectacular view of a wet Mrs. Griggs. "And you didn't come get me?"

"Yeah, right. Like you would know what to do if a MILF like that offered the pussy on a platter. You know Fistina and Palmetta are the only women for you."

"Fuck you, Smit."

"Naw. Smitty don't do that Brokeback shit, bro." There he went, going all third-person. "Maybe you lookin' to move to West Hollywood."

I sighed, wondering why I even bothered. "What I need is a fuckin' job so I can move the fuck away from you."

3

Glover

Mona arrived late to my apartment in her gold Volkswagen, honking as usual. The brown-skinned, leggy twenty-six-year-old was the daughter of a successful real estate developer who made his money reinvesting in the inner city. While she usually shunned his favors, Mona wasn't stupid enough to decline his gift of a comfy little condo in Santa Monica. It was his way of making up for her newest stepmother, to whom she was severely allergic.

Mona and I had been best friends since attending West Los Angeles College. When I got on with the downtown state employment office, I brought her along with me. We were as close as sisters and tried to look out for one another as if it were a fact.

"Did Lionel spend the night?" Mona asked as I dug in my purse for lipstick during the drive. "You know how persuasive he can be when he wants something."

"Nah. Trying to keep some boundaries, although he's persistent. Had to push the nigga out the door."

"You know, you really need to stop using the N-word. There was this big discussion about it on TV last night."

"You watch too much TV, Mona."

"Don't I, though?" She smirked. "Anyway, have you guys had the talk yet?"

"No. What about you?" I asked, tiring of the topic. "You still seeing Craig?" With her cute little tapered short crop atop her petite yet curvy frame, Mona was a stunner. When combined with her smooth, sophisticated voice, she was devastating. Craig, an international basketball player, was the latest in a long line of conquests.

"Changing the subject, Ms. McDaniel?"

"Not at all," I lied. "Just curious. Are we on for this weekend?"

"I guess. Have you checked with Charmaine?" she asked, referring to the missing third of our crew.

Charmaine was our co-worker at the employment office. Caucasian by birth, she was pure sister in every other way, having grown up around minorities in SoCal most of her life and sharing a lot of the same obstacles and strife. She kept us in stitches with her comments on who was doing what to whom in the office. Weekends were when we bonded, going out or simply hanging and unwinding.

Traffic was unusually light, so we made it downtown on time. Mona parked next to Charmaine's black Kawasaki and we rushed inside to clock in. When we spotted Charmaine, she had her hands full with a cup of Starbucks and a six-box of Krispy Kremes, but that didn't stop her from running over.

"G-love! Mona!" she yelled, excited to see us after a last minute cancellation had squashed our weekend plans. Her own little pet name for me was a play on the spelling of my name. Very original, even though I hated the fuck out of it.

"Did you guys see those construction workers in front of the *Times* building? Damn. Might have to take a little walk at lunch." Charmaine chuckled to herself, all the while serious.

"Good morning to you too, Charmaine," Mona said dryly. Construction workers were so far removed from her type. While often physically attractive, they tended to lack the social status or sophistication she required.

"Charmaine, are we going out this weekend?" I asked.

"You know, G-love, you've got Lionel, and Ms. Mona here has . . . well . . . I don't know who she has this week, but I've got to play catch up."

"Whatever," Mona chimed. "I really don't date that much."

"I don't know what you call it, but you do do it much."

I fought back a laugh, wondering how these two ever got along, and if maybe I was the glue.

4

Max

I had spent my time in Los Angeles getting acclimated and working odd jobs, but hadn't found anything close to taking advantage of my degree. Today was no different. Smitty and I spent the first half of the day pounding the pavement northeast of town from Pasadena to Pomona. Applications were filled out and some handshakes given, but all we got were promises to call us if something came up. Straight-up lip service. We knew what that meant: resumes in the trash.

And any hopes dashed.

My nest egg was beginning to run low, and the last thing I would do was call home for my momma to spot me. I could hear her soothing voice now, telling me what a mistake I'd made . . . but that it was okay.

And all I had to do was just come home.

I had the evening off from the Denny's on Hawthorne in Torrance, so Smitty and I agreed to get some playing time in if nothing turned up. We changed clothes in the restroom at the last employer we'd visited and got back on I-10 to head to Venice for some b-ball.

We took my Corolla, as Smitty's car wasn't running. His hooptie was always broken, but he always managed to find some sweet young thang to either chauffeur him around or allow him to borrow her ride. They weren't the most appealing of prospects, but Smitty really didn't seem to mind. "I gets minez," he would always say.

Smitty was one of the first people I met upon moving to Los Angeles. It was his damn music that did it. It was my second day there on Venice Boulevard after my cousin Jay had helped me locate my apartment. I was crashing hard after a long night of unpacking and putting away my stuff—until his thumping bass startled me from whatever good dream I was having. I pounded on the ceiling for a few minutes, but that didn't do shit. I threw on some clothes and went running up the stairwell in search of an ass to kick. I banged on Smitty's door, but wasn't expecting to see this skinny little figure looking at me when the door opened. He had the nerve to look like he was the one being disturbed. This five foot four, bird-chested individual in a silk robe was such a sight to behold that my eyes watered up while holding back a laugh.

Instead of scolding him over his volume, all I could think was, *Do you know how stupid you look?*

We'd been hanging ever since.

We managed to get on the court after an hour, losing both games. That didn't stop my friend from talking shit. Smitty, being a little man, *always* had to talk shit. This was true whether it was hooping at Venice or flag football at Leimert Park on weekends. It usually amused our opponents that Smitty thought he was the Second Coming, and I hated to be the one to burst his bubble.

Smitty and I retreated to the Third Street Promenade in Santa Monica to lick our wounds, finding an outdoor seat at a bar and grill. Smitty ordered the chicken strips and fries with a beer. I ordered the fajitas and was nursing a margarita.

". . . next Kobe."

"Say what, Smitty?"

"Next Kobe, Max. I'm telling ya. I'm gonna be the next Kobe. Or at least Tony Parker. Maybe snag a wifey like Eva Longoria, too, now that I think about it. You saw me out there. Ballin'!"

he said, making the shot gesture popularized by Jim Jones' song.

"Sounds like you got your future all figured out. Wish I did," I dryly joked.

"Don't hate on the brother like those fools back on the court. You saw all the elbows whenever I drove? I guess if I wasn't so good I wouldn't have so many haters, huh?"

"Yeah. Must be it," I indulged. "How are the chicken strips?"

"They a'ight. The longneck's helping, though. It cost enough. How's your shit?"

"Pretty good. I need to get paid, though, so I can start eating some high-end shit. Ramen noodles and McDonald's dollar menu ain't cuttin' it, y'know? I want some filet mignon for a change. Maybe some—"

"Prime rib," Smitty continued for me. "Yeah, dawg, I hear ya. I only got an associate's. You're gonna have an easier time with your bachelor's degree, even if it is from the backwoods. Where you went to school again? McCajun? Possum University? Alligator State?"

"Watch that shit. It's McNeese State. You ain't funny."

"My bad," he said, already moving on to future insults. "Look, I just want to get a reliable car. Somethin' dependable. Tired of Mexicans lookin' at me all stupid on the side of the road and laughin'."

"All in due time, Smit. We need to hit downtown next week. Maybe something will break for at least one of us."

"Max, shorties at three o'clock."

Smitty's radar locked on. Two blondes had just sat a few tables over from us. Judging from the growing crowd, they'd probably just left the movies down the street. The taller one wore a short, frizzy hairstyle and was well endowed. She sported a black halter top with a pair of weathered denims. The short one had straight, shoulder length hair with donk for days. She wore a white designer T-shirt with a pair of black shorts that barely contained her ass cheeks. It was a little cool for shorts, especially those shorts, but this was California. I was still adjusting to that.

Diversity at its finest.

"So, are we gonna do this, dawg? The tall one's callin' to me, and I'm ready to scale Mount Everest."

"Smitty, you don't even know if they're game. Besides, we're all sweaty and shit."

"Hey," he grunted with a shrug. "Sweat now, sweat later. Does it matter?"

I wasn't going to admit it, but Smitty was right. It had been too long for me.

And my days of being a good boy had only resulted in pain and disappointment.

5

Glover

New state requirements, along with the plethora of new forms they entailed, had descended on the California Employment Development Department. We were sucking air. Charmaine was in charge of data entry and filing, so the day was wearing even on her usually upbeat, devil-may-care attitude. Mona was confirming employment searches of benefit recipients who sometimes creeped her out, and I was doing a little bit of everything. During our first break, we managed to chat some.

"Shred this one. Send these back. Retain these for five years," Charmaine muttered. "Rules, rules, rules. These motherfuckers are gonna make me go postal in here."

"And you'd be on lockdown so quick," Mona replied while shuffling through the worn *Los Angeles Times* on the table.

"Lockdown? At a male prison, I would hope."

"Please. No prison talk. Mona, we don't need Charmaine's graphic imagination going to her mouth."

"Speaking of lockdown, you about to go away for a stretch with Mr. Moneybags?"

"If you're referring to Lionel, Charmaine, we're having lunch today."

"What I'm referring to is whether Lionel's going to make you an honest woman."

"I'm as honest as they come already, girl. I don't need some man to do that."

"I heard that," chimed in Mona. "Girl, let Glover do her thang."

"Honestly, we really haven't discussed the marriage issue that much. I mean, Lionel appears to be interested, but he's not pressuring me." *Much.* "I mean, he asked me to move in with him and quit my job, but—"

"Hold up! Quit your job?" Charmaine barked out loud enough for half the office to hear. My girl was flabbergasted. "And you haven't skipped out on this place yet? Girl, I would have told everyone in here to kiss my white ass, especially Mr. Marx."

Mr. Marx was the office supervisor, a Grinch of a man. Charmaine hated him with a passion but still needed her job, so she nervously looked around the break room to ensure he wasn't within earshot.

"That's why she's with Lionel and you're not, Charmaine," Mona chimed defiantly. "Glover's not weak and dependent like that."

"Thank you, my sister!" I said with a high five, while Charmaine rolled her eyes and hummed the notes to Destiny's Child's "Independent Women."

The lunchtime crowd at New Japan sushi bar in Little Tokyo was massive. Luckily, Lionel had told me their service was fast once you got in. His work schedule hadn't permitted lunch together as frequently these days, so I was already in line when Lionel pulled up in his Audi. I watched as he casually flipped his keys to the valet, running up to give me a kiss.

"Any problems finding it?"

"Not with your directions, baby," I answered, knowing lustful eyes of single women of many shades were upon him. Without missing a beat, he pulled me along, strolling to the head of the line, where he gained us immediate seating with a mere whisper of his name. Doors and obstacles were a minor inconvenience in this town for the Dunnings, as I had been quick to learn.

I was new to some of the stuff to which Lionel was exposing me, but that made every encounter an interesting experience.

I staked out the safe shrimp tempura lunch, while Lionel went with the raw salmon sushi and veggie rolls.

"You are looking good, woman. How's your day going?" Lionel was giving me that look. Days be damned; he wanted to be sharing the night with me.

"It's going. That's about it. Busier than usual. I missed you last night after you left."

"Really? Is that why you made me leave?" Lionel shifted to his innocent puppy dog look.

"You know how that goes, Lionel. Gotta keep you wanting more."

"Oh, I want all right."

Lionel had a little piece of veggie roll dangling from the corner of his mouth. I leaned over the table and removed it while stealing a juicy kiss. He was quick to accept the kiss, returning one of his own. A slight chill ran down my spine as memories of last night crept back into my consciousness. He was oh so good when oh so bad.

"Is that a new suit?" I asked, admiring the power suit, a single-breasted charcoal number with a white silk shirt and thin black tie. Definitely something my girl Mona would approve of, with her eye for fashion.

"Yeah, I picked it up last week. Antonini Loretta. You like?"

"It's nice. I'm a little less into the European stuff, but Mona would give you kudos if she saw it."

"How is Mona?" he asked; then added, "And Charmaine? They're still carrying on at your office?"

"You know those two. Some things will never change. We're supposed to be going out this weekend. Want to come? It would be fun."

"Uh . . ." He paused, thinking of an excuse. Men. "I would, but I have a presentation for the big boss next week and want to be sure it's perfect. Want to come by my place tomorrow night?"

"Sure. I'm not spending the night, though."

"I got it. Loud and clear. But I don't see why you're so hung up on that," he scoffed.

The waitress came to our table to bring the check and to clean up.

"*Domo arigato gozaimasu*, Keiko," said Lionel in her native tongue.

"Thank you, Mr. Dunning," replied the waitress with just a hint of an accent as she gushed over him. She took his American Express card and left.

"Come here often?" I asked, slightly put off by her friendliness and Lionel's eagerness to accept it. I tried to conceal my displeasure.

"Every now and then, since it is in the area. I meet some customers here for business sometimes . . . kind of like that time at Mariana's."

"Yep, I will never forget that. Is Mr. Brewster still your client?" I smiled as the memory of our first encounter returned.

"No." Lionel chuckled. "Misha at the office has his account now. Remember her?"

"Oh, yeah. The Greek chick? Kinda eager-beaver? Really perky?"

"Yeah, that's her," he replied with amusement. "She's actually running circles around some of our veterans at ol' B and G. Shows initiative."

"Probably not all she's showing," I snarked in a rare display of cattiness. "Cute young thang. That doesn't hurt."

"Haven't really noticed that, Glover. Too busy thinking about this sexy young thing in front of me."

"You always say the right things, Mr. Dunning," I responded, erasing thoughts of fawning, eager co-workers from my mind.

6

Max

I was awakened from a deep, restful sleep by
my T-shirt landing on the bed. "Good morning,"
she said in a language with which she wasn't
fully comfortable.

Accent.

Loved that shit.

It was my new friend, the tall blonde from the
Promenade in Santa Monica.

"Good morning to you too," I replied, wishing I could speak her native tongue, impress
her. Show her there was more to me than good
conversation and good dick. But my sparse, broken Creole French learned at the two Fs—family
reunions and funerals—would be embarrassing.

"Do you remember my name?"

"Velina," I said slowly . . . deliberately, as she'd
taught me last night in between drunken kisses.
"Yes. Good. Very good." She smiled. Velina and
her friend, Kaylen, were grad students at USC.

Things went off well with them. We all wound up back at my apartment, and they were polite enough while Smitty and I ran around cleaning up. We ordered out from the local pizza joint and watched a couple of pay-per-views.

Smitty was his usual crazy self, the life of the party, doing and saying whatever popped into his head. He had us literally falling over laughing while we played cards and finished off a couple of bottles of my finest discount wine. In spite of Smitty claiming "the tall one," things started getting a little hectic between Velina and me as the night went on. A touching of hands, followed by a kiss stolen here and there.

Between laughs.

Between sentences.

At first.

To be honest, I was a little hesitant with the whole interracial thing. I had met some beautiful Chicanas and Filipinas since moving out here, but to me, that was different. It was all brown skin, some browner than mine. Although things were changing, there tended to be a little less "fraternization" between whites and blacks back in Lake Charles.

Old lines, formed by mistrust, failing to completely vanish.

As the little get-together began winding down, Velina was winding up. My reservations and misgivings faded as she filled me in on other parts of the world. Places where old school Western Europeans looked down upon immigrants from the former Soviet countries as if they were "niggers."

Not her word, mine. The sentiment's the same: people locking doors with fears of crime and newcomers taking their jobs. I could've used her in some of my classes. She was a curriculum of world history, sociology, and sex education all in one.

Kaylen, she of the "ass for days," had decided that Smitty wasn't going to be getting any of that ass. She was ready to go home, so I gave Smitty my keys, trusting him not to wreck my shit. Velina stayed over, as we decided to get better acquainted.

My supply of condoms came in handy that night as I immersed myself in Romanian. All of my impromptu cleaning was undone, as the bedroom became the scene of conflict.

East versus West.

Her pussy versus my dick.

Her tongue versus my mouth.

It was hot and passionate as we explored every delicious centimeter of one another, straining to breathe in between sessions.

"Mind if I use your shower, sleepyhead?" Velina was standing there buck-naked, a vivid reminder of what had ended only hours ago.

"Didn't we use it already?" My exhausted ass was still trying to be smooth.

"McNeese? In Lake Charles, right?" Velina asked as she pointed to the shirt she had just discarded.

"What do you know about Lake Charles?"

"My uncle is a professor at LSU in Baton Rouge. That is the capital city in Louisiana near Lake Charles, *yes*?" Her accent thickened as her certainty diminished. Hot.

"Yep, you got it right. Small world."

"It's just L.A., Max. A town of transplants and travelers. Everybody winds up here. I guess you did too, huh?"

"Fo' sho.'" I chuckled with mock swagger.

"Care to join me in the shower?" She winked. "I have class today and have to run home first. So . . . I've got to get a move on."

I was dead tired, but ego was coming into play. "Be right there," I said as I went to scrub her back.

After our shower interlude, I walked Velina to her car, which was parked in front of my patio. We exchanged numbers and a couple of kisses before her RAV4 disappeared down Venice Boulevard toward the 405. I wondered deep down if either of us would be calling the other.

7

Glover

As promised, Lionel was waiting for me after work that Tuesday. I was to spend the evening with him. My Civic was still in the shop for warranty work, so I had been bumming a ride with Mona. Charmaine grinned when she saw Lionel's Audi in the parking lot, and took off running past Mona and me.

"She really needs to stop. Really," Mona said, staring at the cloud of dust kicked up by Charmaine as she beat a path to Lionel's car.

"You know how she is," I replied. "Always full steam ahead. That's why we love her."

"Love? Sometimes I'd love to strangle her," said Mona, allowing a chuckle to escape her pursed lips.

Charmaine stopped at his window. He lowered it with a smile that revealed those pretty teeth.

"Hey, Lionel."

"Hello, Charmaine. How are you?"

"Fine. Look at you, all spiffy and shit."

Not knowing how to respond, he just nodded and continued to smile.

"You know I'm mad at you, right?"

"What did I do?" he asked.

"You haven't hooked me up with one of your boys. What's up with that?" she blasted.

"Well," he sighed, "most of my boys are already involved, and—"

"Okay! Okay! I know! I know! And I understand."

"You do?"

"Really, I do. You just don't want this white girl turning them out. But enough of that. When's the big day? You can't keep my girl over there waiting and stuff." Good ol' Charmaine. She was always good for the occasional embarrassing situation.

That was my cue to save Lionel and end this. I entered Lionel's car from the passenger side and gave him a quick kiss. "All right, Charmaine. Behave yourself," I said, leaning across Lionel's lap. Part of me wondered what my motives were for saving Lionel from her question. Was I avoiding the issue myself?

"Mona, how've you been?" Lionel asked as she appeared over Charmaine's shoulder.

"I've been doing fine, Mr. Dunning," said Mona in her usual crisp clip, her sophistication showing through.

"Ms. McDaniel, will you need a ride to work in the morning?" Mona, being messy in her own unique way, was wearing a dry smile.

Lionel's eyes focused on me. He waited to see if I planned on spending the night with him or if I was going home as usual.

"I'll call you later, Mona," I answered abruptly. "Y'all are too much."

Lionel waved at the smiling pair of Cheshire cats before we made our escape.

With everyone pouring onto all arteries away from downtown L.A., traffic was jammed up as we headed for the Santa Monica Freeway. Lionel tuned his satellite radio to one of his preset talk channels, always needing information. I hated talk radio.

"Your friends are a wild bunch," he joked, switching stations for my convenience. "I don't think I'd get any work done with those two in my office."

"Yeah. They can carry on at times, especially Charmaine. But they take care of business too."

"If you say so."

"I do say so. But enough talk about work. Where are we gonna eat?"

I kicked my shoes off to his amusement. As I stretched, my skirt slid slightly up my legs. Lionel tried to play it off, but I saw his eyes locked on my thighs.

"Don't wreck," I said playfully. "It would take forever for a tow truck to come out in this traffic."

We exited I-10 at La Brea Avenue and made the trip north to my apartment on San Vicente. I had Lionel park his Audi in my parking spot, which was vacant due to my car troubles.

He waited patiently in my living room while I hunted up some warm-ups to wear. While I changed, he loosened up too, removing his tie and shirt. The sight of him in his slacks and undershirt was appealing in a rugged sort of way, but I didn't dwell on it, as we had places to be.

We left for Lionel's house in the Hollywood Hills, skipping the 101 to avoid the traffic, and taking Cahuenga Boulevard north instead. We picked up a quick meal, the shrimp fettuccini dinner with garlic bread and two small salads, which we ordered in the drive-thru at Pasta Ta Go. Even with the stop, it only took thirty minutes to get from my apartment to Lionel's neighborhood, but what a difference it was between the two locations.

Lionel lived in an elegant Spanish-style home nestled in the neighborhoods off Franklin Avenue. Most of the homes were in the high six-figure range, and his was no exception. The walled spread oozed of romance, with its aged oak floors, majestic fireplace, and humongous walk-in closet.

Okay.

The closet wasn't romantic, but it did make moving in with Lionel a very appealing proposal. A woman needs her closet space.

We pulled in past the gate and drove under the carport. Lionel unloaded his papers, laptop, and briefcase from the car while I carried the dinner. While Lionel stowed his stuff, I set the dinner at the kitchen table. I fished a bottle of Cabernet Sauvignon from the cooler and some wineglasses from the cabinet.

Lionel had snuck back downstairs, piping in some Nina Simone over the speakers mounted in the walls throughout the house.

"You are an angel," he stated upon entering the kitchen and admiring the set up. He wore his old college fraternity T-shirt and a pair of shorts.

"I am, aren't I? Ready to eat?"

"Yep. I'm starving."

Over dinner, we went over the day's happenings and unwound at the kitchen table. Lionel had a gallon of cookies and cream in the freezer, and we shared a bowl for dessert.

After stuffing ourselves, we retired to Lionel's bedroom upstairs with the remainder of the wine. As he held our glasses, I seductively stripped for him, leaving my clothes on the bedroom floor. He bit on my neck before I broke away, entering the bathroom where the soulful jazz music had followed us. Lionel watched the waiting suds of the garden tub accept my legs first before completely obscuring all the naughty parts from him. As I slipped deeper into bubbly bliss, Lionel flipped the switch to the whirlpool jets.

"Mmm," I hummed along with the amazing vibrations. "This feels so good."

"Ready to call Mona? Before it gets too late?" Lionel had ditched his clothes, allowing me a view of his delicious ebony physique before it disappeared beneath the stirring waters too.

"I'll call in a little bit. Besides . . . I don't know yet. I may go home tonight."

He waded through the bubbles of the custom-made oversized tub, closer to me. "You know what I've been thinking?" he asked. I couldn't tell if the odd look on his face was from the wine.

"No. What?"

"We haven't taken a trip in a while, so I was thinking. Do you feel like some fun?"

"Of course. I'm always down for fun. Especially with you. What's up?"

"Nothing. I'll let you know more next week."

"Next week?" I cracked open one eye, breaking from my relaxation. "What are you up to?" I asked, suspecting this carrot was dangled to get me to stay the night.

"Be patient. You'll see. Next week."

"Why can't you tell me now?"

"Shhhh. Don't you worry your pretty little head. Now close your eyes. And relax."

I did as he suggested. At that point, I felt Lionel shift in the tub. He placed his powerful hands under my ass, bobbing my pelvis slightly in the water. I struggled to balance myself before he steadied me.

"Relax, baby," he said again. "I got you. Just trust me."

As his head descended into the whirling water between my thighs, I parted. I felt his lips as they softly grazed my mound.

Waves of water, waves of pleasure.

"So . . . so good," I muttered. "Don't stop."

As my eyes rolled back in my head and I began thrashing about, I knew I would not be going home this night.

8

Max

I slept the rest of the day away after Velina left. A just reward for the work I'd put in. Besides, I had a double shift at Denny's waiting for me that evening. Upon staggering awake, I turned the TV on to SportCenter to see if there were any highlights from last night's Lakers' game versus the Hornets, and then went to the kitchen in search of cold pizza. Grabbing a piece, I checked my phone for calls I might have missed while asleep or whatever.

A message awaited me from my cousin, Jay, probably checking my schedule, as he was at the mall tonight. He worked at the TruMale men's store in the Del Amo Mall, across the street from my job, so we hung out on breaks and stuff. Less than a year my elder, he acted much older. This was out of character, as he wasn't known for being the most responsible or reliable person.

I guess Jay felt like he had something to prove by watching out for his small-town cousin in the big, bad city.

"Hello?" "Hey, Uncle Maurice," I answered respectfully to the voice that had picked up.

"Max, that you, boy?"

Thirty-plus years on the West Coast hadn't erased the Frenchman's accent Uncle Mo possessed. It was almost as if he had never left from "Down East," as we called the countryside in Louisiana from where most our relatives had originated.

"Yep, it's me. How are you doing?"

"Doin' good, boy. Doin' good. When you comin' by to eat? I know you don't be cookin' any home-cooked meals at your place. Speakin' of that, you talk to your momma lately?" Uncle Mo loved to pepper you with multiple questions.

"I've been kinda busy, so I haven't—"

"Well, you need to call her. Hold on, I'm getting Maurice Jr. on the phone. Junior!" he yelled without missing a beat.

I could hear Jay mumbling something as he picked up the phone from his dad. Jay was born Maurice J. Chavis Jr., but hated being compared to anyone, hence his preference for the name Jay.

"Whaddup, cuz?"

"Whaddup, Jay. Sorry, but I just woke up."

"It's all right. Just checking to see if you workin' tonight. I gotta close tonight at the store."

"Yeah, I'll be there. About to put this funky uniform on now. Samir's working tonight, though," I said, referring to my manager. "He's pretty easy to work for, so it should be straight."

"A'ight then. I'll probably pass by on my way in. Any new women workin' there?"

"No, cuz. Always tryin' to mack, huh?"

"You know me, cuz. Business, never personal."

As I jumped in my Corolla in my uniform, I noticed the door had a new ding. The car was already showing its age.

It didn't need the added help of my neighbors. Something for me to worry about later, I thought as I turned the key.

I took I-405 south down to Hawthorne Boulevard. While stopped at the light on Rosecrans, I felt bass coming from the car on the side of me. It was this sister in a candy-green convertible, nodding her head to the E-40 playing in her ride. She smiled at me as I checked her out. I was admiring her, as well as the chrome dubs on her ride. Both of them had it going on. I could see myself behind the wheel, driving up Pacific Coast Highway with her at my side. Brotherman thought he was about to get the digits, until I remembered I was wearing my Denny's uniform.

"Shit," I whispered to myself. She lowered her stereo to talk to me just as I began scrunching down in my seat. The light turned green, so I decided to cut my losses, driving away rather than going down in flames. Denny's was coming up, but in my rearview mirror, I saw that she hadn't turned off. I drove into the parking lot, stopping in my usual spot. When I looked back, the convertible was there, just off the street.

Waiting on me.

I thought aloud, psyching myself up, "What am I doing? I'm a good-looking brother, there's a fine-ass woman out there, and I'm sitting here hiding out? *Because of this uniform?* Shit, I ain't no punk! I got a damn job, and she should be lucky just to know me."

I was brimming with confidence when I stepped out of my car. . . . And that was when she saw my uniform.

The last thing I heard was the chirp of her tires as she shifted gears and sped off down Hawthorne in search of someone that obviously wasn't me.

Oh, well. I guess she didn't want to hear about the free Grand Slam breakfast I could've given her.

Her loss. Yeah. That's it.

Who was I kidding? It sucked being treated like this. Even hurt some.

But hurt was a thing of my past. Something I left behind in Louisiana. And the sooner I could exchange these clothes for a nice suit, the better.

Throwing up my hands, I went inside and clocked in. Business was light, which was good for me. Samir was explaining something on the menu in his best dime-store Spanish to this elderly Mexican guy when I returned.

A heavyset brother with a gold tooth, Samir was one of the nicest people I've ever known. He worked his way up straight out of high school, and was promoted to manager a couple of years back. Samir had confessed to some gang-banging in his early days, but was now married and living in Gardena with three kids, one of which was his own. Samir was all about helping brothers get ahead, and I was lucky to have him providing me with some guidance.

"Glad you could make it, Max," Samir said, looking up from the menu he was explaining to acknowledge me. You always knew where you stood with him, and he was never one for bullshit.

"Thanks, Samir."

There were a few tables that needed cleaning, so I got started on them. I did a little bit of everything when I worked this shift, be it cleaning tables or waiting on customers. While on my third table, I noticed Jay's glistening red BMW outside. Jay always kept his pride and joy clean. When he strolled in the door, he had on a shirt and tie with a pair of black slacks. His typical work attire.

"You missed a plate, Country!" he yelled. Jay loved to clown me, but couldn't take it when he was on the receiving end.

"Nah, I left that one for you. You might need the scraps for some of those little crumb snatchers around town that you don't claim." I made that up, but figured it would bother him.

"Awww, you know that ain't me. I know better than to fall into that trap."

Jay was a *true player fo' real*. Twenty-six, with the style, the looks, and the car, Jay also had that straight black shit atop his head, courtesy of the "good hair fairy," that drove the ladies crazy. Due to the hair issue alone, he had a lot of sisters out here wanting to have his baby.

For all Jay supposedly had going for him, he was drifting through life. Jay still lived with his parents, worked in the mall, and dropped out of college after a year at UCLA. Hell, Uncle Mo bought him the Beamer just before he dropped out.

"Jay, do you ever think about going back to school?"

"What made you bring that up, cuz?"

"I don't know. I was just thinking."

"I might . . . one day. I just need to be ready up here when I do," he said, pointing to his head. Jay seemed to be a thousand miles away before he caught himself.

"I hear ya, cuz. Well, I've got work to do. Samir's cool, but he does expect me to work some of the time."

"Yeah, I feel ya. I've gotta get over to my job and get that commission. Oh! Before I forget . . . Pops wants you to come over for dinner this week. You are lookin' a little poor."

"How about this Friday?" I asked, knowing a free meal wasn't something to take for granted. Besides, it was always good to see family.

9

Glover

I finally got my Civic out of the shop, so I made plans to hang with Mona Friday night. We decided to lounge at her crib down in Santa Monica. Lord knows Mona's view was better than mine. I picked up Robin Thicke's new CD on my way to her crib down on Ocean Avenue and was scanning through the tracks as I pulled into Mona's parking lot. The sun was setting over the Pacific as the waves rolled in along the beach. I stayed in the doorway of my car for a couple of seconds, absorbing the breathtaking view.

California. It doesn't get any better.

I walked into the colorfully splashed lobby, past the doorman. He had seen me before, so no questions were asked. Just a simple smile and a charming hello before the elevator opened. I gave the doorman a parting smile as I pushed the number seven button and ascended to Mona's crib.

When I arrived outside Mona's door, I could hear the exact same Robin Thicke CD playing. I let out a giggle over the eerie similarities between us two as I rang the doorbell.

Mona answered the door and probably wondered what was so funny. She wore her usual home apparel: a long T-shirt, this one emblazoned with her dad's real estate company logo, and a pair of black capris. What surprised me was the do-rag, which came to a knot in the front of Mona's head. Mona almost never let anyone catch her with a hair out of place, or out of her diva-wear. If you hadn't kicked it with her like I had, it would be hard to believe that Mona possessed a tomboy side.

I couldn't let the do-rag thing go, so I said, "What's up, thug-life?"

"You are the funny one, Ms. McDaniel," she said, holding back her own laugh.

"You better duck back in before your neighbors see."

"Oh, they've seen me like this before."

"When? Last time the building caught on fire?"

"Get in here!"

Mona yanked me through the door, causing me to almost trip over my own feet.

"I see you got that new Robin Thicke too. Sexy-ass white boy. Matter of fact, I just picked mine up."

"Yeah, Craig bought it for me," she admitted nonchalantly. "He left it with my doorman. He also bought those flowers on the counter over there. He's still trying, but I'm not feeling him. I do appreciate the CD, though, and the flowers do smell good."

I hustled across the carpet, walking over to Mona's counter to get a whiff of the flowers. They not only smelled good, but they were a beautiful collage of colors—purple, yellow, and pink. The card that came with them was lying there, but I didn't want to be *that* nosey.

"Aw, they're beautiful! I think it's really sweet of him to do this for you. You guys do make a cute couple. Are you sure about dumping him?" I gave Mona an accusatory look, trying in vain to make her feel guilty.

"Yes, I'm sure. Besides, we were never really a couple. I made that very clear to him."

Mona had met Craig at an exhibition game his team was putting on at the Staples Center. Mona's tickets to the game were a gift, courtesy of a promoter named Rico. Rico had a thing for her too, but that's another story. Well, Mona strolls in to the practice session to pick up her tickets, wearing one of her cute little designer workout sets, and runs smack into Craig. I wondered if she was going to have the nerve to keep accepting tickets from Rico after this all played out.

I plopped down on her couch and began thumbing through one of Mona's *Essence* magazines. "Are you ever going to settle down, girl? I thought you might do that with that Brazilian dude a while back."

"Who? You mean Romi? I wasn't about to move back to Sao Paulo with him. I was fond of him, though. Besides, we all can't have someone like Lionel, now, can we?" Mona remarked, tired of my sermon and deciding to turn the tables.

"Okay. Touché. Let's move on to another subject besides men. What are we getting into tonight?"

"You hungry? I've got some leftovers in the fridge."

"Nah. I picked up a turkey burger after work. Did you get your hair done?"

"Yeah, girl. I was overdue for a relaxer. Naps were starting to show. I headed straight for Inglewood when we got off. Can you believe that I actually got out of there at a decent time? The stars must be in alignment. And speaking of decent, when are you going to let me do those jacked-up feet of yours?"

"Fuck you, bitch," I replied jokingly. "They're not crusty. But feel free to give me that manicure, girl." Mona was da bomb when it came to manicures. She could probably do a mean pedicure, too, but Ms. Mona wasn't about to go near these toes without a license.

While Mona tightened up my nails, we spent the rest of the night reminiscing and yakking it up. Robin Thicke continued to play as we talked about this great book we'd both read but could not remember the author's name. All was well in the world with us, but that had to change, as the subject eventually returned to relationships, of course.

"Lionel has something up his sleeve for next week, but I don't know what." I was actually thinking out loud.

"You think he's going to pop the question?"

"I don't know, Mona. Real talk, I'm not sure that's what I want. Maybe he's not who I want," I mumbled, letting a random silly notion get the best of me. Mona's mouth dropped to the carpet, but she tried to play it off. "That's not what I mean," I gasped, trying to take it back.

"Girl, you know I'm wary about any kind of commitment, but it sounds like you've got a lot of issues yourself."

"Yeah, you're right. I just want to be certain that it's real for me if it comes to that. God, I wish my mom was here. She could relate to this."

"Oh?"

"Yeah," I sighed, treading on a subject I kept to myself. But it was Mona, so I continued. "She parted ways with her family over someone that was too good to be true. My dad."

"I'm familiar with being disillusioned, girl, but you can't let that eat you up. That was their life, not yours."

"You're right. But this kind of talk makes me realize how much I miss her." I'd begun crying and hadn't realized it until Mona reached over and handed me a tissue. She gave me a long hug. No words needed.

"Mona, you know what would be good now?" I said, removing my damp face from her shoulder.

"No. What?" She didn't know where I was going with this.

"Ice cream. Lots of it. My mom used to fix me ice cream and it would make everything better. Is Ben & Jerry's still open this time of night?" Even with my droopy red eyes, I managed to crack a smile like a spoiled kid.

"Girl! You know damn well I'm not going out looking like th—" She sighed before giving in. "Oh, let me get a hat or something."

Mona was a true friend.

10

Max

Friday, I made my way to my Uncle Mo and Aunt Lucy's home for that dinner they'd promised me. They'd lived in the same two-story house in Carson for more than twenty years. A retired shop foreman, Uncle Mo had the means to move out to the suburbs, but chose to stay where his heart was. He had been through everything from the Watts Riots to the L.A. uprising and wasn't budging. He had a certain pride about him and refused to let any trends dictate his life.

When I arrived, I saw his new gold Caddy parked beside Jay's Beamer. The big Deville was Uncle Mo's treat to himself. With the driveway full, I parked along the curb, careful not to park too close. I was barely out of the car when the wind carried the smell of fresh greens my way. Aunt Lucy was throwing down. My stomach began growling on command at what was in store.

Jay, Uncle Mo, and I sat around getting our grub on, as Aunt Lucy finished up in the kitchen. Fried chicken, mustard greens with salt pork, turnips, potato salad, and buttered rolls.

High blood pressure heaven.

Aunt Lucy was always the last one to the table, but she never wanted a hand with the cooking. If Uncle Mo's home was his castle, then the kitchen was Aunt Lucy's own little private tower. A native of Opelousas, Louisiana, my Uncle had met her at a zydeco dance back when he lived in Compton.

"You need to bring your ass here more often, Country. We normally don't eat this good. They like you," Jay whispered in my ear as he pulled a roll apart.

"You need to cut that 'country' shit out. You have more of a twang than I do, Junior." He flinched at the "Junior" reference, but I was enjoying the good and free meal too much to put up with Jay's foolishness.

"F—f—fuck you, country-ass nigga." No one outside the family knew Jay used to have a stuttering problem as a child. It was under control now, but if you knew what buttons to push, it would come back.

Uncle Mo had just devoured a chicken leg down to the bone and was glancing over at Jay and me. I knew what was coming.

"Maxwell, you call your momma yet, boy? She called here the other day. Her and your Auntie Lucy talked for a little bit. That lady there," he said, shaking his head, "she miss her boy."

"No, sir. I haven't called her yet. I'm gonna call her. I promise." I was starting to feel bad, but wanted to wait until I had good news to share, and not just my hardships.

"Yeah, baby. You know she already think somethin' gonna happen to you out here," Aunt Lucy chimed in as she sat at the table.

"How's your job search comin' along, boy? You and your little neighbor still lookin' for work?" Uncle Mo didn't particularly care for Smitty. Again, that defensiveness over anyone not family or overly familiar to him.

"Yes, sir. We're both still looking for decent jobs with benefits and a reasonable starting salary. We're going downtown next week. The business district, employment office, and all that. I thought it would be a little easier than this, but I'm not giving up."

"Well, son, nothing good ever comes easy. And there's so much competition out there in this economy. I'm just glad it ain't me. You need to convince your cousin Junior to finish school and try to get a good-payin' job too. That boy there, he spend too much time chasin' tail when he needs to be takin' care of business." Uncle Mo spoiled Jay to some extent, but he wasn't a pushover. Having put in much effort thus far, he didn't plan on taking care of Jay his entire life.

"Aw, Pops! I'm tired of you puttin' me on blast." Jay excused himself from the table and went upstairs to his room. Aunt Lucy frowned at my uncle, but he ignored it.

Here I was really looking forward to dessert, but the look from Aunt Lucy urged me to go talk to Jay. I guess I could get some dessert with my take-home plate. I excused myself from the table, bounding up the stairs and down the hall to Jay's door on the left.

"You know I'm missing dessert, right?" I yelled. When Jay didn't answer, I pushed the door open and entered. Jay was on the computer, pulling up his MySpace page. He wouldn't even look at me.

Yep, pissed and embarrassed.

"You all right, cuz?"

"Yeah. They don't need to send you up here. I'm not some fuckin' kid. Fool's always on my case." Despite my love for cuz, Jay was a prime example of what I didn't want to become.

"You know he loves you, though. They both do. You're truly blessed, man."

"Yeah, I know. That's why I'm gonna do them a favor and move the fuck out. Maybe move in with one of them for a while," he said, referring to his Top Friends on his MySpace page. Nothing but women. That was Jay. Their pictures ranged from classy models to wannabes who left nothing to the imagination, but they all were bangin'. I wondered if any of them had equally impressive personalities.

"You know you're welcome to move in with me, cuz," I offered.

"Thanks, man. I'll think about it. Get back to ya. Think I'm gonna crash now, if you don't mind."

"Nah. Not at all. Talk to you later, cuz."

"Yeah. I'll probably stop by your place tomorrow."

And with that, I was dismissed from Wonderland, a place where a grown man refused to do just that—grow up.

11

Glover

Saturday night was our time to hit the town. We'd been hearing about this new club on the Strip called Drama. The name was appropriate for this town, where everyone is either an actor or aspiring to be one. We just hoped there would be no drama when we arrived there.

Charmaine rode her motorcycle from the Valley and met up with Mona first, their plan being to pick me up in Mona's ride. Charmaine grew up around Crenshaw, but had moved out to the Valley with her family during high school. Despite that, she was still L.A. to her heart.

I was drying myself off when I heard the cackling outside the door. It was time for the sisters to get rowdy. I wrapped myself up in the towel and let them in.

"Hey now! It's time to partay," Charmaine yelled as she danced past me. I could tell she'd begun her celebration on the way here.

Mona sauntered in next with a simple "Hey." "Make yourselves comfortable, ladies. I'll be ready in a minute."

"Bitch, please. Your ass is gonna take more than a minute,"

Charmaine said with a ditzy laugh at her own remark. She always had a lovely way of putting things. Sometimes she was right.

I looked back over my shoulder and gave Charmaine the evil eye. I smiled just before yanking the wet towel off me and throwing it dead in her face. As I slowly carried my naked ass into the bedroom, I could hear Charmaine spitting.

"You're lucky I didn't have a drink in my hand," she scolded.

"You've had one too many already," I replied as I closed my bedroom door.

While admiring myself in the mirror, I made a mental note to get my highlights redone soon. I put my hair up and went with simple femme fatale wear: black silk halter top and designer jeans, topped off with my black Jones New York jacket.

"What do you think?" I asked of the chicas. Mona was sitting on my sofa and looking through my photo album, while Charmaine was thumbing through my magazines.

"Brilliant," Mona said matter-of-factly. She was going with some china-doll shit that only she could pull off: a form-fitting, collared dark blue sleeveless dress with wild splotches of red in it. Mona accessorized it with gold bangles on both arms.

"What she said," Charmaine mimicked. "Can we go now?" With her reddish-brown hair teased, she went with black as I did. A short black skirt, which I'm sure she wasn't wearing on her motorcycle, was topped off with a black sleeveless blouse.

It was ladies' night at Drama, so we got in free. The men were paying that night, so they were out to recoup their thirty dollars in either phone numbers or something a little more immediate and physical. Charmaine would probably refer to that something as "ass." Typical as most establishments, Drama used to be a techno club that I had visited once before, but it had changed with the wind. It was interesting to see how different management would come in and put its stamp on the same spot.

Drama promised to deliver a hip hop/dance feel, but for a mature set, and it was living up to it. Charmaine and I nodded our heads as we worked the crowd, exchanging furtive looks and giving consent to future dances with certain ones. Mona was in diva mode, so her head-nodding and conversation was limited this night to only the rare few she deemed worthy of her time.

There were such good-looking men in the place trying their damndest to get that holler. I was involved, so I politely smiled while deflecting their requests for the digits. Some of them I regretted denying, but I wasn't into games, despite the temptation.

Charmaine got out on the floor and began causing a scene with this brother who wore a blonde fauxhawk atop his head. Must have been an athlete.

While Ms. Charmaine was content to be at the center of all things Drama, Mona preferred to work the edges in a more subtle fashion. This was Mona: all eyes on her as she glided around. A fantasy in their midst, men turned away from their dates to sneak a peek when Ms. Thang came around. It was a bold confidence Mona possessed in this environment that made even the most secure women call her a bitch. I have to admit, I would probably be right there with them if I didn't really know Mona or was insecure about myself.

Which I wasn't.

"Oooo, your eyes." I was snapped out of my club-gazing and self-adoration by this light-skinned brother in an expensive pinstripe suit. He stood at my side, smiling.

"Huh?" I said, bewildered.

"Your eyes," he stressed over the pounding beat. "I just noticed them. What are they? Hazel?" He had apparently been staring at me for a while.

"Yep, hazel. You got it. What's your name?" I figured it was best to take control of this situation. It usually caught them off guard, made them less aggressive.

"Terry. I'm from Cleveland," he said over the music.

"Hi, Terry from Cleveland," I teased. He was cute, but I was only being nice at this moment.

"Have you ever been there?"

"Nope. Never been there, Terry. What brings you here?"

"In town for a television producer conference. Staying at the W in Westwood, but I'm flying out tomorrow. You never did tell me your name." He was so busy trying to remember his lines that he'd almost forgotten to ask. I felt some guilt for giving him this much time, but like I said, he was cute.

"Glover," I answered honestly, noticing my drink was getting all watery on me. Time for another one.

"That's an interesting name. May I buy you another drink, Glover?"

"Nah, I'm not drinking anymore," I replied, lying through my pretty teeth.

Terry continued talking, but something else had my attention. With his height, he stood out.

Craig was in the club.

He had somehow spotted Mona and skirted the edge of the dance floor, past a still-dancing Charmaine, to get to where Mona was standing. Of course, Mona was in the company of someone else just then. Craig didn't look too happy, and interrupted her conversation. With Craig towering over both of them, Mona excused the startled young gentleman as she and Craig proceeded to get into a heated discussion. The heat appeared to be one-sided, though.

Craig pointed and flailed his arms, while Mona stood there, unemotional, arms folded, with one of her eyebrows raised.

Charmaine noticed Mona's situation from the dance floor and was walking toward me.

"Hey, are you listening to me?" Terry asked, breaking my concentration by grabbing my arm. "I'm trying to give you a moment of my time and buy you a drink, and you're just blowing me off. Both my time and my money are important."

"Um, Terry? First, don't ever presume to touch me. Second, I'm seeing someone, so you might want to try those stale-ass lines on someone else. Okay? Oh, and your suit is too big for your build. Makes you look like a little boy trying on his dad's clothes."

Terry stood there dumbfounded for a second, flashing a fake smile then storming off. I'm sure I heard the word "ho" as he disappeared into the crowd.

"Who was that, G-love?" Charmaine asked, catching the end of my encounter.

"Some loser," I replied. "What's up with Mona?"

"You see that shit too, huh? Craig's going off."

"Let's get over there before something stupid happens," I urged.

Charmaine and I hastily moved through the crowd toward their location. As we got closer, the music was still too loud to hear what was being said. Just as we closed in on them, Craig raised his hand as if to hit Mona, then suddenly dropped his massive arm and stormed off.

"You okay, Mona?" Charmaine asked with a look of relief on her face.

"Yes. I am fine. It's Craig that's not. I guess he finally understands what 'over' means." Mona had her ice queen face on. The entire incident really didn't seem to faze her.

I asked, "I guess you're ready to go, huh?"

Then Mona surprised me.

"No. Why? The night is still young. Craig is the least of my concerns." Mona said it in her most dry manner. The diva rolled on . . . for a little while longer.

Mona began walking off to continue her rounds when Craig returned. His little walk hadn't cooled him off, as he still looked pissed. *Roid rage.*

In the middle of the club, with everybody now watching, Craig stood dead in front of her. Security began rushing toward him, but he paused them with a wave of his outstretched hand. I guess spending the night in a jail cell wouldn't be good for his career. Instead of hitting her, he snatched a beer from somebody's hand and poured it on her head.

"You stupid bitch!" he uttered before exiting quickly in the direction away from security. A hush fell over the ground level of the club. I could almost hear the DJ breathing.

Now it was time to leave.

On the drive home, Mona didn't say a word. I'd offered to drive, but she'd declined. Craig had actually succeeded in embarrassing her, I guess. She would be over it by tomorrow, though. Charmaine was pissed off because she couldn't find her dance partner after Mona's scene and wouldn't be getting the digits. And I was just left with the unsettled feeling that other than Mona's incident, I had been enjoying myself just a little too much.

So much for there not being drama at Drama.

12

Max

I woke up early Sunday morning and did some major cleaning. My funky clothes needed to be washed, and the apartment was a mess. I straightened things out around the place then decided to tackle the laundry. But first, I remembered my promise to my Uncle Mo.

Adding two hours due to the different time zone, I figured she'd be back home. Orelia always attended the early mass at Saint Henry's then hung around chatting with the other parishioners. Barring a church barbecue or fair, you could set your watch to her.

"Hello?"

"Hey, Momma."

"Max! How's my baby doing?" she asked. I'd given up trying to stop her from referring to me that way. I would always be her baby, even when old and gray.

"I'm fine. You just got back from Mass?"

"Yeah, baby. I saw Mrs. Duplechein in church today. Remember her? She used to do the sewing for us. Anyway, she asked how you were doing. I told her you were in California. She said a prayer for you when I said that."

Holding back a chuckle, I replied, "Yeah, Momma. I remember her. Her boy still in jail?"

"I think so, baby. She don't talk much about him, so I don't ask. You know how that goes. You know your cousin Huey died?"

"Who?"

"Huey. Auntie Suzette's stepson's boy," she rattled off . . . somehow. "You never met him, but I know I mentioned him before. Well, he had a heart attack just last week. Way too young, that one. I went to the wake."

"No, I don't remember him, but that's too bad. How are you doing, Mom? Uncle Maurice said he spoke with you."

"I'm doin' just fine, baby. Just the old arthritis and gout every now and then. I hadn't heard from you, but I didn't want to bother you with that mess. How's your money lookin'?"

"I'm okay. Still looking for a full time job. That's all," I admitted, groaning internally. "Me and my neighbor are going downtown this week. I hear the state's hiring."

"Downtown," she mumbled. "Just be careful down there. I hear they have winos and drug addicts that try to mess with folk. Maybe you should carry some Mace or one of them Taser things." I had to snicker. Momma had a habit of excessive worrying at times.

"No problem, Momma. I'll be on the lookout when I go," I assured her.

"How was your meal at your uncle's? I know Lucy can put too much salt in her food sometimes." There she went, the old competitiveness flaring up.

"It was fine," I answered swiftly before catching myself. "Well, it was good . . . just not as good as your cooking."

"Oh, you're so sweet," she gushed. "That's why I'm gonna fix you a big ol' meal when you come home."

"Thanks, Momma. It may be a while, though. I plan on making a go of it out here," I said, planting my flag in the ground. "Once I get permanently situated, I'll probably be able to fly down . . . to visit."

"Just don't be showin' up on my door with one of them fast California women on your arm. You need to get a good girl from right down here, not one of them siddity little wenches."

Time to go. The last *good girl* she approved of had ripped out my heart.

"Momma, you need to stop. Lake Charles has plenty of its own 'fast' women—and some siddity ones too." I thumbed through the yearbook of my mind, coming up with a few faces that matched both those descriptions.

"Well, I guess you got a point there."

"Momma?"

"Yeah, baby?"

"I love you."

"I love you too, baby."

Despite my terseness at times, I really did love her. It was just that she reminded me of my failings every time I had no news for her. She was also my escape valve from all this, so I resented it to some extent. Other people would be lucky to have a parent that cared so much and could do for them, but I was a man, and part of me needed to feel the desperation, as if pushed into a corner, to spur me to better myself.

Cutting through the bull, maybe I needed to prove it to my ex.

Rub it in her face.

On the real.

Take that, Lake Charles. How ya like me now? Holla!

After taking that brief mental vacation, I grabbed my laundry and headed out the door. On my way

to the laundry room, I caught Smitty lurking near
the pool, waiting to gawk at Mrs. Griggs, no doubt.
Couldn't fault him. For an older woman, she was
finer than most of the young things in the complex.
And with her husband being away on lock for several years, she fed into many of our fantasies.

"You about to wash?"

"No, I just like carrying clothes around in a
fuckin' basket," I teased him.

"Wouldn't surprise me. You a strange one, Maxwell."

"Whatever. Are you washing, or you gonna
stay here hoping Mrs. Griggs shows?"

"I'ma wait it out. If she don't bring her ass
down soon, I'll join your little laundry party."

"Suit yourself," I said, knowing I had two more
loads to haul down.

Smitty eventually got around to washing his
shit too. Being his usual prepared self, he ran out
of laundry detergent. I remembered a brand new
box I bought being in my trunk, so we walked out
to the parking lot, where the familiar red BMW
was just arriving.

"Uh-oh, Cousin Junior's in da house!" Smitty
yelled out when he saw Jay's car.

"Shhhh. Call him Jay, Smitty," I hissed back.
I regret the day I told him about the "Junior"
issue.

Jay finished his texting then exited his car.

"Whaddup, fellas?" he hollered as he came over. He wore one of the new Lakers jerseys with the warm-up pants, perpetrating, no doubt. The circles under his eyes were probably from a night of partying.

"Whaddup, cuz?" I replied while digging in my trunk for the Tide. Smitty gave Jay a wary nod.

"Washing clothes? You can do mine next."

"I'll wash that Beamer for you, Jay," said Smitty. "But you gotta leave it with me for the day. Whatchasay?"

"I say yo' little skinny ass better look like Vida Guerra or Meagan Good before I would even consider it. And last time I looked, that ain't you."

Smitty didn't find Jay's comments that funny. I just shook my head.

"Went out last night, huh, Jay?" I guessed, changing the subject to something more appealing to my cousin.

"Yeah, cuz. That's why I wasn't able to roll by. I had to hunt up a new suit. Let a true player fill you wannabes in on what went down last night."

As Jay droned on and on about his latest exploits, I tuned out. Instead, I thought back to his immature outburst at the family dinner the other night, realizing again that I didn't want to be that dude.

13

Glover

It took until Tuesday for Mona to loosen up again. Charmaine and I had exchanged whispers here and there since the drama at Drama, but we avoided the subject when in Mona's presence. Charmaine had felt bad even when she carelessly mentioned beer.

Lionel called me before lunch, wanting me to meet him at his office over in the central business district, or CBD. All he said was that he had something to discuss with me. I wondered what it could be, but decided not to dwell on it, as I'd know soon enough. Due to my short lunch hour, I hoped he'd at least have something tasty waiting for me.

As I drove up Grand Avenue toward Lionel's office in the Gas Company Tower, I thought about the changes the area had been through. The homeless had all but disappeared, having been "relocated" to other parts of downtown by design. That left the area more palatable for the business conducted around here, but at what cost to the people that found shelter from the elements amidst these tall buildings? The professionals milling about on their cell phones as they crossed the streets and overhead walkways to drive off in their Range Rovers and Mercedes wagons were probably oblivious to people having to live like that. Of course I wasn't. I was old enough to remember those first years after my dad left us.

I pulled into the parking garage adjacent to the architectural wonder in which Lionel worked, taking the special elevator up to the fortieth floor, where Barnes & Greenwood was headquartered. Lionel hooked up with them straight out of Stanford and made a name for himself in no time. For being one of the few minorities there, Lionel was considered a real "team player" and trusted confidant. I wondered at times if the outcome would have been different if Lionel didn't have the old L.A. Dunning name to back him up. Probably not, as he was so driven.

The contemporary-styled lobby bustled as usual with what I called The Suits, older white men in dark blue suits with red ties, as they either welcomed their clients or rushed out to meetings. It was never too late to change their ways, but at least Lionel didn't fall into that stuffy, traditional trap. My baby was a trendsetter and trailblazer, destined to have his name added to the corporate logo before long.

I went to the receptionist's desk, about to ask her to call for Lionel. I saw his office door was open, so decided to see myself in instead. I had been here before, and they weren't stuffy enough to keep me from seeing my man. I was close enough to Lionel's office to read his nameplate on the door.

"Hey!" I yelled, almost being knocked aside.

"Oh," she said, equally startled but less pissed off. It was that eager-beaver chick, what's-her-face. She'd flown out of Lionel's office like a bat outta hell and ran right into me. She didn't look too happy.

"Misha, right?" God, I hoped I was right with the name. I extended my hand. That's me, Ms. Courteous when I want to be. No need for an office scene.

"Yes! You remembered my name!" she bubbled. "How are you doing, Glover? Lionel's in his office. Sorry about almost bowling you over." *Almost?*

"That's okay. Accidents happen." *Bitch. At least she knew my name.*

"Well, I've got to run. Lunchtime," she rapidly commented, pointing at her watch for emphasis. "Nice seeing you again."

And with that, Misha hustled away, awash in her normal perkiness.

I stepped into Lionel's office to see my baby standing by his window, looking out onto the city. He was wearing the tie and suspenders set I'd bought him last Christmas.

"Well, hello, sir. Hope I didn't interrupt anything. Your friend almost ran over me on her way out."

"Nah, baby. Misha was pissed with her salary review and was venting to me about it. She can be high-strung at times," said Lionel with those pearly whites glistening. Misha didn't seem pissed to me, but perhaps she was good at concealing stuff to outsiders. Made good sense in the business world.

"*Oh, really?* I didn't know she confided in you like that. Am I gonna have to keep an eye on her?" I joked, perhaps feeling some wariness about pretty, ambitious kittens like Misha.

"Not at all, babe. Come here," said Lionel as he outstretched his arms. I walked behind his desk to kiss him, but he cut it short.

"What's up with that?" I asked, denied my sugar.

"The door's open, baby. I don't want anyone around here tripping. That's all."

"How about if I did this?" I asked, discreetly passing my hand between Lionel's legs, where I brushed against his manhood. Lionel jerked suddenly and protested a little, but figured no one could tell we were doing anything else but hugging. As Lionel began to harden, I suddenly stopped. I didn't appreciate my kiss being cut short, so got my revenge.

"I hope you had lunch delivered, because I don't have much time."

"Oops. Well, I didn't have anything delivered except for what's on my desk there," he replied, pointing over my shoulder.

On Lionel's desk were airline tickets, as well as brochures. I saw the words "Miami" and "South Beach" and went crazy.

"Lionel! No! Is this the secret you mentioned the other night?"

"Yeah." He chuckled, sounding sexier than usual. "You like?"

"Do I like? Of course!" I jumped in his arms again, getting the kiss he'd intentionally put off before. "Um, when are you planning this for?" I asked, catching my breath.

"This weekend. We fly out of LAX Friday and return Monday evening."

"Monday? But I have to work."

"Guess you need to go back to that office and tell them you need Monday off, huh? Or you could just quit . . ."

"Nope. Nice try. I'll take Monday off."

"Good. Now we'll have some alone time. No distractions, just rest and relaxation and time to talk about us."

That last comment bothered me slightly, as I knew what that "talk about us" entailed. I needed to start acting my age and shake off these irrational doubts that plagued me.

"I look forward to it," I answered with as honest a smile as I could muster.

14

Max

Friday night had me dancing around my living room in my drawers to Al Green's "Love and Happiness" with a hot iron in my hand. As I spun around the rickety ironing board, I placed a perfect crease on the sleeve of my shirt. Having some ends in your pocket and someplace to go will do that to you.

After picking up our paychecks, Smitty had tightened me up with a fresh haircut. I'd showered, and my Kenneth Cole cologne was just right. I wanted the ladies to smell it, not choke on it. Jay, who was going to be our driver, was selecting our destination. His volunteering was a rarity. We usually went in separate cars, giving Jay the freedom to break out and get his "whap-whap" whenever he wanted. Knowing Jay, he probably wanted to use my apartment or something.

Speaking of Jay, he arrived bearing gifts. Heinekens in hand. Maybe I misjudged him this time.

We all agreed to go kinda casual for the night, so no suits. I ignored the "kinda" and tried to do some Kanye shit—a black sweater vest atop a white dress shirt with rolled-up sleeves, my most expensive denims, and some black Chuck Taylors. Oh, and a loose black necktie

"What the fuck?" Jay asked at my failed experiment. We'd said no suits, and he still wore one. Fuck him and his hatin' ass.

"Just give me a beer," I said as I locked up and led him upstairs to Smitty's. Whatever me and Jay had on, Smitty, true to himself, rocked a bright-as-hell silk shirt with black slacks and shoes. Fool looked like he was ready for *Dancing with the Stars* rather than the club. So much for stealth. I guess it was best that the *womens* knew we were coming from a block away. It gave them time to prepare—and run for cover.

"Awww, my eyes!" I screamed before Jay could beat me to it.

Smitty slammed the door on us—until he found out we had beer.

We killed the Heinekens while telling the traditional tales of the women we'd had and of the ones we hoped to get. Smitty's stereo had the walls shaking with Keri Hilson and that new album from Tha Dogg Pound, but I wanted to hear some Lil' Wayne and some classic UGK. I stumbled downstairs and grabbed a couple of their CDs for Smitty to jam. Jay couldn't help but come with the "country" cracks, but it didn't faze me. I had my buzz on and I was in L.A. Haters be damned.

Jay let us in on the destination once we were rolling. We were on our way to hang with the beautiful people at El Ami in Hollywood. Normally, we had a slim chance of getting in the joint on a Friday night, but Jay went to high school with the brother at the door. That made our chances a lot better. Well, that and forty bucks that we'd thrown together. Jay never said they were good friends in high school.

The beautiful people were in effect, and the food was damn good too. I didn't need anything weighing me down, so I had a bowl of gumbo in the dining room. Not as good as home, but not that watery stuff that some places called gumbo either. Smitty was tearing up some fried chicken like he hadn't eaten in days. Jay had moved on to the lounge, where the ladies were.

"Ay, Max, that's all you're eatin' tonight?" Smitty asked as he sucked on a chicken bone.

"Yeah, dawg. Just enough to soak up some of that beer. Gotta stay light on my feet. Don't want to be belching around my future wife, y'know?" I joked, knowing she wasn't to be found as long as I continued my hit-it-and-quit-it ways; one day, perhaps, I'd be over what had happened back in Louisiana and ready for something real.

"I guess you got a point there. You ready to mingle?"

We split up to cover more area. Smitty headed toward the bar, probably for another drink, while I ventured into the crowded lounge. I spotted Jay immediately. He was seated on a barstool, with an audience of not one, but two women. One sister, with a cappuccino complexion and pretty little braids running down her back, wore a tight, backless light blue dress. The other one had one of those cute permy-fros to go with her golden-delicious self and red dress. I was about to slip by when Jay motioned me over.

"Hey, cuz," Jay said, brimming with confidence, as he should, for what he'd landed. "I want you to meet my two friends here. Diane and Brandi, this is my cousin, Maxwell. Maxwell, these are my friends, Diane and Brandi."

I could tell Jay was running game when he called me by my full name. Diane, in the blue dress, shook my hand and then slowly let it go. The lingering touch and eye contact as our hands parted spoke to me. Her nipples popping up through the fabric of her dress spoke louder. Brandi gave me a little wave while communicating with her friend via smiles and the unspoken cues known only to women. I'd been given the approval and wasn't going anywhere.

The brief conversation went well, until Jay told me to take a walk with him to the bar.

"Cuz, they are ready!" he said, barely away from their ears.

"Bet," I said, noting the obvious.

"I need to fill you in, though. They think we're in the NFL."

"Say what?"

He put his arm around me, pulling me into his web. "I told them we both play football and return to L.A. when our season ends."

"Why do you have to make up shit? Man, look at us. We ain't built like pros." I was up for the action, just minus all the extra fake bullshit Jay seemed to excel at. If someone didn't like me for me, then fuck them.

"What?" he said, feigning innocence. "They don't know shit about football. We could be kickers for all they know. All they see is the promise of being part of our world. Well, for one night at least."

"You don't think people fall for that shit, do ya?"

"All the time, cuz. All the time. This is L.A., nigga. Everybody lies. It's all about whether your story is better than the next nigga's. Your country ass will never survive out here if you don't learn that. And quick." Jay's smooth demeanor soured temporarily as he channeled his inner ass-hole.

I paused to glance back at Diane and Brandi, who were still smiling and waiting patiently for us. As I continued my trip to the bar, I envisioned Diane riding me all night, inhaling her sticky sweetness, probing her wetness. Wondered how it would feel to be in the throes of passion with her and to hear her screaming my name. But would it be me making her scream, or simply a falsity spun by Jay?

As Jay ordered a final round of drinks, I tapped him on the shoulder.

"Where are we supposed to go with them? One look at my apartment and this is over."

"Relax. I've got Pops' credit card, so it's time to get that room. After these drinks, we're outta here. I might even let Brandi drive the ride. Yeah," he said, admiring his plan. "Then I'll ride her."

"Hey, what about Smitty?" I asked, my lust diminishing long enough for me to remember my friend.

"Fuck him. Besides, there's not enough room in the ride for all of us. His runt ass can catch a cab with his radioactive shirt."

"That's foul, cuz." This was one of those times I really didn't like my cousin, despite him being family.

I looked around our vicinity, but didn't see Smit. This was wrong.

We returned to Diane and Brandi with their drinks, continuing where we left off. I talked, but didn't contribute to Jay's lie. Sensing I was holding back now, Diane took a sip of her drink and pulled me into her. She kissed me hard, opening her mouth to share her tongue, as well as the sweet coconut rum. I kissed her back, my tongue meeting hers as our bodies came together. She was more intoxicating than the liquor I'd had tonight.

Next thing I knew, the four of us were heading out of El Ami and straight for Jay's Beamer, which was parked across the street. Jay had his arm around a giggling Brandi, while Diane was skipping toward the car with me willingly in tow. Jay hit his remote, disarming the alarm and unlocking the doors. He appeared to be serious about letting Brandi drive. I looked at Diane's ass as she bent over to enter.

But I couldn't dog my boy like that—or put up with any more of Jay's lies tonight.

I could've just called Smitty if he'd paid his cell phone bill, but . . .

"Hey, I just remembered. I gotta run back inside."

Jay locked on me with his eyes, implying, "Don't do it."

"My agent's in there and we gotta . . . talk about my new deal," I said weakly, tossing Jay a slight bone. Weak. Real weak. "I'll catch up with you guys later."

The ladies erupted in a series of groans and gasps. I could read Jay's lips as he silently mouthed, "Punk ass." Diane got out of the car and tried to convince me to leave with them. I let Jay stick to his story and apologized to Diane before the three of them drove off down La Cienega. Diane did give me one last long, wet kiss and placed my hands on her ass in an attempt to sway me.

It almost worked. I don't know where my strength came from.

I did get her number, though.

Now, I not only had to locate Smitty and explain why we had to cab it home, but I had to figure out how to get back inside El Ami. Looking at the line now gathered outside, I knew it would take more than I had to get back inside.

I was left with the smell of Diane's perfume on my shirt to give me some solace.

Yeah.

Some solace.

15

Glover

Florida. The sunshine and palm trees—minus the smog.

I lowered the window to feel the breeze. "Beautiful," I whispered as we crossed Biscayne Bay en route to the Palms Hotel & Spa.

The limousine was waiting for us upon touchdown at Miami International. No surprise, as Lionel was the master of organization. Our flight in from LAX had been quiet and uneventful, allowing us to get a nap in.

With my digital camera, I snapped some pictures of the tranquil waters. The driver slowed just enough to indulge my tourist moment. Lionel sat across from me, his mind solving whatever puzzle was before him at the moment.

This trip was going to be different from the others. I could tell.

We arrived at our exquisite hotel, checking in and having our bags delivered to our ocean-view suite. I'd felt like a little girl all the way up to our room, but once the attendant received his tip and left us alone, that was over.

It was time for Lionel to make me feel like a woman.

"One question. Am I going to have to wait any longer?" I asked, my hand still resting on the door I'd just closed.

Lionel responded immediately by pinning me against the door. I couldn't escape. Gripped the door handle anxiously. Stroked the polished chrome as if it could respond.

"No," he answered. "No more waiting."

"Oh," I gasped as Lionel's body pressed into my ass. I felt him swelling as I steadied my legs. My grip on the door handle tightened, while his tongue slid up and down my neck and across the edges of my ear.

His tongue flicked into the center, weakening me further. "Glover, are you gonna give it to me?" he whispered.

"Yessss," I panted.

"How do you want it, baby?" he asked, knowing how crazy-hot he was making it for me. My pussy throbbed, my legs quivered, causing me to buck uncontrollably against him. He leaned into me harder, flattening me against the door. With it not giving, I had nowhere to go but to grind harder into him. His breathing became ragged.

Lionel removed his shirt and began fondling my breasts before reaching under my T-shirt to undo my bra. I released my grip on the door handle and reached back to undo his pants and grip something more useful. As the pants peeled off and dropped to the floor, I took his dick in my hand. From its swollen head to the base of its shaft, I stroked its contours.

Strong.

Curved.

Needed.

Ready.

I turned around and pushed Lionel onto the king-sized bed. The rest of him fell back, but his dick remained at attention, not wanting to be parted from its owner.

For I owned that shit.

I threw my shirt off and fell on top of Lionel's sleek, hard body. His left hand found its way inside my shorts, where his fingers took root inside me. In and out they slid, while he took one of my breasts in his other hand, succulently teasing my nipple. I kissed atop his head as he sucked harder and harder, making me gush and swell in all the right places. I was whipped into an uncontrolled frenzy and quickly pulled off my shorts and thong.

"I've never wanted you more than I do now," he uttered as he rolled me onto my back.

"Take it. Take me."

And he did. Entered me as I willingly accepted all he had to give.

Needless to say, we wound up staying in the room the rest of the day and into the evening. Other than ordering room service, the lovin' continued into the night with few words spoken.

Upon being awakened by housekeeping Saturday, we were reminded to hang the DO NOT DISTURB sign. We had some breakfast on the beach with the Atlantic Ocean rolling in behind us, then set out to explore South Beach.

Lionel's thoughts still seemed to drift somewhere between here and some secret place he refused to divulge. Beyond sheer satisfaction, my thoughts went to how this trip would change things for us.

After a cab ride over to Washington Avenue in South Beach that evening, Lionel decided to show his stroke by getting us into the VIP section of a club called Mirrors. Don't get me wrong. It was impressive and I had fun, but I would have preferred something more intimate, with maybe some salsa dancing. Perhaps I hadn't fully recovered from Drama, and was expecting a beer to be dumped on someone.

We spent Sunday evening having a quiet dinner to put a perfect little red ribbon on our trip. Lionel must have coughed up some serious money to have the restaurant to ourselves. Sometimes he tried too hard to impress me, but I'd given in to his ways for once. I was having a nervous feeling about this, though, fear of my mother's experience casting an unnecessary color on what was supposed to be the best chapter in my life.

We had fried calamari for an appetizer. Lionel had the stuffed, marinated pork chop, while I dined on a petite filet. Nothing like a hunk of beef to get my strength back up after all the weekend's activities.

"Had a good time, baby?" he asked before taking a sip of his iced tea.

"A great time, honey, although you didn't have to do all this. I'm in heaven here. Pure heaven."

"Good. I'm glad you're in heaven, and you know what? I don't want you to come down . . . ever."

I noticed our waiter standing in the distance, watching our table curiously. I was focused on him, so I failed to notice the small box Lionel had placed before me on the table. When I looked back, all I heard was "Glover, will you marry me?"

My world froze.

I knew this was coming, but I had tried to put it out of my head.

"Glover, did you hear me?"

The too-good-to-be-trues, I secretly named them. Where desires meet disaster. But this wasn't my mother's life. And Lionel wasn't my father.

"I'm—I'm sorry. Yes, of course I'll marry you!"

I welled up and let the tears come forth. As I bawled like a baby, my thoughts were of my dear mother. The waiter came forward from his vantage point and brought out champagne as the rest of the staff stood around us and applauded.

We were returning to Los Angeles tomorrow, officially engaged and ready to take the next step.

16

Max

I was tempted to call Diane over the weekend, but decided it was best to put that whole production behind me. Man, I needed a lady out here on the regular. Someone to keep it real for me, and for whom I could do the same.

I never gave Smitty the whole story about Friday night. I felt terrible about almost going along with Jay, and I didn't want Smit to know what an ass he was. Jay was blood and had done right by me since I moved here, so I knew we would be talking eventually.

Just not now.

The late shift at Denny's came and went Monday with no Jay and no problems. Although dead tired, I forced myself awake the next morning. It was my off day, so no better time to resume my job search. This time we would focus on downtown.

After getting the cold out of my eyes, I pulled my best interview suit from the closet. It was still covered in plastic from the dry cleaner after my last futile attempt. I fished my black dress shoes out of the back of the closet and dusted them off.

On my coffee table, I arranged my resumes along with some generic cover letters. I'd printed a map from Map quest, circling places I planned on targeting. While searching online, I'd noticed the State of California was hiring as well, so I had to hit the Employment Development Department also.

I stepped out of my door with briefcase in hand, ready to take on the world. The navy blue with gray pinstripes was hitting, with my burgundy silk tie and white Perry Ellis showing from beneath.

Smitty was waiting by my car, holding a folder containing his paperwork. He was pacing there in his white but-ton-down, salt-and-pepper slacks, and gray-and-black tie. He'd joke about it, but I could tell he was uncomfortable dressed like this.

The things we do to get paid. At least it was legal. Right about now, I was prepared to put on a chicken costume if a nice crib and some money in the bank came along with it.

"Check you out, Maxwell. Lookin' like you own the fuckin' company."

"One day. One can hope, my brother."

Getting a late start, traffic was smooth coming in on I-10 heading east. We planned to bum-rush the CBD and try to get into as many places as possible. More planning and networking would have been a good idea, but I was getting desperate. And desperation was just what I needed to step up my game.

I glanced at my map of downtown again, focusing on the circles I'd drawn. Smitty had his own list he was following, so the plan was to go straight through lunch then meet back at the car that afternoon.

My aim was to just get a foot in the door, maybe at an entry-level position, then work my way up to management. I wasn't picky about the type of business. I just knew I didn't want to return home to Louisiana as some kind of failure.

I hit up the Gas Company Tower first. Its unique architecture stood out, like money was comfortable being inside it. From my research, I knew businesses like Nalcon, Intrix, and Barnes & Greenwood, which I'd heard of in college, were housed in there. I tried not being impressed or overwhelmed by the success amassed around me, but I couldn't hide the grin plastered on my face.

All I needed was a chance.

I went over to the building index and formed a plan to cover as many businesses as possible in here. I was sure to face a lot of rejection and maybe get thrown out by security, but it wouldn't kill my spirit. I began with Nalcon on the forty-eighth floor. Might as well start at the top, or near it.

I did some people-watching downstairs as I waited for the elevator to descend. A middle-aged Asian woman in a black business suit politely smiled at me as she walked by. From her smile, I couldn't tell if she was simply being friendly or whether she was acknowledging the outsider in their midst. The elevator opened and I boarded it along with five other passengers: present were a Hispanic courier with a radio on his hip, a middle-aged Hispanic gentleman in a gray business suit, a thin white lady in a red business suit, a younger tanned white girl all in blue, and a bald brother in an olive-colored suit.

"'Sup," I said to the brother, acknowledging him. Good to know there's hope out there.

"Hello," he said weakly. Okay.

Judging by his suit, he was doing really well—or he was fronting and in debt. I first noticed him when we were down in the lobby. Mr. Clean was posted up, holding a conversation with the girl in blue. I wasn't being nosey, but could tell he was trying to calm her down about something.

I guess they'd made up on the ride up, because they stole a quick kiss before getting off together on the fortieth floor. Office romance, I presumed. Whatever.

Nalcon accepted my resume and allowed me to complete an application. Nothing promised, but then again, nothing squashed either. Other businesses in the building, like Barnes & Greenwood, weren't hiring, or least told me that. All I could do was hope the phone call would come.

I was drained by the time the afternoon rolled around, but Smitty still looked energized when he met me by the car.

"I got an interview next week!" my little friend taunted. He'd already loosened his tie and looked like he was ready to celebrate. I was ready to crawl back under my covers. Can't say I wasn't happy for him, but his success magnified my lack of results today.

"Congrats, man," I said, giving him a lazy high-five. "With who?"

"West-tel, dawg. Mail and file, but it pays lot more than what I make now at Costco. And I can move up. I know I still gotta get past the interview, but it seems almost like a sure thing, y'know. How'd things go with you?"

"Nothing certain, bro. But enough about me; let's get out of here and celebrate!"

I yanked off my tie and threw it in the backseat of the car along with my briefcase and jacket. We were down Sixth Street and already clowning when I remembered that I hadn't picked up a state employment application.

"I guess I can pick that up another day."

"Man, you better pick up that app now. Remember, the deadline is this Friday. And you see how mugs is outta work. Besides, that may be your lucky break."

"Sure. Lucky." I chuckled. "I'd forgotten about the deadline."

I turned the Corolla around and headed for First Street. To my right, I spotted the *Los Angeles Times* building first, then saw the employment office in its shadow. Smitty decided to recline in the car while I ran in to pick up an app.

The office was almost empty when I walked in. No employees in sight, which reminded me of the office back home. If applications were handy, I would have simply picked one up and headed out the door.

They weren't, though.

I waited at the counter for a couple of minutes, hoping Smitty wasn't fucking with my radio outside. I was about to head out the door in frustration when I caught a glimpse of someone zipping by in the back.

"Excuse me!" I hollered in the general direction of the blur I saw. The blur slowed then hesitated.

And what a blur it was.

Out walked this gorgeous piece of womanhood. Around five foot six, light brown, with the eyes to match, she wore a gold jacket and skirt that really showed just how fine she was. Her brown hair had some highlights in it, with this stray piece that dangled over one eye. Don't know if it was intentional, but it pointed almost perfectly to this little beauty mark on her cheek.

Yep, I was taking it all in.

No longer a blur, she opened her lovely mouth, asking, "Can I help you?"

"Um," I fumbled, blanking out for a second. "Hi. I need an application."

"For . . . ?" The look on her face told me she didn't have time for this. I was on the receiving end of a little bit of attitude.

"For the state jobs," I answered, hoping she knew what I meant. "I was told they could be picked up at any of the Employment Development Department Offices?" I phrased my statement like a question in hopes that it would make a light bulb go off in her head.

"Oh, okay. I don't normally work up here. The girl called in sick today and another one quit. I'll try to find it for you." Her tone softened. Good. She probably had her mind on other things. She looked behind the counter and came up with the application in hand.

"Thank you."

"You're welcome. Don't forget, it needs to be in by this Friday." Aww. The beautiful one could be courteous and helpful when given a chance.

"Oh, don't worry. I won't forget. I need some work," I said with a chuckle.

"Well, I hope you find the work you're looking for," she playfully replied. No she didn't. The remark seemed almost flirtatious.

Almost.

But the rock on her finger told me otherwise.

Oh, well.

Strange, though. I would have thought someone with ice like that on her finger would be waving it around more. I'd caught a glimpse of it when she came up with the application and it almost blinded me.

"Later," I replied, excusing myself. For my own amusement, I imagined her eyes on me as I headed out the door.

Yeah. Right.

Cheap thrills mean nothing.

I looked back to confirm that I was just being a silly little kid.

Correct.

There was the empty counter again. The blur had gone back to being a blur, and I was left a simple idiot.

17

Glover

I returned from Miami officially engaged. Really engaged. And I had the ring to prove it. All of Lionel's planning stood revealed. He had more than the proposal mapped out, as I found out later that evening. We had gone for a walk on the beach after dinner. Following the surf and sand, we returned to the room, where we made love.

I'll tell you now, I've never faked an orgasm my entire time with Lionel—until that night.

As Lionel cradled me in his arms, I cried. They weren't tears of joy, as Lionel probably figured. As I lay there, emotional, he informed me of his (and his mom's) wedding plans.

Catalina Island.

It was the first place Lionel had taken me. He had already talked it over with his mother, Adele, and she was on hand to arrange everything for us once we selected a date. Hell, she would probably rent the whole fucking island. I knew she would have preferred a traditional church wedding with bells and all, being a Dunning, but Lionel knew how I felt about churches. My mom was supposed to be here for this.

"When do you want to do it, baby?" he'd asked.

I was still numb as I stared down at the diamond on my finger, and I blurted out, "No time like the present." What happened between my mom and dad wasn't me. This was going to work.

We were to be married in three months.

When the limo returned me to my apartment late Monday night, I had no idea of the rollercoaster in store for me on Tuesday.

I returned to work to find that one of the girls had walked off the job the day before and another was out sick. My desk overflowed with stacks of files, and I was to be wed in three months.

Tuesday felt more like a Monday than Monday ever could.

Mona and Charmaine rushed to my desk before I even had a chance to put my purse down.

Mona squinted at me disapprovingly. "Bitch, you came in last night and didn't even call to tell me? Let me see that ring!"

I held it up for them to see. Charmaine was silent for a full four seconds.

A new record.

Four.

Three.

Two.

One.

"Oh my gawd! OMG! OMG! OMG! The size of that diamond. Do you know how much this must have cost?"

"I do," Mona chimed in. An avid collector/ recipient of diamonds and such, she probably did know.

"C'mon, y'all. It's just an engagement ring," I said, trying to convince myself. The immense piece of ice on my hand was a sobering reality that made me more self-conscious the more I tried to ignore it.

"Okay, okay. Enough about the ring. How many times did you do the nasty? Do you have a date set? We want the dirt." Charmaine cackled with delight. Mona actually agreed with her this time.

"I'm not answering your first question, you nasty wench. As for your other question, well, the wedding's going to be in Catalina . . . in three months."

"Oh," they answered in stereo, caught off guard with the announcement. Mona and I exchanged looks that spoke of our conversation at her condo that Friday night.

"Whew. All this work." I sighed in an effort to change the subject.

"C'mon, Charmaine. Let Glover catch her breath. We'll holler at you later, girl," Mona said, letting me off the hook for now.

The rest of the day was less than peachy. Mr. Marx, the office supervisor, was on the warpath with us being understaffed. In addition to playing catch-up on my own desk, I was expected to fill in wherever needed. That, combined with the jet lag, did not make for a happy Glover.

Yep, a lot of shit on my mind.

Lionel called me from his office to see if I was up for lunch. I took a raincheck, needing to clear my desk as well as my head. Besides, we had a lifetime ahead of us. In a futile attempt to catch up, I decided to work through lunch. Charmaine and Mona, having no such notions, trekked off to do some shopping.

Lunch came and went in a blur. I was deep into my work while simultaneously lost in thought.

Did I love Lionel?

What's an extra stapler doing on my desk? Who's been sitting here?

Did I really love him?

These files don't belong here. But where do they belong?

He never gave me any reason to doubt his love, so what was wrong with me?

Now, why couldn't somebody return this call? That is pure lazy.

I guess I had issues.

"Excuse me!" he yelled as I stormed past the front of the office. Somebody had come in from off the street.

Damn.

I didn't work the front and wasn't up for the grief that came with it. I slowed down, considering whether I should keep on walking to the other side of the office. He didn't *really* see me anyway. I moved too fast when I got wound up.

That wasn't my style, though. I broke off from the direction I was heading and approached the front counter.

The voice belonged to one pretty good-looking brother. He was medium brown, not as tall as Lionel, but with some little bulges beneath his white dress shirt. I wondered briefly about another bulge that might lurk in his navy blue slacks.

Briefly.

He looked like he'd had a rough day at the office. Believe me, I felt him on that. I felt his tired eyes all over me as I approached, but he had something different in his accompanying earnest smile. Seemed a little less "wolflike" than most men, if there is such a thing these days.

Strangely, it reminded me of the first encounter with Lionel.

"Can I help you?"

"Um, hi. I need an application." He seemed a tad slow, and I had work to do.

"For . . . ?"

He told me he was looking for the state employment applications. I apologized for not knowing where things were and explained about our being short-staffed and stuff. I really don't know why I volunteered all that info. I found the application and handed it to him, reminding him of the Friday deadline and options for online filing.

"Oh, don't worry. I won't forget. I need the work," he replied with that smile. He laughed, but it didn't hide the exhaustion behind it. Poor thing.

"Well, I hope you find the work you're looking for," gushed from my mouth before my mind caught up. Why did I say that? My intention was to just be courteous, but it came out playful, almost kittenish. His facial expression didn't change, so I was relieved I hadn't embarrassed myself.

Unless that was his poker face.

"Later," he said as he took the application from my hand and departed. My eyes went to lock in on his ass, but his shirt had come out of his pants in the back, blocking the view of his bum. I lingered at the counter for a second more for less than noble reasons. I was grinning—until I looked down at the weight on my hand.

And on my soul.

Time to be a big girl again, as reality kicked in. He did have a nice smile, though, and I appreciated the brief escape from my issues, but it was time to finish the task I was doing prior to "smiley" interrupting me.

I moved on to the back, taking one last peek before he made it out the door.

Hmm. I never got his name.

Good.

18

Max

An entire day passed and the woman from the employment office was still on my mind. Still. I never got her name. That was good . . . I guess.

Last night, she was washing my Corolla in a T-shirt and thong. Everything was in black and white. Suds and ass everywhere. Then she blew bubbles at me.

In slow motion.

I'd been watching too many videos.

I considered telling Smitty about her, but felt pretty immature about the whole thing. Smitty would have either laughed his ass off or gone inside the place for a look-see. No, he probably would've done both.

But enough with the distractions. I needed to finish the application before tomorrow, and there was no time like the present. I walked over to my iPod boombox and found tracks by Vassy.

Nothing like the smooth vibe of "Loverman" and imagining she was singing seductively to me, to spirit me away from all my concerns and cares. I found a pen and plopped down on the couch, grooving to the song.

Might as well start at the beginning, with my last name.

Guillory. G . . . U . . .

My cell rang, breaking my concentration. So much for being free from distractions.

I didn't recognize the number, but hit the TALK button.

"Hello?"

"Hi. Max?" It was a female voice that I couldn't place. Maybe a call from one of the companies I'd visited. I flew off the couch to turn down the stereo.

"Yeah—I mean yes, this is he."

"It's Velina. How are you?" I heard the smile in her voice, although it was a nervous one.

"Fine. I'm fine," I replied, regaining my cool. "And you?" I plopped back down and rested the phone on my shoulder, determined to complete my application and return it today.

"I'm okay, Max. You know, I've been thinking about you. I was wondering if you were going to call. Probably not, huh?"

"I was planning on calling you. For real. I've just been busy with work and all." I don't *think*

I'd told a lie. That night, while fun, was whatever it was. No hopes, no promises.

"I see. I thought maybe we could see each other. Talk some more. I like talking to you. You're a very nice man."

I'd reached the line on the application to check off "married" or "single." I began thinking about the ring on the employment lady's finger.

Never got her name.

Not good.

"Max? Are you listening?"

"Yeah . . . I'm sorry. I'm trying to fill out something. That's all."

"Sooo?" she stressed, the Romanian accent asserting itself. I must have missed something she said. Uh-oh.

"So?"

"So, can we see each other tonight?" Damn. I'd missed that completely.

"Tonight's bad, Velina," I replied. "I'm about to head out the door. Not sure what time I'll be back. Raincheck?"

"Raincheck?" she said, her mind processing the slang. "Yes. Raincheck would be good, Max." I was the last person who needed to be giving out nookie rainchecks.

"All right. I'll call you. Maybe we can catch up this weekend or something?"

"Yeah. That'd be nice," she answered, as all enthusiasm was gone with the wind. "Take care, Max."

"You too."

Grabbing my keys, I ran out the door with the application, realizing how absurd I was to move Velina to the left for a fascination with an engaged stranger. I immediately returned to grab my resume before exiting a final time. The Santa Monica Freeway awaited.

I made it downtown without getting pulled over by five-oh. The employment office was bustling with activity this time. I guess everybody was showing up at the last minute.

No blur in sight.

Another sister at the front counter. Good looking as well.

Did they grow them in here?

I waited nervously in line, feeling like I was back in high school and waiting for my prom date to come down the stairs. I moved up to the counter.

"May I help you?" Her words rolled out so crisply. Damn, they put a polished sister up in here.

"Yeah," I said as I looked beyond her, hoping for a glance. "I'm dropping off the application for the state job openings. I wanted to make it in before tomorrow."

"Okay. Do you have a resume also?"

"Right underneath," I pointed out while still looking other places.

"All right. Do you need anything else?" She looked at me suspiciously. I hope she didn't think I was a crazy or something.

"No, that's it. Thank you."

I pushed off from the counter and walked away, cursing to myself for being so silly.

19

Glover

My alarm went off Friday morning. Always interrupting me from my fantasy, except this time I was close to making out his face. Perhaps the fact that it was definitely not Lionel was a harbinger of things to come.

I had to be at work in an hour, so I didn't have time to dwell on it. I threw my T-shirt in the dirty clothes hamper, donned my shower cap, and then jumped in the shower.

I stood there under the spray with my eyes closed. Water rolling down my body as steam clung to the air around me. Trying to wake up yet still dazed, until a sharp whoosh of cold air hit me. Goosebumps mounted. Then I felt them.

A pair of hands came up slowly from behind me and grasped my hips. I knew I had to be to work, but this . . .

Mmm. What was I saying?

I didn't open my eyes for fear of it disappearing. Maybe the dream hadn't ended. The hands . . . his hands slowly worked across my stomach then headed upward, tiny circular motions along the way. At last, they caressed my breasts as I bit my bottom lip. The water splashed me on the outside. His hands then plunged deep between my legs. My own splashing had begun in earnest. As I felt fingers enter me, all I could think of was a face.

And a smile.

From behind me, a deep voice whispered, "Forgot about me?"

I spun around in shock to see Lionel's face. He was right. I'd let him stay the night and had forgotten him in bed. I really was in the shower.

And this was real. No dream.

After insisting that I drive myself over Lionel's objections, I made it to work a little bit late. Mr. Marx had put Mona working the front until our personnel problems were solved. Charmaine was still bitching when I came in. My mind was still focused on the guilt I felt over fantasizing about a stranger while forgetting my fiancé was there.

"G-love, I'm gonna plant my foot in that white motherfucker's ass," she said, blissfully unaware of where my mind was at.

"Charmaine, you're white. You could just say 'motherfucker,' y'know," I offered, not having the time for this.

"Oh, hush. You know what I mean. Mr. Marx told Mona that she was gonna be up front for a whole week. A whole week! Now, does that make any motherfuckin' sense?"

"Whoa. I need to get started at my desk, and you need to go easy on the caffeine. The DMV has a few openings, and I have to get to work on these files, so I'll see you later," I said as I eased away.

"You do that, girl. I'm not bustin' my ass for anyone today. It's Friday and I just got paid. Direct deposit is a blessing, but too bad I already spent it." With that said, Charmaine marched off with a smile, having lifted her own spirits.

I sat down at my desk, poring over files of potential hires to pass on to the DMV. Then a stray thought hit me. I left and walked up front. Mona must have taken a break. I went over to the application bins. Embarrassed, I glanced around then ducked behind the counter, where I rifled through the most recent state employment applications. They were date-stamped prior to being entered and scanned into the system, so it was easy to go through the recent ones. For all I knew, the particular one I was looking for may not even have been turned in—and I didn't have a name to go on. I was busted when someone behind me spoke.

"Looking for something, Ms. McDaniel?" Mona stood over me accusingly, even though she hadn't a clue. She liked making people uncomfortable, and I was easy pickings right now. Hell, I was probably blushing.

"No big deal," I replied as I managed to keep a straight face with my hand in the cookie jar. "Just looking over the apps for those state jobs."

"Oh, yeah. Today's the last day. I hope they're finished bringing them in because I have to send them off to Sacramento later on. We got some online, but people really started pouring in yesterday with the paper apps. Including this cute brother."

"*Oh?*" My eyebrow rose. "I'm surprised you didn't try to make him your newest slave. What was wrong with him? Too short? Gold tooth?"

"No. Other than that whole 'broke college student' vibe, there was nothing wrong with him physically. Around six foot, tight little bod 'n stuff. Nice smile too. Just the nervous sort. Kept looking around like he was casing the place or something."

"Oh, I see. Nice smile, huh?"

Bingo.

20

Max

I went by Del Amo Mall Friday. Something I had to do, I suppose. I'd gone by Denny's to check the work schedule and found out I was working the weekend. Samir took care of a brother, but he had to put me on the weekend schedule sometimes. Besides, it would keep me out of trouble. Nothing like good, hard work to clear a man's head. I drove across the street, spotting Jay's Beamer in the mall parking lot. He must have opened the store this morning.

We hadn't spoken since the night at El Ami, and my weak ass was beginning to feel bad. I didn't agree with what Jay did, but I didn't want to let stuff end on that note.

He was blood. My mom had taught me the importance of your peoples. I bopped on by the food court and took the escalator up to level two, where TruMale was located on the left.

There were a few customers browsing the racks and one at the register, but no Jay in sight. He was either in back or on break. I decided to hang for a second, digging through shirts on the sale rack. I had found a nice extra-large when I heard Jay's voice. He was at the register, now ringing up the customer I'd seen before. Jay had to have seen me when he returned, but he wore his "work face," all about getting that upsale, whether it be a pair of socks, a tie, or an extra shirt. I waited for him to finish the transaction before approaching the counter.

"Whaddup, cuz?"

"Whaddup with you, Country?" His intention was to bother me, but it wouldn't work this time.

"Nothing. I was on this end checking my schedule and saw your ride. You stayin' outta trouble?" Stupid question on my part, but it helped to break the tension between us.

Jay smirked and shot back, "You ever gonna get in any trouble, Country? Man, I'm ashamed to call you my cousin sometimes. That was some foul shit, nigga."

"Foul? How was I foul? You were the one up there lying 'n shit. Then you—" I paused, as I was starting to talk loud and there were still customers in the store. "Then you tried to ditch Smitty. You know that was cold, man."

"All right. All right. You got me there. I had no choice, though. I mean, you saw how they looked. What was I supposed to do, leave that ass for someone else? Cuz, you should have been there," said Jay with a big grin that told everything as he stroked his goatee with pride.

I stopped my imagination, as I didn't need to be thinking about the three of them doing it big at the W—and my lonely ass standing outside El Ami.

Jay tensed in the middle of his bragging. New customers had entered the store, but they weren't shopping. Four dudes, either bangers or affiliated, laughed among themselves while throwing hard glares at Jay. The gang situation out here was one of the things to which I'd never adjust. Call me simple, but Blacks and Latinos killing one another over territory or colors just didn't make sense.

"You know them?"

"Nah, I don't pay that shit no mind. I probably know their women, though."

"Man, you're crazy. I wouldn't fuck around with that if I were you."

"Hey, may I help you?" he asked aloud of the four, challenging them to buy something or leave. Their joking ended. For a tense moment or two, I thought something was about to pop off.

Acting as if they hadn't heard him, they simply started up with the jokes again and walked back out. No eye contact or acknowledgment. As if they knew it would fuck with Jay worse.

"That was something," I offered as the situation defused.

"They'll be back."

"You ever thought about it?"

"What? Joining a gang? Shit, Pops would've stomped a hole in me if my momma didn't. Lucy don't play that. She's real O.G."

"Whatever, cuz. Hey, look, I'm gonna run. I gotta go home and get some sleep. You be careful, okay?"

"Always, cousin. Always," said Jay with a laugh, strolling over to assist a customer.

A female customer.

Jay would always be Jay.

On the way home, I passed up my place when I realized I was riding on "E," and filled up at the Union 76 just up the street. The gas prices out here were murder. I grabbed a turkey sandwich from inside, which I ate on the drive back to the apartment.

After I returned, I headed straight for the bedroom to catch some Zs. I threw my clothes on the chair and clicked on the nineteen-inch on my dresser. I sprawled across the bed while watch-

ing *The Price Is Right* crowd scream for someone to bid higher on a vacation package. I clicked
the TV off just as I prepared to go unconscious,
and turned on my side.

Then I saw it, a flicker of light from my answering machine, just as my eyes closed. I suddenly
reopened them. I was going to let the message
keep until after my nap, but decided against it. It
might be something important. Besides, I didn't
know how long it had been blinking. I pushed the
button and waited for the machine to play.

It was a woman's voice.

"Ummm, this is the California Employment
Development Department downtown. I am calling for Mr. Maxwell Guillory. You completed an
application recently for one of the state openings. I know you may not be interested in this,
based on your qualifications, but the DMV has
some openings to fill as well. Please call if you
would be available to come by our office on First
Street this Monday around eleven A.M. for a pre-
screening interview."

21

Glover

I was pulling some stupid, crazy shit, and spent all weekend trying to talk myself out of it. It didn't work. Friday, I went through the applications that had been dropped off the day before. I found three applications that matched what I was looking for. Mona had no idea that she'd helped me out with this.

Monday was the day. I showed up to work wearing my royal blue three-piece skirt set. Of the three applications I pulled, two of them agreed to come in for the DMV "prescreening interview." I hadn't heard from the third. The interview was a half-truth anyway. With my job, I had the authority to do some interviewing for the DMV openings, but never actually had. I usually reviewed the files of registered job seekers, forwarding those that might be compatible with the employer's needs. The applications that I pulled and reviewed were for people seeking higher paying state jobs. I didn't want to block that, so I just made copies of the two applications. Even though my intentions were less than noble, I did plan on forwarding my pre-screening results to the DMV.

My first interview was set up for 10:00 A.M. I had cleared my desk and told Mona that I was expecting some interviewees. Mona had replied with a "Huh?" followed up by her more traditional "Whatever."

She was still less than enthusiastic about working the front, but did come get me when the ten o'clock showed. The first interviewee was a twenty-four-year-old brother. He wore twists in his head and was polite as hell. He wasn't the person I was looking for, but I thought he would be a great hire based on his interview.

While I interviewed him, I could see Charmaine making faces at me behind his back. She couldn't wait to run up when I was finished.

"Girl, what in the *hell* are you doing?"

I playfully replied, "I don't know what you're talking about."

"First your ass shows up here dressed all professional, then you're holding interviews? Girl, you *are* up to somethin'. You *are* gonna fill me in, right?"

"I'm not sure myself, and you're probably better off not knowing. Can't I just be doing my job?"

Charmaine shot back, "Bitch, *please*."

Mona walked up and interjected, "Ms. Mc-Daniel, your *next* interview is here." Mona then dropped one of those looks on me. Her eyes told me that she had a better understanding of what had gone down Friday than she let on. She was still in the dark, but could see the light under the door. She felt played, but wasn't sure how.

I walked out to greet the final interviewee then escorted him back to my desk past a suspicious Mona. After I offered him a seat at my desk, we began to get into the interview.

"I'm glad you received my message last Friday. I've reviewed your state application, but why don't you tell me some more about yourself . . . Mr. Nelson."

Number two was another good candidate, and I was going to forward his information as well.

Two good candidates.

Maybe that was some consolation for making a fool of myself and trying to scheme. For someone normally confident and in control, I had been doing some stupid shit as of late. Here I was, engaged to be married but trying to create a "situation" to meet the brother with the nice smile from last Tuesday. Serves me right that neither of the two interviewees was him. I wasn't even positive he had returned his application.

While finishing my interview with number two, Charmaine and Mona had gone on to lunch without me. My odd behavior was probably their hot topic.

I felt foolish and dejected as I threw my purse on my shoulder. I decided to do lunch at the little diner across the street that had great specials, needing the walk to clear my head. I punched out, dragging my feet as I headed for the front door. I was frowning at a scuffmark on one of my pumps and didn't see the door swinging open.

Bang!

I bumped heads with someone, catching a glimpse of a gray pant leg and black loafers in the instant before it happened.

"I'm sorry, ma'am! Are you okay?"

"I'm fine. I'm—"

It was him. The smile was there, and the eyes didn't seem tired this time. He wore a gray suit, looking all *GQ*ed and debonair.

"I got a call Friday for an interview and I know I'm running late. Is Ms. McDaniel here?"

"That would be me. I'm the one who called. You must be number thr—" I caught myself. "I mean you must be Mr. Guillory." His was the application that I hadn't heard from.

"Right. Call me Max," he said, sticking out his hand to shake mine. I reciprocated, holding his hand a little longer than usual. He was smiling as much as I was.

"I'm going to lunch right now. Care to join me, Max?" I asked, feeling wonderfully reckless and free for a change. Now I anxiously awaited his answer after putting it out there.

"Okay," he answered.

Hallelujah.

"It's the least I could do, since I ran into you, Ms. . . ."

"Glover. Call me Glover," I answered for him, suspecting our lunch conversation would be a lot less formal than our appearances.

22

Max

I'd tried calling the employment office once I got over the shock of my message. I was too late. It was closed for the day. The DMV wasn't what I had in mind, but I couldn't be too choosy. I worked the weekend at Denny's, so I was to call the employment office first thing Monday morning. Thing is, I hadn't looked at Monday's schedule. Just my luck, I was scheduled for that morning. Samir, being the man, agreed to let me off early so I could make it downtown in time.

Now I sat at lunch with the blur, who had finally slowed enough for me to fully appreciate her.

Her name was Glover and she looked as beautiful as ever. Too bad she was taken. Too bad for me and good for whomever the buster was.

Still mindful of my budget, I ordered a grilled cheese and fries, while she had the soup and salad.

"Again, I'm sorry about running into you. I knew I was late, so I was rushing. I'm still new here, so I'm afraid to try shortcuts when traffic backs up."

"New? New to L.A. or new to California altogether?"

"New to California. I'm from Louisiana. Do you have any people from there?" I asked, wanting to know more.

"No. Most of my family is from Virginia, around Arlington and Fredericksburg. Me and my mother moved here when I was a kid . . . before she passed away. Why'd you ask about Louisiana?"

"No reason really. You resemble a lot of people from there," I answered, realizing that the perceived familiarity may have been what attracted me to her initially. "You have lovely eyes. What are they? Light brown? Hazel?"

"Whatever you want to call them, Max," she replied, those lovely lips of hers curling into the perfect smile. She reached over and helped herself to one of my fries, but the sight of that ring on her hand brought me back down to Earth. We hadn't discussed any business yet.

"I called this morning to let you know I was coming in, but the girl who answered didn't know what I was talking about."

"That doesn't surprise me. I should have left my direct number for you. You're looking good today," she said, admiring my suit. My best one.

"You mean compared to the other day when you saw me," I teased. "I was a little rough then. I'd been all over downtown that day and was worn out."

"Trust me, you were fine that day," Glover stated playfully as she adjusted herself in her seat. Made it hard for me to focus on my purpose here. "Tell me, would you really be interested in one of the openings at the DMV?"

"Real talk?"

She laughed at my slang, making me self-conscious. Even if she were on the market, maybe she was too sophisticated for me.

If.

"Yes, real talk," she answered.

"To tell you the truth, I'm hoping for more money than probably what they're offering, but you have to start somewhere. What made you call me?"

"What made you come down here for the interview?" she shot back. Glover seemed rattled for a second, hesitating as if avoiding my question. Women sure could be hard to read, and this one was no different.

"Ms. Glover doesn't want to answer my question, huh? What happened to 'real talk'?" I teased, feeling more comfortable around her.

"No, it's not that! It . . . it's just that I'm the one who's supposed to be asking the questions here. That's all." Her playfulness shown, I was really feeling her. And I think she knew it.

"Okay. I apologize. Can I ask one more question, ma'am?"

"Oh my, such a gentleman. Yes, you may, sir," she replied, enjoying the game as much as I was.

"How did you get your name? A girl named Glover. It's different."

"Yeah, it is different. I was named after my great-grandmother. And to correct you, that's a woman named Glover," she chided. I nodded my understanding while lost in her eyes. "Max, is there a special someone in your life out here . . . or in Louisiana?"

I swallowed hard, shocked by such a personal question coming from her.

If I didn't know better . . .

There I went with such foolish thoughts.

"No, nothing here. Just going through the motions right now. And the last serious thing ended a long time ago back home. We all can't be as lucky as you," I said, eyeing that sparkling rock again. Seemed the lovely lady in front of me offered no change in my luck nor a cure for my past hurt.

"Oh. Okay," she said, smiling even though it was apparent I'd bothered her with that remark. Not quite sure, but maybe the ring was a front to keep the wolves at bay. Was I having lunch with a player?

More importantly, was I playing myself?

"By the way, you owe me for that fry you took."

"Maybe I'll have the chance to return the favor in the future." Our eyes met and I knew I was playing a dangerous game.

"Just make sure the fries are hot. I hate cold fries."

"How about frozen? Or maybe just warm. That's okay?" she clowned, making her eyes cross.

"Are you usually this silly?"

"No, I have you to thank for that. Thanks."

"For what?"

"Just for being here. I know the only reason we're sitting here is because of the interview, but you've really helped me forget about some things that are going on right now. So I just want to say thank you." I watched her lips in slow motion.

"Things are going that bad right now?" I inquired, wondering if I was just a timely distraction as she'd stated, or if maybe there was more to her call. Like maybe she felt that spark too.

"No, just complicated. You're someone without a vested interest, so it's easier for me to say it to you. That's all."

I knew not to push the subject. If she wanted to open up, she would do so on her own. I sat back in my chair, easing up on the moment. Odd that we never got around to what I would consider real interview questions. I'd heard of business deals done over a round of golf, but this didn't fit that. I may have been a little bit *country,* as Jay would call it, but I don't think things are this different in California.

"What do I do now? About the opening," I clarified. "Do you need me to go back to the office and sign something?"

"No. I'll forward your info to the DMV; then it'll be up to them. Your application for the state jobs was put in the system and sent off to Sacramento last week. And that's it," she said with a sigh. It was like she didn't want lunch to end. Our plates already cleared, I put the money on the table.

"Well, at least let me walk you back to your office."

As Glover walked ahead, I surveyed the curve of her hips through the tight blue skirt she wore. I wondered how it would have felt to the touch.

We walked back across the street, stopping in front of her office. The look she gave told me this was it. No following her inside. This was the place to say good-bye.

Finality.

Both of us smiled, standing there, absent words.

"Thank you," she finally said. I wanted to silence her again, take this stranger in my arms and feel those lips, but instead I gave her a polite, professional handshake.

"Sorry about your mother," I offered oddly.

"Huh?"

"You mentioned your mother passing away."

"I did, didn't I? Well, thank you. Again." Confusion had overcome her, but the smile was genuine.

She disappeared through the door and was gone like a blur—again.

23

Glover

I did everything I could to keep myself busy. Anything to keep Max off my mind. I was spending Saturday with Lionel, so the ladies decided on a sleepover Friday night. We held it at my apartment this time, since the last few were either at Mona's or Charmaine's.

Charmaine brought the drinks, Mona brought the movies and music, and I cooked the dinner. I'd brought some of my secret baked chicken to work one day, and they had been bothering me ever since. I bought the fresh chicken and left it marinating Thursday night, just like my mom had taught me. I'd learned the recipe while standing at her side as a little girl and had committed it to memory. People loved my version, although it could never touch hers. I cheated with the store-bought potato salad, but did toss a fresh green salad with a raspberry vinaigrette dressing.

Mona showed up in jeans and a T-shirt, with her shades atop her head. Her overnight bag dangled over her shoulder as she held the DVD and CD selections. She went straight to work on the entertainment, putting on some Keyshia Cole while setting the movies atop the TV for later. Charmaine, in her jogging suit, banged on the door less than five minutes later. After putting the drink mix and alcohol down, she helped Mona set the table. With the chicken fresh out of the oven, we barely allowed it to cool before getting our grub on.

The three of us waddled to the living room on full stomachs. Charmaine stopped for a second, letting out a tiny belch that was followed by a giggle and an "excuse me." After that display, she staked out the couch as her territory. Mona and I sprawled out across the Persian rug I'd picked up from the swap meet.

"Mona, what movies did you rent?"

"Why?" Mona answered, feigning innocence.

"Aw, shit. She done gone and rented *Mahogany* again," Charmaine screamed.

"Mona," I dared, "tell me you didn't rent that again."

"What's wrong with *Mahogany*, y'all?"

Charmaine answered, "Nothing, if you like watching that shit again—"

"And again!" I chimed in. "Okay, Mona. We gotta watch something else tonight. It's fun to watch Billy Dee's radical, protestin' ass, but not tonight. Okay?"

Mona rolled her eyes then gave up. After that debate, I think we all needed some tension relief. I got up off the rug and went into the kitchen.

"Ready for drinks?" I called out. They didn't answer. I heard them as they whispered, but shrugged it off and made some chocolate martinis. As I carried them out, Mona and Charmaine grinned at me.

"Glover, we've been wondering," Charmaine began. "Do you plan on asking us to be in your wedding? It'll be here before you know it, and you haven't really brought it up. We noticed you've been kinda *distracted* at work . . . with interviews and all."

The two of them snickered, thick as thieves.

"What the fuck is so funny?"

"Nothing," Mona offered. "You just seem different since you came back from Miami. Like your mind is somewhere else."

"I'm going to be married in less than three months and you're wondering why I'm acting strange? Damn! Wouldn't you be?" I scolded, my defensiveness all too apparent as my voice rose.

"Easy, G-love. We're not tryin' to come at you like that. We just noticed the way you were acting the other day, when you were interviewing those dudes. That and how you never talk about the wedding and stuff. It seems almost like you don't want to be married. And that's your business too."

"Hey, if it is my business, then why are y'all all in it like that? What am I supposed to do, run around singing and shit?" I asked, lashing out at my friends. It was more a reflection of my frazzled and conflicted emotions than any real antipathy toward them.

Mona and Charmaine sat there, blinking and looking embarrassed. The room was silent as the CD player switched to another disc. Rafael Saadiq came on.

I knew exactly what they were getting at, but I didn't want to deal with it now. Embarrassed? Ashamed? Confused? I would agree to all those assessments of me.

Mona chose to break the silence. "Glover, there's no need to blow up like that. We were just worried about you. We didn't mean to upset you, girl."

"Yeah. Real talk," Charmaine said, reminding me of Max at the worst possible moment.

"I'm okay. Just under a lot of stress. And it was stupid of me to forget, so please forgive me. Will you guys be in my wedding? Please?"

Charmaine was the first, her answer rushing out of her mouth. "Hell yeah! You think we would pass up the chance to walk down the aisle with some of Lionel's friends? Sheeeeeeeeeeeeed!" We all laughed at her impression of Senator Clay Davis from *The Wire*.

"Charmaine, do you have something else in you besides white?" I asked, curious.

"Well, if you must know, my dad's Native American and my mom's Italian. I took my mom's last name, Fulda. My dad was never really around much."

"I know all about that, Charmaine," I remarked, with thoughts of a man too good to be true who got my mom to forsake her family. "My father skipped out when I was little. I couldn't even tell you where he is now. And here I thought you were just another crazy white girl from the Valley."

"Fuck you too, bitch," she said with a smile. "Now you know that I'm just a half-crazy white girl. Or would that be a crazy half-white girl? And watch that 'Valley' shit. You know I wasn't raised there."

"Okay, okay! A half-crazy white girl from Cren-shaw."

Mona was uncomfortable. Our talk about fathers bothered her. Unlike us, her father stayed in the picture. The problem was that Mona thought him an asshole as well, especially after he left her mom.

I broke the tension with, "So, are y'all gonna drink your martinis or what? It's the least you could do, since you're gonna be in my wedding and eating all my cake 'n shit. Now, give me some love."

After the big group hug, we moved on to other things, including watching Mona's other rental, a Will Smith movie that none of us minded in the least. As we wound down in the early morning hours, Charmaine snored loudly from under her blanket. Mona was in my bathroom putting on her night mask and pajamas, so I got up to bring the glasses into the kitchen. I stood there alone in the dark, placing items in the dishwasher, when I almost jumped out of my skin.

"We saw you the other day."

I jumped up, startled.

Mona.

She stood behind me in her silk pajamas, scaring the hell out of me. The glowing green shit on her face didn't help.

"Huh?" I asked, my pulse rate beginning to slow.

"Me and Charmaine saw you Monday. In front of the office with your friend. Wasn't that the cutie I told you about?"

Damn.

"Yeah," I answered calmly. "He was one of the interviews. He got there late." In spite of the darkened kitchen, I still avoided eye contact.

"Just be careful, Ms. McDaniel. All right?" Nothing else to say, Mona abruptly turned and walked off.

24

Max

"Ay! Ay, man! Open up!" Smitty banged on my door to no end. One day, his loud ass was going to get evicted and I'd be there to help him move. I wasn't doing much Friday afternoon. Just hanging in my boxers and not expecting any company.

Paradise to many.

I had barely opened the door when Smitty barged in. He wore a suit, so I knew what that meant.

"You got the job at West-tel, huh?"

"You damn right!" he exalted, brushing imaginary dirt off his shoulders. "Wallace Lewis is now gainfully employed. They even take care of my parking and shit. Damn, you still in your drawers?"

"They look good to me."

I spun around toward the voice I'd just heard, seeing an overly thick sister in my doorway. She had a lollipop in her mouth, looking at me as if I were her next piece of candy. She wore a white blouse with a pair of tight denim shorts. Her gold earrings dangled just below her brand new ebony weave. It was Zena, one of Smitty's jump-offs. She worked with him at Costco and must've given him a ride downtown. Removing myself off her dessert menu, I scurried off to my bedroom to put something on.

"Oh, don't put nothin' on, on my account. I'm just enjoying the view, Max." She laughed, husky like a smoker, as she closed my apartment door behind her.

"Hi, Zena," I said over my shoulder as I retreated.

Zena made herself comfortable, having never been inside my apartment. As I put on some clothes, I hoped she wasn't putting her feet up.

"You tryin' to make me jealous up in here?" Smitty asked of his woman.

"Smit, you know I'm just havin' a little fun with Max. You know he can't do nothin' for me, boo." From my room, I could hear the two of them sucking face or something. I decided to hurry up, lest they take it to another level on my furniture. Those two carried on like lovebirds when they were together, but both of them did their own thing when apart. I think they both liked it that way.

Smitty hollered, "Hurry up, Max. Put some clothes on your ass and shit. We're gonna get our celebration on."

I threw on a pair of jeans and my white Nike tee and laced up my black Airs. I could still hear Zena giggling in the living room while I tightened up my hair in the mirror and donned my watch. Fully clothed, I ran back out to join them.

"Where is this celebration supposed to take place?" I asked.

"Me and Zena were thinking about going by Hometown Buffet to celebrate. They got shrimp scampi on Fridays. Zena likes that, and I like the fried skrimps." I groaned before Smitty continued. "But Zena changed her mind," he said.

"Yeah, I want to go to Roscoe's instead, baby. We ain't been there in so long," Zena said as she licked her lips. She was through with her lollipop. I wondered what she did with the stick. She better not have dropped it in between my sofa cushions.

"I don't want to cramp your style 'n shit. Why don't you two go on?"

"Nah, you my boy. Besides, I wouldn't have the job if it weren't for you. You drove us down there that day, remember? C'mon. Zena's drivin'."

We drove up Venice Boulevard toward the Santa Monica Freeway in Zena's baby blue Impala rolling on twenties. She had the windows down, sunroof open, and her stereo blaring Day26. All eyes were on Zena as Smitty leaned over the armrest beside her. Marking his turf to any busters that might be watching, I suppose. Smitty still had his suit on, savoring the moment. I decided to enjoy the ride, watching the mini marts and residents as we drove by.

"We're going to the Roscoe's on Pico, right?" I asked over the music once I had my bearings.

"Starting to learn your way around, huh, Maxwell? Zena, you should have seen this fool when he first got out here. He had his little maps and shit and had to plot out everything before he turned his car on. Now he thinks he knows his way around here better than me."

Zena smiled at Smitty as she threw her lollipop stick out the window and fetched a new one from the center console in one smooth motion. How many of those did she have in there?

"Smit, have you told Costco yet?" I asked.

"Nah, I was thinking about just bouncing on them without word, but that would be unprofessional. I'm gonna put in my two weeks' notice."

"Yep, my baby's a professional now," Zena chimed in as she looked in the mirror to merge onto the freeway. "Hey, Max, did Smitty tell you about my sister, Niobi? She broke up with her old man last week."

"Oh." Here it comes. I knew something was up.

"Yeah. Anyway, she's lookin' for a new boo. She's a little bit smaller than me, but just as cute. I know you ain't gay, so I was thinkin' about bringing her with me next time I came over. You two would make a cute couple. I know you from down south and all, so you probably ain't used to sophisticated women like us. You probably used to them slower country girls back home," she proclaimed assuredly.

"Yeah. Sophisticated. It's been an adjustment."

Smitty didn't say a thing. He had quietly slid back over to his side and kept looking out his window. Admiring the view, my ass. He knew this was coming.

"Smitty, baby? Ain't y'all barbecuing next week?" Shit. He told her about that. I guessed it would hurt too much if I hurled myself out the car door now.

Smitty, acting surprised, replied, "Yeah, baby. We got a reason to 'cue now."

Mental note: kick Smitty's ass.

25

Glover

After learning my best friends had discovered me making a fool of myself, I still slept pretty well. It must have been the chocolate martinis that helped. Upon waking, I fixed a big breakfast for my girls before they headed out. Charmaine was going back to the Valley and Mona was off to Santa Monica. There wasn't a further mention from Mona after her revelation last night, sparing me further humiliation. That left me clear to go see my future husband, Lionel. Knowing that was just what I needed to help me make sense of my feelings, I wasted no time.

I took one last look at myself in the mirror as I drove through Lionel's gate. Just to think, I would be living here soon. As nice as it was, I remained uncomfortable on a certain level. Kind of like a stranger in a strange world, with all its accoutrements of money and status that I didn't particularly crave. Being married to a Dunning would bring a lot of stuff with it.

Before I had a chance to park, Lionel was at my door. Once I got out, he kissed me deeply, passionately. As if he needed me in order to live. At that moment, my silly fears diminished.

As our lips parted, I copped a feel on his ass.

"Nice to see it's still there," I joked. "I haven't grabbed it in a while."

"I missed you. Wish you were here last night, but I know you had plans with your girls and all. I need to be patient, though. We're going to be with each other every night soon enough."

"Yep. Just don't be expecting a home-cooked meal every night."

Lionel gave me a gentle elbow. "What's wrong with my woman cooking for me every night?"

"Nothing's wrong with it," I replied. "I'm just wondering what woman you're talking about."

"I see we're going to have to negotiate the terms of this marriage, huh?"

We walked inside through the kitchen, passing through the living room with its vaulted ceiling, before walking out back at poolside. Lionel had a table out there, and we sat, enjoying the refreshing breeze from the north. A small tree was providing perfect shade for us. A perfect day next to the perfect man. So why had doubt taken up so many of my thoughts?

Lionel went back inside and came out with a couple of Snapples. He knew that fruit punch was my favorite.

Stocking up for the Mrs. already.

He twisted the top open on my bottle. "My mother wants to know if you're available Wednesday. She's trying to put the plans together."

"I can make it after work I guess," I replied, dreading this part of the affair.

Lionel's expression changed for a second. Something on his mind. He sat next to me.

"You know you can leave your job at that place. I've told you that before. Answer me this: Do you plan on working there after we're married?"

"I'm not sure, baby," I said as I sipped my Snapple. "We'll see." I wasn't coo-coo for Cocoa Puffs over my job, but disliked the notion of being beholden to someone else for my well-being. There once was another man with everything that promised another woman the moon and stars. Now her daughter was in an eerily similar situation.

"I'm not going to push that. Lord knows it wouldn't help. You're just so damn independent, but that's one of the things I love about you."

"Are you coming with me by your mother's?"

He chuckled. "No, I know better. I plan on just showing up at the wedding looking good. I'll leave all the details to you women."

"You mean to your mother, don't you?"

"C'mon. I already talked to her about this. This is our wedding and she understands it. Totally. Y'know, you need to give her a chance, baby."

"Okay. You're right. I'll give her a chance. She is going to be my mother-in-law after all."

"Have you thought about moving in yet? I've got all this space, and it's so lonely over here."

"Buy a dog, baby. You know I want to wait."

"Well, we're *almost* there."

"Almost ain't the same. Once I'm living here, you'll probably be wishing for your single days. You know I've been eyeing your walk-in closet."

"That's cruel. Once we're married, I'll give you a view of it from a different angle."

"Are you being a nasty boy?"

"Me?" he replied, those pretty teeth of his showing.

"Yeah, you," I answered as we came together to kiss again.

26

Max

Zena left her Impala with Smitty the next day. Probably his reward for conspiring to hook me up with Niobi. Smitty had some health club guest passes that were about to expire, and we both had the day off. I needed to relieve some stress, and hitting the weights was the right idea. I could tell Smitty was allergic to working out just by looking at his scrawny ass. He wouldn't admit it, though. He just wanted to push Zena's whip in front of some honeys.

"Damn, boy. You're gonna put more weight on there?" he asked as I added some plates on the bench press. Having quit after ten minutes of struggling, he'd decided to be my spotter and protect me from injury. Yeah.

"Just a little bit more. You not getting tired, huh, Smit?"

"Nope. I just don't want you hurtin' yourself."

"Oh, okay. Hey, what's up with that Niobi shit? Wasn't cool, man."

"Aw, dawg. That was Zena's idea. Niobi saw you one day when she and Zena came by my crib. I'm not in this shit, bro. Honest. Now, if you and Niobi happen to hook up, then that's your business, bro. That loco motherfucker she was foolin' with got put in the County."

"And you want me messin' with his woman? I may be new out here, but I ain't stupid."

"Nah, man. He's gonna be gone for a long stretch. Plus I heard she's a freak," Smitty added with glee. I was about to lift the weight, but stopped.

"You did her, Smit?"

"Hell no! Zena would kick my ass—no, she'd bust a cap in my ass."

Two women walked past, breaking our train of thought.

"We're not gonna be able to hang like this anymore soon, man," I lamented.

"I'll be doing those banker's hours in a few weeks. You will be too soon. Just you wait. Heard anything yet?"

"Smit, remember that day downtown, when I went in the employment office?"

"Yeah."

"I met somebody there."

"She broke and unemployed too?"

"No, fool! She works there."

"That's what took your ass so long! You coulda came to get me, bro. Afraid I was gonna steal her from you, huh?"

"She's not mine to steal. Big ol' rock on her hand, all blingin' and shit."

"For real? Then why you still cryin' over her? Something else must have happened. Talk to me, dawg."

"Something else happened, but I'm not sure what. We had lunch, but it was supposed to be an interview. I never asked her about the ring. I figured it was none of my business. The problem is I can't stop thinking about her."

"You sound like you're sprung and you haven't even smelled it, let alone tapped it. What's she look like?"

"About this tall, light brown, light brown eyes, fine as all hell. Name's Glover."

"Glover? What the fuck kind of name is that?"

"Trust me. If you saw her, you wouldn't be complaining about the name."

Smitty worked up the courage to lift again. We traded places, with him hemming and hawing before sitting down. I stood over the bar after reducing the weight to something manageable for him. Or a sixth grader.

"How'd you guys wind up going to lunch? And why didn't you tell a brother?"

"She called me. Strangest shit. She pulled my app and called me about some jobs at the DMV."

"Maybe she wanted to give you a driving test, Maxwell," he joked in between straining to lift the weight bar.

"I would think it was maybe a coincidence, but I'm not sure. I get this vibe when I'm near her."

"That vibe's called a hard-on, fool. I get that vibe often around women. It's a reflex. Trust a player on that. Did you get the digits?"

"Nah, I don't even know if she's about that. Don't want to make a fool of myself. Everything could be about business. You know I need a job. I don't want to fuck anything up by playing the pimp hand. I leave that shit to you."

"Sounds to me like she's up to something, bro. Be careful you don't get played. Seriously."

"I won't, bro."

"Max?"

"Yeah, Smit?"

"Could you get this weight off me?"

27

Glover

Wednesday was here before I knew it. In spite of my promise to Lionel that I would go by his parents' house, I really didn't want to be bothered after combating rush hour traffic. A promise was a promise, though, so I kicked off my shoes and rested my eyes for five minutes before venturing back out the door.

Bel Air was only five miles away, but it was several dollars from my station in life. The view of the million-dollar homes (and their equally impressive gates) made for a scenic drive as I wound my little Civic through West Sunset Boulevard. While passing the intersection at Whittier, I recognized Mona's dad's car at the red light. I had forgotten he lived around here still. I caught a fleeting glimpse of him behind the wheel of his Bentley, with the new Mrs. Stevens seated beside him.

Damn. The woman looked to be about my age, maybe younger. He'd found his fountain of youth somewhere between those thighs. They had so much in common, I'm sure. Hope he was getting his money's worth.

Coming upon the ivory walls of the Dunning estate, I reflected on the beautiful Mediterranean design. Lionel told me the estate had been built in the 1930s. For as big as it was, it had an understated elegance about it. Lionel's parents bought the place about ten years ago when they moved from Ladera Heights. Lionel's father was a prominent attorney in L.A. who had recently retired, and his mother, Adele, was one of those society types who loved having her name in print. The fact that Lionel was marrying me had to be killing her, but she was one to honor her son's wishes.

Usually.

The gate opened for me when I pulled up. I assumed somebody was watching my car on some security monitor. I drove around the half-circle, careful not to scratch the Mercedes, and parked by the water fountain. I'd really wanted to change into some sweats after work, but stayed in my work attire. No need to give Adele any ammunition.

The demure Spanish woman greeted me at the door then walked me through the foyer, past the double spiral staircase. A canvas portrait of the Dunning family rested on the wall above the left stairwell. I glanced at it, wondering sarcastically if they were planning on having another painting done to add me above the right stairwell.

We continued toward the back of the first floor, proceeding down a hall. The light disoriented me as we flowed into an enormous open room lined by an entire wall of glass. The sun poured in from all around, glistening off the marble floor on which I stood. It was beginning to set, but it seemed as if it were midday in here. The glass wall looked out onto a palm tree—lined pool below. The room was almost bare, save for an antique table and a few chairs, but it was large enough to host a ball.

Lionel's mother stood with her back to us, surveying the grounds. There was a reason she'd picked this location to receive me. This was Adele's turf, and she wanted to let me know it. A grand scale, and I was just a little pebble in her eyes.

A pebble that happened to be marrying her dear son, though.

"Aw, Glover," Adele said, turning as if startled by my arrival. "How are you, my dear?" Adele was a dead ringer for Eartha Kitt, but wore her hair in a short salt-and-pepper afro. She stood before me in an embroidered, multi-colored tunic, with gold sandals. We walked toward one another, giving a gentle embrace followed by the customary kiss on the cheek.

Adele held my face in her hands and stared at me with an adoring smile.

"I'm glad you made it." She then turned briefly to my escort and said, "That will be all, Iris." With that, Iris smiled and disappeared back up the hallway from whence she came.

"How are you, Mrs. Dunning?"

"I'm fine, Glover. Please, call me Mother, or at least Adele. I hope you will come to think of me as that over time. I know I could never replace your dearly departed mother, and I would never presume otherwise. I just want you to know that I am here for you."

"Thank you," I said, internalizing the urge to bristle at her mention of my mom. Adele was right, though. She could never replace her. "How is Mr. Dunning?" I asked, referring to the more pleasant of the two.

"He's doing very well, Glover. He's somewhere on the property, probably outside looking to change the landscaping. He's always trying to stay busy since retiring. Come over here. I have some ideas to run by you." Adele led me to the antique table.

"I have a couple of sample menus from the caterers, as well as some wedding dress samples. We're going to need to get you fitted. You're a size fourteen, right?"

"Uh, no. I'm a size ten." *Bitch*.

"Oh, I'm sorry. I was close, though. Do you like Vera Wang's designs, or Escada? I see a lot of that these days."

"I *love* Vera Wang. I just wish I could afford her stuff."

"Nonsense, child. Vera Wang it is. When do you want to be fitted? We don't have time to waste, and I'm already going to pay extra due to the late notice."

"I don't know. As soon as possible, I guess. Do you have to call the store?"

"Store?" she repeated, petrified. "No, dear. I'm going to call Vera. Your dress is going to be an original. I can't have my son's bride in anything less." Adele let out a chuckle over my amateur moment.

"That's okay. Really. A store-bought dress is expensive enough, but an original? I can't pay that kind of money back. "

Adele ignored me and continued, "I'll need a list of guests for the invitations. We'll also need

to get your bridesmaids and matron of honor
fitted. I have two locations on standby down in
Catalina. Are you positive about getting married
there? There are some really beautiful sites up
the coast, and Catalina is so, so . . . I don't know."

"I'm sure about Catalina, Mrs. Dunning. If you
don't like the location, then don't worry about
it. I can take care of it by myself," I said, waving
my arms as was my tendency when irritated. I
tensed, prepared to back away from the table we
were standing at and leave if this suddenly went
south.

"No, dear. I don't have any problems with your
choice," she said, not changing her stance in the
least. "I'm just trying to help you explore your options. That's all. Tell me, do you like paté?"

We explored my "options" for another hour.
I had to be to work in the morning, so I used
that excuse to end the agony. I dreaded having to come back, but put off that thought as I
sped away. I'd left my cell phone on the seat,
and picked it up to call Lionel, sure he'd want to
know how I made out with his mother.

I'd pressed the MENU button, finding his number, when I came to a red light. I stared into the
light for a few seconds before hitting the CLEAR
button. I then reached into my purse for a folded
piece of paper and started dialing again.

"Hello?"

"Did I wake you up?"

"Um, nah," he said, lying through his teeth. "What's up?"

"What are you doing tomorrow?"

"Nothing."

"How about dinner this time? On me."

28

Max

Late at night, the call surprised me. I was more surprised by the voice on the other end—and the invitation.

She trusted me in her apartment. Her private space.

I was scheduled to work that night, since Samir had taken me off the weekend schedule for our barbecue. But I begged and pleaded my way off, as I couldn't pass up the opportunity to see Glover again. I owed Samir my first born for this one.

When she gave me directions, I discovered she lived on the same end of town. When I first moved out here, I'd even considered moving into the same apartments where she stayed. Delicious irony, it would've been. They were just a bit pricier than what I had in mind. In spite of my familiarity, her directions were perfect anyway.

On the way there, I picked up a bottle of Zinfandel and a single yellow rose from the Albertsons on South Sepulveda. That was after I got a haircut that I really didn't need. Wasn't sure what to expect, but I felt the overwhelming need to look my best.

When the door opened, I realized my decision was the right one. I stood there in the hall and checked out Glover. She wore a yellow top and black pants, with black slip-on sandals. By her shoulder, I could see a glimpse of her black bra strap. A small gold chain draped her neck, just below that pretty face of hers. Her lips were covered in gloss that I was dying to sample—right off them, of course.

"Are you going to come in, or are you going to just stand there staring?" she asked, leaning against the open door. Her smile told me I amused her.

"Both options seem pretty good, but I think I'll come in." I strolled past Glover, stealing a glance at her backside as she closed the door. The snugness of her pants made it easy. She wore a thong.

Damn.

When she turned to welcome me officially, I leaned in, giving her a short, platonic hug and kiss on the cheek, still in the dark as to what she was expecting. I caught a whiff of her perfume as

I pulled back. Made me want to camp out on her neck, wake up to her. Women placed that shit in all the right places to drive a brother crazy.

"Welcome to *mi casa*, Señor Guillory. No problem with my directions, right?"

"None whatsoever. Oh, this is for you," I said, handing the yellow rose to her. I hadn't planned on it matching her outfit, but hey.

"That's so sweet! Thank you." She came closer and placed her right hand over my shoulder, where it came to rest around the base of my neck. Slowly, gracefully, she pulled herself into me, planting a soft kiss on my cheek. Her lips lingered there for a moment before she returned to her own space. My heart begged her to stay, made me want to pull another flower out of thin air just so we could repeat it.

"You brought wine too? Let me take that." She sashayed into her kitchen with the bottle in hand. "Make yourself comfortable. Dinner will be ready in a minute."

"Can I take my shoes off then?"

She chuckled. "Sure. Just don't funk up my apartment."

As I sat, I noticed some pictures by her television set. One of the photos was of Glover as a child at the beach. She was with a woman whom I presumed was her mother. Another was Glover in a graduation gown. The same woman was with her in the photo.

"Is this your mother in these photos?"

"Yeah, that's my mommy." You could hear the light that entered her voice. "Those are some of my happy times."

"You were cute in your little swimsuit. The other picture is of your high school graduation?"

"Yep. That was the last picture of my mother . . . before she passed away. We were like best friends."

"Hearing you say that makes me think about my momma. We're close, but it kinda makes you think. I guess we take tomorrow for granted sometimes."

"Tomorrow's never promised, Max," she offered, emerging from the kitchen with plates in hand. "Food's ready. I hope you like pasta. You can put on some music while you're over there."

I found one of Glover's light jazz CDs and inserted it into the CD player. I liked her taste. Definitely a sophisticated lady, but still down to earth. Glover ran back in the kitchen to wrestle with the bottle opener and the Zinfandel.

"You got it?"

"Of course. Just have a seat," she replied while obviously struggling. I liked her toughness.

She'd gone to great lengths to prepare the meal—fresh salad, fettuccini Alfredo with shrimp, and hot buttered garlic bread. I don't know if my wine was the right one for the dish, but she didn't complain. Over the small talk of dinner and watching one another from across the table, the bottle dwindled down quickly. I regretted not picking up two, but it loosened me up enough to begin really speaking my mind.

"Glover, what's going on? Really. I see one thing, but I'm feeling another. Would you help a brother out?"

"All right, I'll come clean." I watched her set the wine glass down before her. Noticed her clench her napkin several times and release it as she sighed. "I intentionally pulled your application and called you. This is not the normal kind of thing I do, you understand. I'm acting completely out of character, because I'm usually straightforward."

"Be that way now," I pressed, figuring I had nothing to lose.

"Okay. I'll spell it out. I'm feeling you, but you know that already. I'm also engaged—to a wonderful man," she robotically added, as if obliged to say that. "It means we can never be anything more than friends. That's why I can't be straightforward. I barely know you, but I feel so at home when I'm around you. I should have been straight with you from the jump, instead of acting like a schemer. I'm sorry, Max." All of that seemed from the heart.

"No apologies needed. At least we've got that in the open," I said, finding it impossible to hide my deflated spirit. "What's his name?" I asked, being a glutton for further punishment. Did I really care who her fiancé was? Probably not.

"Lionel."

"Lionel must be something. He's got you and he's able to afford a ring like that. Yep, he's very lucky." I took my glass, guzzling down the remainder of my wine.

"Are you upset with me? You have every right to be. I would understand it if you never talked to me again."

"Okay, it's my turn to come clean. I saw the ring the first time I met you. I hoped it was just for show or to keep dudes off your back. You've been on my mind ever since I met you. At least now I know where we stand, and I can live with that. Hell, I don't have a choice really." I smiled because it was the only thing I could do. I wanted to demand that we have our interview now, list all my qualifications and why she should be with me, but that job was already filled by a *fuckin' Lionel*. She had stoked dormant fires in me, but I was crippled from acting on them.

"Again, I'm sorry, Max. I know I'm wrong for what I'm about to say, but I still would like to get to know you better . . . as a friend. I can't explain it, but there's something there that I feel I would regret to no end if I didn't explore it. Maybe I'm just buggin', and feel free to tell me if I am. Would you be okay with that?"

"Yeah," I said, trying to mask the pain and resentment as I convinced myself. "I would like that. I don't have that many friends out here, and one can never have enough friends. Shake on it?"

I extended my hand across the table and Glover took it. Our eyes met in understanding, despite what our brains and hearts debated. Logic was trying to tell the heart what to feel, but it was only a game, for the heart feels what it wants. Lionel was definitely a lucky man if he held even half of Glover's heart.

"Max?"

"Yeah?"

"You didn't get the DMV job. They hired someone else. I found out late this afternoon. I did forward your info to them like I promised."

"I knew you did. No matter what else, I trust you. Thanks for trying, though."

"Would you like some ice cream for dessert?"

If I could eat it off you. "Sure."

"It's cookie dough. Is that okay?"

"Yep."

"Good. It's in my freezer. The bowls are in the cabinet on the left and the spoons are in the second drawer. Bring me some too."

"You've got a lot of nerve," I said dryly as I got up, walking past her and into the kitchen. True to her word, everything was where she said it would be. We stayed in the safe zone, trading jokes at the table while eating dessert.

As we wrapped up, Glover's phone rang. I could tell it was one of her girlfriends. Even though she spoke briefly, I chose that time to leave. She walked me to the door, where we hugged again. I held my breath as our chests pressed, fearful of any further rush I might get from her scent. The atmosphere was different from when I'd entered.

"Did you pick up that Oriental rug at the swap meet?" I asked, pointing toward her sofa.

"It's a Persian rug, and yes, I did buy it there. How did you know?"

"My boy Smitty has the same one in his apartment," I said. "Speaking of him, we're barbecuing this Saturday. We'll be out by the pool and stuff. Nothing crazy. You're welcome to come." Stupid of me, but I had to see her again, for the heart not only feels what it wants; it does what it wants.

"Thank you. I'd love to come," she said, accepting my offer.

"Good. It's at my apartment. I would give you the address and stuff, but you already have it from my app. Good night." With that said, I turned and walked away. I had to get back at her for the ice cream thing.

"Good night to you too, smart ass," I heard Glover laughingly say as she closed her door.

I was filled with all-consuming thoughts of Glover, knowing deep in my heart that she wasn't totally committed, despite what she'd said. Maybe it was just that I wasn't as sold on it as I should be, both disappointed in the present but foolishly hopeful for the future as I walked to my car. What was it about me that demanded pain and heartache whenever I connected with someone? Shit.

A little too much thinking for me, as I didn't see the dark-colored Audi speeding toward me just as I stepped off the curb.

"What the fuck!" I yelled as it barely missed landing me in the hospital or worse, continuing at speeds unsafe for an apartment complex parking lot. Probably a drunk, I guessed, as it kept going. Still alive to daydream on what might have been with Glover, I got in my car and drove away.

29

Glover

I didn't intend to rush Mona off the phone that night, but Max was about to leave. I was going to see her the next day anyway. When I told her I had company, she assumed it was Lionel.

I didn't tell her otherwise.

In spite of two late evenings in a row with my future mother-in-law, I had a spring in my step by the end of the week. Friday was busy, having spent a lot of it on the phone with Adele, going over wedding planning and scheduling. It was becoming apparent that this was going to take up more time than that of my job itself. Lionel's request to quit was beginning to seem more inviting.

I put off the usual evening with my girls, deciding to go it alone. I wasn't sure if I knew myself anymore. I went jogging through my neighborhood with only my MP3 player for company.

Time for some quiet reflection, I figured. It was stupid of me to accept Max's barbecue invitation with so much stuff going on right now, but I had to. I had to see him again, had to prolong the conversation, both spoken and unspoken, that we had going on. Was it more about that "something" I'd found in Max that led me to want to foolishly extend this? Or was it more about what was lacking with me?

Lionel is going to kill me, I kept thinking as I pushed on in my run.

I slept in late Saturday morning, sore from my jog. It felt so good to simply lie around and not think about anything. However, I began to stir as the hours went by, reaching out from under the comforter to pick up my phone from its cradle. I dialed the number off the piece of paper again, continuing my folly in spite of having the perfect man ready and willing to commit to me.

"Hello?"

"Hey. It's me."

"Oh, don't tell me you're calling to bail on me."

"No, no," I answered, emerging from my down cocoon into the daylight. I squinted as my eyes adjusted. "I was calling to see if you're really okay with me going by there."

"Of course I'm okay with it. I wouldn't have asked you. Friends, right?"

"Right," I answered, reaffirming my part of the lie we were agreeing to.

"Then hurry up and bring yo' ass over here," he teased. "Feel free to bring the rest of you too, 'cause it ain't bad either. We're about to start 'cueing."

"All right, I'm coming." I sat up, taking in the full day.

"That's what I'm talkin' about. Before I forget, bring your swimsuit. My apartment may not be as posh as yours, but we have a pool too."

"I'll think about it, Max."

"My apartment number is 105. My white Corolla is parked right outside. If I'm not there, I'll be out by the pool. A'ight?"

"A'ight," I mimicked. "See you soon."

"Don't keep me waiting."

I hung up the phone and climbed out of bed. I got in a good long, catlike stretch before walking over to my dresser. I didn't know how anyone else was going to be dressed, so I spent twenty minutes in front of the mirror like a silly schoolgirl. I finally selected my outfit and laid it out on the bed. I also selected some swimwear, my navy Anne Cole tankini top with the white bottom, stowing them in my tote bag along with my cell phone. Afterward, I skipped into the bathroom to get my act together.

I arrived at Max's complex two hours later and stepped out of my car, wearing white linen shorts, a tan sleeveless top, and white canvas tennis shoes for the tired old feet. My Calvin Klein tortoise shell shades kept the sun out of my eyes, and my CK tote bag draped my shoulder. Only one chance to make a first impression, so I might as well go in coordinated.

There were two units near Max's car. One was on the second floor, and the other was just below it. Both of their patio doors were slightly open, and I could hear music coming from both as well. I figured that Max's was the ground level unit based on his apartment number. I walked through the hallway to the interior of the complex, finding his unit. I took a deep breath and knocked.

No answer.

Maybe the music was too loud. I waited then knocked harder before a heavyset man greeted me with a smile.

"Hello. I must have the wrong apartment."

"You must be looking for Max," he said with an extra-wide grin. "He's by the pool with the food. C'mon, I'll walk you there. He's been expecting you." The brother certainly was the friendly sort. What exactly had Max told him about me?

"By the way, pleased to meet you. Samir," he offered, his large hand engulfing mine.

"Glover. Do you live here too, Samir?"

"No, I live over in Gardena. I'm Max's manager at Denny's. He's a good worker. Yep, my boy's gonna blow up one day. Soon. Just you wait and see." His smile reflected an almost fatherly pride in Max. I knew about his work history already from his resume, imagining for a second how much ridicule I would sustain if I did something to ruin my engagement to Lionel for this newfound friend. But Max was just a friend.

We'd both agreed to that.

Samir led me to the courtyard, where Max was manning the barbecue pit by the pool. I finally had a decent view of his broad shoulders, protruding from the black muscle shirt he sported. A small gathering stood nearby, talking and joking amongst themselves.

Upon seeing me, Max's eyes lit up and he ran over. He put his arms around me, squeezing oh so tight as he lifted me off my feet. His energy and muscles both felt good.

"Hey, lady! You made it, huh?" he cheered. I liked the enthusiasm and attention he showered on me.

"I said I was coming," I answered calmly as he set me down, although my heart was moving a little fast at the moment.

"Daaamn!" someone from the gathering yelled. One of his friends, I assumed, a little skinny fella in a pair of denims and a grey Raiders T-shirt. A heavy sister with a lollipop in her mouth gave the little dude a massive elbow, presumably in response to his outburst. She cast a nasty look at me with her beady eyes.

Lord, don't let there be some shit up in here.

"Glover, let me introduce you to some people. This is my boy, Smitty." Smitty was shorter than me. Nice enough, though. I could tell he was a character, a male version of Charmaine. He was quick to shake my hand—in a very safe manner. His chest was probably red from the elbow he'd received.

"This is his girl, Zena." Warrior princess, she wasn't. She smiled, but her beady eyes didn't look any happier than before.

"This is Zena's sister, Niobi." She was a smaller version of the Lollipop Kid, and lurked in the background. She was cuter than her sister, but wore a dead serious scowl on her face. Not even a fake smile. She made it apparent I was unwelcome here.

Like I really cared. Mona would proud of me.

A boom box rested on one of the patio tables. Next to it were aluminum pans filled with barbecued sausage, hamburgers, ribs, chicken, and kabobs. Coming primarily to hang, I wasn't that hungry, but the food was lookin' hella good.

"You're looking beautiful as always," Max heaped upon me. "Excuse my smell. I'm all hickory and shit."

"I don't mind, Max. You're the chef today, so I'll forgive you. Do you have somewhere I can put my tote bag?"

"Yeah. My apartment's open. People have been going in and out of there, so you may want to put it up in the bedroom. Samir walked you from there, right?"

"Yes. He's a nice person. Thinks very highly of you. I guess I kinda do too."

We exchanged a glance as he fought a blush. I tilted my head so my eyes could meet his. Max stood there, transfixed, with a bottle of barbecue sauce in his hand.

At that moment, one of the partygoers broke our brief moment with, "Hey, Max! That's your girlfriend, dawg?"

Max snapped out of it, casting a glance his way. "Nah, dawg, she's not mine. She's just a friend," he replied. No matter my situation, those words bothered me.

Max paused as he looked back toward me, seeing bare fingers on my left hand. Thrown for a loop in mid-sentence, his eyes widened. They moved up from my hand, where they were met by my smiling face.

I hadn't planned on leaving my ring off; it just worked out that way. I accidentally left it on my dresser when I was trying on clothes in front of my mirror. I was halfway to Max's place before I realized it was absent. I almost turned around, but decided it might be best to leave it off if I planned on swimming. Explaining a lost ring to Lionel would be worse than Max's confusion, which was actually cute at the moment.

"I'll be back. I'm going to put up my bag."

"Hurry back. Don't make me come looking for you."

"What if that's what I want?" I teased, looking over my shoulder. I loved playing around with him, but somewhere beneath my words I felt that maybe I could be serious. I had to get a grip. Zena's and Niobi's eyes were on me, whispering as I watched them out of the corner of my eye.

Max's apartment had the look of a college student's, albeit a lot neater. Still, a far cry from the situated, stable opulence of Lionel's place. Not that I should be comparing the two anyway.

I found Max's bedroom and stowed my tote bag on the side of his bed, where it wouldn't be too visible. The bedroom was immaculate. Not what I expected from a single young man. I still had a lot to learn about him. I ran my hand across the top of his bed and walked over to his oak dresser.

Sitting on his dresser beside his Mason ring was a framed picture. It was of Max and his mom, from his college graduation. I smiled over our similarities just as sounds in the living room startled me. Somebody had entered the apartment. I hurried out of Max's bedroom thinking—perhaps hoping—that he'd followed me inside.

"Well, if it isn't Ms. Siddity. Look at this here, Niobi." The Lollipop Kid and sis had some shit on their collective mind. Being a lady, I tried ignoring them as I walked by.

Niobi mumbled, "Who the fuck does she think she is? Sorry-ass bitch."

"Excuse me? I heard you talking about a sorry-ass bitch. Someone I know?" I was about to get "ignit" with these pro-wrestling heifers and possibly get drove by them, but the sista wasn't backing down. First thing, that lollipop was going straight down Zena's throat.

"Girl, you steppin' to Max like that in front of my li'l sister. That's disrespectful, and we don't play that shit. Maybe that's cool where you from, but not around here."

"Excuse me? Is Max your man?" I asked of Niobi, looking at her with a crazy smile and half-laugh, catching her off guard. I could tell she was about to lie the way she paused and looked away as she prepared to answer. Something I learned in my job. I didn't think Max to be the type to invite me if he really had an interest in Niobi, but let her think I was about to wild out anyway. My mom didn't raise no punk, and I prepared to take my beating if it came to it.

"There y'all two! Honestly, I can't take you anywhere. All frowned up like somebody stole your lunch. I told both y'all to chill." It was Max's friend, Smitty, fast-talking to diffuse things. "I need to make another beer run. You wanna drive me, Zena? You know you're almost out of lollipops, baby."

Zena and Niobi loosened up, storming out of the apartment. Before they left, they gave me parting looks, with Niobi motioning to her head with her hand, like a gun going "Pow!"

Smitty started walking out behind them, then paused. "Sorry about them," he said with a shrug. "They're all talk . . . most of the time. Zena called herself hooking Niobi up with Max, but Max ain't havin' that. Not even if you weren't here with all your sexiness, girl. You know you got my boy buggin', right?"

"Be gentle with him, though. He don't get it that often and you . . ." He mocked wiping sweat off his face. "You *foin* as hell, girl. You damn lucky I'm with Zena, 'cause I'd make you forget all about Max. Have you worshipping in the Temple of Smitty."

"No, no. We're just friends. I'm engaged and—"

"Riiiiiiiiiiight!" he jeered, cutting me off. "I saw how you two look at each other. Don't shit a shitter. See ya later." Smitty shot out the door to catch up with the two headbusters. He enjoyed making me squirm, and I probably deserved it for the bullshit of which I was trying to convince myself.

I let out a huge sigh, exhaling mightily before heading out the door. I didn't know what I was getting into when I came here, but I was definitely hungry now.

30

Max

I invited Jay to the barbecue, but he was a
no-show. Probably out scheming as usual, but
it didn't really matter. I had other concerns on
my mind. Glover had been gone for a while and
hadn't returned from my apartment. Maybe she
was serious about wanting me to look for her.
Nah. I learned to limit most of my fantasizing
when she broke it down to me. No need to get my
hormones riled up.

Just then, Glover appeared in the courtyard.
Her shades were off, so I was able to peer into
her pretty brown eyes again.

"Everything okay? Thought you'd gotten lost."
"Everything's fine, Max. Thanks for your con-
cern, though."

"I fixed a plate for you over there," I said, motioning to one of the nearby patio tables. "Figured you'd get hungry eventually, and can't have
you starving on my watch."

"You not gonna join me? What kind of host are you anyway?"

"Okay. I'm finished 'cueing anyway. I'll fix a plate too."

Relieving myself from my duties at the pit, I joined her at the table.

"Did you have any other plans this weekend?" I asked, relishing the close space I shared with her.

"Not really. I cleared my entire schedule just to come here. I had to taste your barbecue."

"Well? What's the verdict?"

"It's good. Share your secret?"

"Beer."

"What? You get drunk before you start?"

"Cute. You sooo funny. I pour it over the meat while it's cooking. Just before I dab the sauce on."

"I should have known. You're an alcoholic. Probably full right now."

"I don't hear you complaining about the food."

"You know I'm just fucking with you, right?"

"Yeah, I know. That's why you've got some sauce on your face."

"I do? Where?" she asked, feeling embarrassed.

"You know I'm just fucking with you, right?"

"Max?"

"Huh?"

"Stop."

"Okay. What do you like to do for fun? I mean, besides giving people a hard time and making them squirm."

"You're cute," Glover said with a chuckle. "I like to listen to music and chill out sometimes. I like to travel when I can. I like hanging with my friends most of all. They're important to me. Kind of like family."

"Sounds a lot like me. I used to be a party person. Now I'm content to just hang out. Maybe I'm growing up, or maybe it's just that my priorities are changing. I guess a move to a city like Los Angeles will do that to you also. Whew, it has been an adjustment."

"The hustle and bustle?"

"Just the unfamiliarity of it all. I'm on familiar turf back in Louisiana. The place isn't that big, so you get a feel for things and people really quick. You know where you stand. Here, I'm a little slow to trust. So much is not as it seems, y'know?"

"Me included, right?" Glover said as she rested her hand under her chin.

"No, I wasn't including you in that statement. This is a place where so many people come to reinvent themselves. Fresh starts. I guess I'm included in that group."

"So, what do you want to change, Max? Better yet, what *would* you change in your life right now?"

"Well, I would have my career on a roll, whatever that is. A nice house with an ocean view and someone special to share it with."

"Having someone special is important, Max. Trust me on that."

Trust.

I trusted her. I wanted her to be that someone special, but couldn't bring that up again.

"Did you bring your swimsuit?" I asked, avoiding the waters I found myself sailing in.

"That's for me to know and you to find out."

"Hey, nudity is cool too. The pool is heated, but you still might be a tad cold."

"Always the joker. Are you ever serious?"

"Most of the time. I just like seeing the life in your face when you smile."

"You're the one with the nice smile. Real genuine and sincere. It's refreshing."

The mutual admiration society continued its meeting for the next hour and was only adjourned as some of the partygoers moved on. Smitty returned from his beer run. He was busy keeping an angry Zena and Niobi at bay, until he moved the remainder of the party upstairs to his place. The sun was setting in the west as clouds began rolling in.

"Do you want to go up to Smitty's?" I asked, sensing a change in the flow of things. "It's up to you."

"No, not really," she said, taking a final look at Zena and her sister. She pushed her chair away from the table and walked lazily around the courtyard. I watched her as she took a wine cooler from the ice chest. "Is that a Jacuzzi on the other end of the pool?"

"Yep, and it's working this week, too. I knock these apartments, but they're really pretty nice. I wish they had a gym, though. Even just a small one."

"You could come by and use mine sometime, Max. Don't want you losing that muscle tone, now, do we?"

"That's a no-no. Friends aren't supposed to talk about each other's bodies. Not even if they're as fine and sexy as yours."

Glover responded with a grin. She came over, taking my arm in hers. "C'mon. Show me your place before we come back for that swim. I need to change anyway."

"So you did bring a suit." I grinned like a little kid at Christmas.

We strolled to my apartment, where I gave her an informal tour of my tiny abode. I sat on the arm of my sofa while Glover looked through my photo album. She took great delight in laughing at photos of my developmental years, filled with bad haircut and clothing ideas that we all thought were "da bomb" at the time.

"I need to shower before we head down to the pool. I smell just like that pit. Make yourself comfortable and remember to tell any females that you're my cousin if they call. Okay?"

"Any other orders? Shall I wash dishes or anything?"

"No, that'll do, madam. You know you can hang upstairs if you want while I shower. I won't be long." I pointed up at the ceiling, as we could hear the muffled sounds of music and dancing overhead.

"Nah, I'm not really up for seeing *certain* people. I'm here to have fun, and the company down here is just fine."

"Did something happen with Zena and Niobi? They didn't try to start any shit, huh?"

"Nothing I couldn't handle. They were just being catty in their own special way. I'm not causing any problems with you and Niobi, am I? I don't want to assume I know the answer."

"Niobi? Nah. Zena calls herself trying to set me up with her crazy sister, but she knows I'm not interested. You're cool. Trust me. There is nothing going on there and never will be. So you're gonna sit tight?"

"Yep. Get your ass in there and shower before I change my mind. You know a sister doesn't want to get her hair wet anyway."

"A'ight! A'ight!"

I walked into my bedroom, tossing my smoke-infused attire in the dirty clothes hamper. A cold shower would be a good idea, but I needed this shower primarily to get clean. I quickly sudsed up so I wouldn't keep Glover waiting too long.

My bathroom door was partially open, so I called out to Glover that I would be out soon. She responded, sounding much closer than the living room where I'd left her. It was probably my imagination. As I turned off the shower, I reached for my towel to wipe the water from my eyes.

I heard rustling sounds coming from my bedroom. It was Glover. Through the crack in my door, I saw her changing into her swimsuit. As I dried off, I was unable to take my eyes off her. She had to have heard the water stop, expecting me to emerge eventually. My eyes followed every inch of her, from her shoulders to her hips, as she removed her top, followed by her shorts.

"Told you I wouldn't be long," I shouted from inside the bathroom, giving her some kind of warning—and to feel less voyeuristic.

"Hope you don't mind. I left my bag in here and started changing." She didn't pick up her pace or anything. She slowly reached for the clasp on the front of her bra and let it drop to the floor. Her bare breasts exposed, I stirred as I gazed at her lovely brown, erect nipples. She had to know I could see her every move. She had to know that I was watching.

And wanting very badly.

"That's okay. You had to change somewhere . . . and I'm in here hogging the bathroom," I joked.

Her panties dropped to the floor. That round bootie right there, just waiting.

My every instinct was to rush out there and take her. To put her on my bed and know ecstasy as I'd imagined way too often.

No. For someone on the receiving end of betrayal in the past, it wasn't worth the drama of being with another man's woman.

My swim trunks were in there with her, so I waited for her to finish. Besides, I had a serious hard-on that my towel would not have hidden. She had to have seen me, but I didn't ask. On one hand, I felt like a perv. On the other, I was a lucky witness.

When I knew she was finished, I exited the bathroom. Glover stood at the side of my bed, looking almost as good in her swimsuit as she had while unclothed. The top was navy blue. It covered some of her tight stomach, but revealed enough to make you want to see more. She had these cute little white bottoms that she nervously tugged at. Women. Why try to hide what we want to see? I politely smiled and went to my dresser.

In my mirror, I watched her as she folded her clothes on my bed. As she did this, I saw her eyes slyly watching my every move. I found my black swim trunks in the middle drawer and pulled them out.

Glover excused herself from my bedroom, but had to pass me on the way out.

As she walked into the living room, she asked, "Do you want me to leave a crack in the door?"

She was fire. And I was already sweating from the heat.

I exited the bedroom and we grabbed some drinks, a Smirnoff for her and a Corona for me, heading out to the pool. As the sun faded, the outdoor lights would be coming on shortly. We had been holed up in my apartment longer than I expected, as Smitty had already moved the barbecue pit and cleaned up at poolside.

I owed him.

We placed our drinks on the ground near the edge of the pool. Glover slowly lowered herself into the water as I held her hand. When she was completely in, she began backstroking toward the far end. Following in Glover's wake, my head was visible by her feet as she paddled. She intentionally kicked water in my face the closer I got. We came to a truce, stopping to tread water when we reached the far side.

"This chlorine's kickin'. You know you owe me for another relaxer," she offered. "You're the one who talked me into this. Denny's pay you enough to take care of my next hair appointment?"

"I would say fuck you for that Denny's crack, but you might take it literally, Ms. Look At My Big-Ass Ring. We can't have you trying to freak me in the pool. I don't swim that well, and you might drown me in more ways than one."

Glover swatted her hand, sending a wave toward my face. After clearing my eyes, I dove below and came up under her. She playfully screamed as I picked her up and dunked her with a large splash. We wrestled around in the water for a minute, until we wound up face to face in each other's arms.

The laughter slowly faded as our eyes locked on one another. Glover's hands trembled as she pulled me against her, our wet bodies forming a seal. I slid my hands against the small of her back. She seemed to be in great pain. I just wanted to make it all better. We were heading somewhere we had been fighting with all our might.

I put my finger under her chin and lifted her head up. Her eyes revealed great confusion, like part of her wanted to run off, while the other part wanted something else.

Me.

I leaned over to finally kiss those lips . . .

Bloop!

A large raindrop fell onto my nose. I flinched in surprise, enough to break the fragile mood that was set. Then several more fell—cold rain pouring from a sky that had just opened up.

Glover relaxed her grip on me. Her head lowered again as she whispered under her breath, "God's crying." It was barely audible.

"What did you say?" The rain picked up. A freak storm, I guess. And they say it never rains in Southern California.

"God's crying. My mom used to tell me that when it rained. She used to say that somebody was doing wrong somewhere. Some stuff she brought from Virginia."

"Let's go in before we catch pneumonia."

We retreated inside my apartment. I gave her a towel to dry off with and one of my shirts to don. We were back in friend mode.

The way it should be.

31

Glover

It came in slow at first. Bump . . . bump, bump, bump. Bump . . . bump, bump, bump.

Not my usual alarm beep. And I hadn't visited my dream date either. Maybe I was still dreaming. But why was I hearing rap music in my sleep? I barely listened to the stuff.

I opened one eye and was startled. I wasn't dreaming. It was morning. From the strange noises in between beats, I knew I was hearing a Timbaland song.

What the fuck was going on? I opened both eyes.

Oh, shit. Max.

I remembered fleeing the rain and eating popcorn during an old movie before falling asleep.

I was lying atop him on his couch. He was still asleep. My head was on his chest and he had one arm around me, while the other hung down onto the floor in an awkward position. I began looking around, trying to figure out where the music was coming from. The walls were vibrating.

My movement awoke Max from his slumber. He stirred and said, "Good morning, beautiful." That smile of his was showing.

"Hey." I pulled myself closer and kissed him. Instinct. No thought.

Max, while caught off guard, responded favorably. Our eyes closed as we used our tongues, guiding each other in sensuous circles. I put aside any guilt over Lionel, instead focusing on how electric this felt. Morning breath was never so good as it was now. We continued kissing as we sat upright on the couch where I straddled him, pulling his head into my chest. I ground into his crotch, giving him a morning lap dance. As his face nuzzled deeper, he reached up and unbuttoned my shirt.

Correction. His shirt.

I wore his property while wanting to be owned by him as well. As I wore his shirt, I wanted him to . . . wear . . . me . . . out.

The only thing wrong was that damn music that kept pounding through the walls. Who was doing that so early? I worked my hips harder, determined to ignore it, as Max's morning bulge rose with the sun to say good morning against my clit. Then it happened.

At first I didn't make it out. Couldn't over the music, but when the volume dropped, I heard it again. It was a phone.

My cell phone.

It was in my tote bag and ringing. I blinked my eyes and looked toward Max's bedroom, where my bag was. It was ironic, as I wanted to go to the bedroom, but not to answer a fucking phone. The music had stopped. I looked back down at Max, noticing the serious look on his face. He brought his hands back down to his sides.

"What time is it?" I asked nervously.

"You need to get that, right?" he asked, disgusted.

"Yeah, I guess I do."

He let out a long breath, biting his lip from whatever he had to say. I ran my hands through my matted hair and climbed off him. I already knew who was calling.

"Hello?" I hurriedly pulled my cell from the bag, but tried to sound normal.

"Hey, baby! Where you been? I've been trying to reach you since yesterday."

"I've been hanging out with Mona. Had to do some shopping yesterday. Looking around for things to put on the gift registry too." I hated lying.

"And here I thought you were looking for your honeymoon outfit. Damn. I miss you."

"I miss you too, babe."

"Where are you anyway?"

"Um . . . I'm out running errands."

"Sure is quiet. You're in the store?"

"No, I'm in the post office. I was about to pick up some stamps. I was looking for change when you called."

"Oh. Do I get to see you today?"

"Yeah. Well, let me get off this phone. The battery's getting low and they don't want you using the phone at the counter."

"All right, baby. Love you."

"Love you too. Bye."

I turned to see Max leaning in the bedroom doorway. If we had both been in here a minute ago, we would have been . . .

"Damn, girl. That was a pretty impressive story. Lionel, right?"

"Do you even have to ask?"

"No," he answered. I didn't like his tone. "But wanted to confirm it, though. That post office thing came pretty quickly. Almost like you're used to doing this."

"Max, I'm speaking to my fiancé. How in the *hell* do I explain that I'm at another man's place, wearing another man's shirt, that I spent the night with him, and that I was about to have sex with him if he hadn't called and interrupted?"

"I thought it would have been more than just sex between us." Max's voice rang with hurt.

"Oh, stop that!" I yelled out of frustration. "Max, you know what I'm saying. I would apologize for what I started on the couch, but I'm tired of doing that. I wanted to kiss you and I did."

"It was a good kiss, too. It was going a lot further than that and you know it. I guess it was meant for the phone to ring. If we ever go there again, I want you to be mine and mine alone. None of this 'post office' shit."

I stood there fuming for a second, not saying anything, and unsure of whom I was angrier with, Max or myself. I'd already done something stupid, so I decided to avoid saying something stupid as well. "I understand and don't blame you. I think I'll put my clothes on now."

"I'll be in the other room," Max said as he began to close the bedroom door for me.

"Max?"

"Huh?"

"Who in the hell was playing that music this early in the morning?"

His smile returned. "That was Smitty. Remind me to tell you about that on our next date."

"What did you just say?"

"That was Smitty."

"No, no. The other thing you said."

"About the date? Oh. Well, I kinda counted this as our first date. After all, I did spring for the popcorn last night. You're not keeping my shirt, though."

The smart-ass was right, though. Max and I saw each other several times over the next few weeks, sneaking in a lunch here and grabbing some fast food there.

Sometimes we didn't eat.

Just talked.

On one occasion, we even broke down, holding hands while taking in a matinee.

I was leading a secret life. Here I was, the bride-to-be, having feelings for another man and stealing away to spend as much time with him as with my future husband. We wrote it off as a complex friendship, sure to avoid situations that would take us back to a dangerous place.

The thought was still there, but once I was married, that would all be over, and I'd be left with a rich set of memories.

The person I felt the worst for was Lionel. He was a good man and didn't deserve this. I was just too scared to come clean with everything, clinging to the notion that I could make things work with Lionel. I was a chickenshit, while my fiancé was completely oblivious.

32

Max

I was deluding myself—and loving it. Guess that makes me a fool. Things had come close to going over the edge with Glover. She was supremely confident and used to being her own woman, which included making her own decisions. The problem was that her decisions, if acted on, would wind up being destructive for both of us. She'd admitted to having some doubts about her upcoming marriage, but was still committed to seeing it through. She also confessed that some of those doubts may have stemmed from her parents' failed relationship. And I agreed to respect her wishes, despite those insecurities. With all that known, I still chose to see her several times over the following weeks. I enjoyed getting to know this fascinating woman, but vowed to never let it get any deeper than it had already gone.

Time would tell if we would both be strong enough to resist temptation. One thing I'd learned from my time with Glover was that if things were different, I could see myself with her for the rest of my life.

Smitty had been at his new job at West-tel for a few weeks now, and I missed hanging out with him on the weekdays. He seemed to be getting his life on track, borrowing my car a few times when his hooptie was uncooperative. Nobody was prouder of my boy than me. I wasn't hearing much from Jay these days, that night at El Ami having strained things. With all the changes going on in my life, that probably was a good thing, as Jay's advice about Glover would be to exploit her vulnerabilities, then hit it and quit it, no doubt. But Glover and I were about more than that, and I'd never be Jay, despite being blood.

Missing Smit, I decided to see if he wanted to hang this weekend. We hadn't thrown the football around at the park in a long time, so I called him Saturday to see what he was doing. He was washing clothes, but would come get me when he was finished.

I heard a knock on my door and figured it was him.

I opened the door to a fist in the face.

My eyes watering, I crumpled to the floor while holding my nose. Though difficult with all the pain, I could still see. A bald, dark-skinned brother stood over me. I thought I was about to be jacked, but didn't see a gun in his hand.

In my head, I imagined Orelia, back in Lake Charles, writing the headline for my obituary:

MY FOOL SON WENT TO CALIFORNIA AND CAME BACK DEAD. I TOLD HIM. LORD, I TOLD HIM.

The man wore all black. Judging by the Rolex on his wrist, he had no reason to rob my poor ass. Then I recognized the look on his face.

This was personal.

"Uh-uh." He shook his head. "It's not going to be that easy. Get up. I'm going to have some fun with you."

"Lionel," I stated with certainty as I picked myself up. I didn't have to guess who this was. My nose still stung, but it wasn't broken—not for a lack of trying on his part. I prepared to return the favor.

"Good guess, bitch. Not as dumb as you look. Should've run you over when I had the chance," he spat, reminding me vividly of that night outside Glover's apartment. "What makes a broke-ass, down-on-his-luck motherfucker like you think you can get away with this? Do you know who you're fucking with? Do you?"

After all my trials and tribulations out here, the "broke" comment set me off the most. I tensed to lunge at him, everything speeding up as my adrenaline surged. Just then, a large howl came from the hallway, distracting us both. Lionel turned toward the noise, but it was too late. Smitty's little five-foot-four-ass launched in the air and came through the open door like a flying squirrel, landing on Lionel's back.

The two of them spun wild, with one of Smitty's arms wrapped around Lionel's neck, choking him, while the free hand punched upside his head. As they flailed about, one of Smitty's legs clocked me. I fell back onto the floor, watching Lionel's attempt to dislodge Smitty from his back. The two of them formed a mad, cursing mass of flailing arms and legs, knocking down pictures and smashing my lamps. So much for attempting to keep the place presentable.

For what seemed like an eternity, probably less than thirty seconds had passed. With the element of surprise ended, Lionel dislodged Smitty, flipping him right onto my coffee table.

"Hey!" I yelled as my friend came down with a crash, sending glass shards flying into the air and all across the floor. My coffee table was split clear in half. The move Lionel made could almost be called a thing of beauty—if it weren't my boy and my place getting destroyed. I got back to my feet.

"Broke ass?" I was far from a thug, but my right had dropped a couple of busters in my time. As Lionel turned toward me, I smiled. I wasn't about to sneak him. I wanted him to see this coming. I put my all into the hook. As my fist shot toward the side of Lionel's head, the strangest thing happened.

Lionel's head wasn't there when my fist arrived. In one fluid move, the brother sidestepped, delivering his own blow to my gut. I seized up, dropping to one knee, but I was getting tired of being his bitch. I lunged at him, finally connecting. I aimed for his head again, but caught him in his neck. Not as planned, but it did send him stumbling back into my couch. As he went to block, I charged at him.

Smitty was trying to remove himself from the coffee table debris as he rose off the floor. I gave Smitty a look to stay out of it. The pained expression on his face told me he was happy to oblige.

I punched Lionel in his eye once before he kneed me in my gut. The knee knocked what little wind was left right out of me. I fell onto the floor, hoping we both were out of steam. No luck.

Lionel bounced up off the couch as if it were a trampoline, landing on his feet like some kind of cat. I was still balled up in the fetal position on the floor.

"I think you get the message," Lionel muttered, touching his own face for damage assessment. Vain motherfucker. He then turned to stroll out my open door.

Before leaving, he pulled out his wallet. Reaching in it, he took out a dollar bill. He balled the crisp note up, throwing it over his shoulder as he disappeared. It landed in the middle of the wasteland, between me and my injured friend.

Smitty, sitting up now, rubbed his smarting back.

"Damn, Max. What was that Tae Bo ho shit he was using? I need to go to those classes. He whipped your ass with that UFC shit."

"Fuck you," I groaned. "He sucker punched me. I thought it was you at the door."

"Ding-dong, it wasn't me. At least he left a tip to pay for the shit he broke. Nigga can't be all that bad, even if it is just a dollar," Smitty said, trying to make light of a bad situation.

I leaned across the floor and snatched up the money. Then I staggered over to the apartment door and closed it. Looking into my hand, I partially unfolded the bill and hurled it down again in disgust. The man had no respect for me.

And with all I'd done, maybe he was right.

"Was that ol' girl's—"

"Yeah, Smit."

"You gonna tell Glover about this, dawg?"

"Nah. She's got enough on her mind. Damn, he seems familiar," I muttered.

"Maybe he whipped your ass in a different life."

"No, I'm serious. Maybe I saw a picture of him at Glover's." I kicked my broken table leg aside.

"Max?"

"Yeah, Smit."

"This ain't no dollar he threw. This is a Benjamin. Fool just threw away a hundred-dollar bill like it was nothin'."

"I noticed. Fuck him and his money," I said in disgust, my body acknowledging my aches. "You want it, Smit?"

"Hell, yeah. Do you still want to play football?"

"Nah."

"Good, 'cause I got some shopping to do at the swap meet now," he said, waving the Benjamin in the air.

Smitty's jokes aside, it kept nagging me that I couldn't remember why Lionel seemed so familiar beyond today's encounter or his attempt at making me road kill that night outside Glover's apartment. That annoying feeling would be there beyond the bumps and bruises I suffered today.

33

Glover

A weekend went by without hearing from either Lionel or Max. I called Max once, but decided not to leave a message. He was probably working or doing his own thing. I wasn't his woman, so it was none of my business. That's what I kept telling myself.

It was more unusual not to hear from Lionel.

Mona and Charmaine could tell that something other than marriage preparations was going on with me. I had become secretive and distant with my best friends, feeling they'd only remind me of how stupid I was at a time like this. Maybe I still wanted them to think of me as "the responsible one."

Monday would bring with it new developments. Charmaine came in late and got written up by Mr. Marx. She almost walked out before I calmed her down. Mona kept to herself that day, not wanting to draw Mr. Marx's attention. She knew to steer clear when appropriate.

I spent most of my day returning calls and doing follow-ups. As I completed a call, I prepared to check on Lionel.

For all I knew, something could have happened to him. I had the button depressed on the phone when it rang, jarring me.

"Good morning, this is Ms. McDaniel. May I help you?"

He chuckled. "Don't you mean Mrs. Dunning?"

"Hey!" I said, breathing a sigh of relief. "I was just about to call you."

"Yeah. What you doing?"

"Work. Same old, same old. I haven't heard from you. You okay?"

"Yeah, baby. I've just been busy. I need to talk to you about things."

"Okay . . ." I said with a pause. "When?"

"Now. I'm down the street."

Lionel showed up at my job within minutes. I took an early break and walked out to greet him in the parking lot. He sat on the hood of his car, his weekday business attire absent. Instead, he wore a button-down shirt and jeans, his eyes hidden behind dark sunglasses.

He wasn't alone.

His cousin Jacob, who was his best man, sat inside the Audi. Jacob looked up from whatever he was doing, flashed a quick smile, and then went back to texting or whatever. Jacob knew something, but chose to stay out of it. I took a seat next to Lionel on the warm hood, hoping the darkening clouds overhead weren't an omen.

"You're off today? I didn't know."

"Maybe if you'd called, you would've known. I had to get fitted today. I'm taking a lot more time off as the wedding date approaches. You still want to get married, right?"

"Yeah, baby," I answered, visibly shaken by his odd question. He had to have noticed me repositioning my hands to steady myself. "What's up with that?"

"Nothing. I just feel we have choices we need to make before we're married. Actually, I made my choice when I asked you to marry me. Maybe you need to clear up some things." Lionel avoided eye contact, only periodically glancing at me when trying to emphasize his point. During one of his glances, I saw a bruise under his shades.

"Lionel, what happened?" I asked, instinctively reaching toward his face. He turned away and gently pulled my hand down.

"It's nothing. I had an accident the other day. No big deal."

"Jacob, what happened?"

Jacob turned his attention to me long enough to shrug, then went back to ignoring us.

"Lionel, what do you mean by *choices*?"

"Just what I said. I think that you might have some issues you need to resolve. You have some choices you need to make if our future is going to be as bright as it can be, baby. You seem distant at times; it's hard to catch up with you, and I know my mother hasn't heard from you in a few weeks. We're running out of time. I'm just here to give you a heads-up."

He knew about Max.

My heart raced, feeling a churning mix of fear and embarrassment in the pit of my stomach that made me violently ill. He knew, and was virtually coming out and telling me he knew. The shock on my face was evident, even though he continued to look down at the pavement. I was speechless. Of course, he didn't need me to say anything. He wasn't here for a response; he was here to make a statement.

"I have to get back to work, Lionel," I said weakly, not used to being called out for cheating emotionally, if not physically. My normal nature was to argue and fight back, but how could I? Lionel hadn't done anything. He'd been perfect and I'd been tarnished. Rather than assert my independence as I liked to brag, I behaved like a sheep.

"I know. We gotta roll anyway. I have to check on some other things for the wedding. You know, we never decided on where to honeymoon."

"I don't know, Lionel. I guess we need to decide . . . soon."

"It'll be your call. I don't care, as long as I'm there with you. Let me know what you decide. I love you, baby."

"I love you too."

I hugged Lionel firmly, strangely enough feeling some relief with things being out in the open. I followed that with a light kiss before he left with Jacob. Lionel's words were with me the rest of the day. I needed to talk to someone about this.

But not Max.

I needed my sister, Mona.

Upon my return to the office, I told her that I needed to talk. Mona, already curious about what was up, simply nodded her head. She had nothing to say about it, until she told me to follow her home after work. She probably thought I would get emotional and didn't want to see me bawling at work.

On the drive west to Santa Monica, I had many second thoughts, but erased them from my mind.

Mona was my best friend, and I felt guilty for shutting her out the entire time. She was far from perfect, but never felt she had to hide things from me, or that I would unfairly judge her. Of course she had her diva persona, but that was usually reserved for others, or when in public.

At her condo, I waited as Mona fished her key from her purse. Spilling my guts and getting all this out in the open would do me some good.

"Did you sleep with him?" she asked while turning the key.

"What?"

She entered her unit, holding the door for me. "Did you sleep with him?" she repeated oh so crisply. "The cute, creepy guy you've been hanging with in 'secret'."

Damn her. Mona figured it out then had the nerve to insult him.

"He's not creepy," I answered in as stern a manner as I could.

Mona laughed. "Touched a nerve, huh? Relax. I'm just messing with you. He was just so nervous when I saw him at work that time. So . . . you did sleep with him."

"No! I didn't sleep with him."

Mona muttered, feigning disgust over my admission, "Sheesh. I knew you didn't have it in you. You hungry?"

"No, I'm all right. Lionel knows . . . I think."

"Oh. That's bad. So it's over between you and Lionel?" she asked. Without waiting for an answer, she walked into her room to drop her purse.

"No. Lionel gave me a 'chance' to make up my mind when he came by the office. He didn't sound very happy."

"Would you be? Well, I don't see why he's that upset. It's not like you slept with what's-his-name. What is his name anyway?"

"His name is Max. Maxwell, actually. He's from Louisiana."

"Oooh. Trying to get a bit of southern hospitality, are we?"

"Anyway," I muttered with my hand up for her to pause. "I didn't sleep with him, but it's not like I didn't want to. I know that's fucked up, but he does something to me. It's different from when I'm with Lionel. We click on so many different levels. And that's without the sex. I can only imagine how it would be if we—"

"You sure you're not just running from your upcoming commitment? People have been known to do that. You wouldn't be the first. Maybe Max is just an excuse to avoid thinking about your marriage, an outlet for whatever frustrations or issues you may have."

"I don't think so, but I can't be sure. How did you figure it out?"

"Easy. The way you've been acting at work gave it away. You've been different since that day we saw you in front of the office with what's-his-name. Charmaine thinks he's a sexy beast, but she wouldn't tell you that."

"So, you guys have been talking about me, huh? I guess I deserve it."

"Yeah, you do, but don't sweat it, Ms. McDaniel. It's come time to make a decision, because I doubt Lionel would understand your continued 'friendship' with . . ."

"Max. His name is Max. Got it? You're right, though. I think something happened between him and Lionel."

"Like what?"

"Maybe a fight or something. I haven't heard from Max, so something must be up. Maybe I should go by there, make sure he's okay."

"And draw yourself right back in?" Mona offered.

"But if Lionel hurt him, I—"

"Stop!" Mona shouted, startling me. "Glover, it's none of my business, but you've made up your mind, despite your fears. Just let it go. For real. You're not the first person that's found themselves torn between two, or even three people. But you've got something in Lionel that most of us would die for, myself included. Don't fuck this up, girl."

We stared at one another, Mona probably regretting being so blunt with me. But I needed that. She'd provided something that maybe my mom would've if she were here.

"You're right," I said.

34

Max

I'd stopped off in Gardena on my way to Denny's. It was rude of me to show up on Samir's doorstep without calling, but I had some issues and needed someone with wisdom and experience to hear me out. Samir and his wife, Yvette, were always an example of what I could have in life, so I knew they were the ones to seek out.

I had only been by Samir's once, but knew I was at the right place— a modest single story home they rented. I'd seen enough pictures to know the kids in the yard by heart. The two little princesses, Asia and Sage, had formed a circle around li'l Shaun, kissing on him. Li'l Shaun was wiping his face and trying to run away. I stepped out of my Corolla and hit my alarm. The kids jumped at the sound.

"I know you! You work with my daddy!" Asia screamed out as I stepped onto the porch. Samir must have heard the noise outside. He came to the door just as I was about to ring. As he opened the storm door, it creaked on its hinges.

"Oh no," he groaned. "Don't tell me. You quit?"

"No, not yet anyway," I said with a smile. It was nice to feel wanted.

"Whew. You caught me off guard. Had me thinking the worst."

"You know I wouldn't just up and leave you without any notice. You've been too good to me. Besides, I wouldn't be showing up here in my uniform if that was the case."

"You've got a point. Come in, boy." Samir opened the door. Back to his relaxed self, he led me to the living room. I sat down in the oversized leather chair, while Samir sat on the end of the love seat across from me.

He looked toward the kitchen. "Hey, Yvette! Max is here! Can you get us a couple of beers?" Sounding like she was washing something, Yvette grunted an acknowledgement.

"That's okay, man. I'm about to go into work anyway."

"I don't want to hear that, Max. You're a guest in my home. One brew ain't gonna do anything to you anyway."

"All right."

"Something wrong, bro? I mean, you usually don't drop in. Kinda out your way. Somebody fuckin' with you at work?"

"Nah, nothing like that. I wish it were something less complicated like that. Remember the barbecue we had at my apartment?"

"Yeah. I had a good time. Been meaning to thank you for the invite. You threw down with the 'cue too. This got something to do with your lady friend?"

"Yeah."

Samir leaned over and whispered, "That's a fine-ass woman, Max. Sho' nuff." He cut his remarks abruptly as Yvette came out with two Bud longnecks in her hands. Yvette, a legal secretary for one of the local TV ambulance chasers, still wore her work clothes, but sported a pair of fluffy slippers.

"Hey, Max. How you doing, baby? Samir, be sure to use them coasters on my table," she instructed before heading back to wash.

Samir made sure Yvette was out of earshot before he resumed with, "She ain't pregnant, huh?"

"Nah, man. It's not like that. I need some advice, though. I'm feeling her, but there's a problem."

"She got a man."

"Yep. How'd you know?"

"Lucky guess." He shrugged. "Man, you get used to that. Goes with the turf. For everyone that's worth it, there's someone trying to lock that down. That's why finding that special someone is all the more important. I did with Yvette. You think she's that someone?"

"Think so. I still have some doubts, though. Her man paid me a visit. She's engaged, y'know."

"What? Oh, shit. That's not good, man. He's beefin'?"

"Nothing major. I cleaned up most of the mess already."

Samir squinted as he examined my face more closely. "Uh-huh. Your nose still swollen. Max, you got a bright future. I don't want to hear about you on the news. Promise me that."

"I promise."

"Boy, boy, boy, that's not cool. Have you . . . ?" He made that face.

"No, we haven't."

"You love her, Max?"

"If not, I'm heading that way. But it's something I don't want to consider right now. That's gotta be a two-way street, y'know."

"I can tell she cares for you, but you need to be real with her. She needs to do the same, son. Somebody's gonna wind up getting hurt more than they have been if you don't do that."

"You're so happy with your family, Samir. I hope I can have half of what you've got one day."

"You'll get yours, Max. When it's right, you'll know, and nothing gonna be able to stop you."

35

Glover

Lionel was right about me having to make choices. My little therapy session with Mona helped solidify my decision. Max and I needed to air everything out and leave it behind us.

Part of me still fought it, so I decided on a compromise between my conflicting sides: I would see Max one last time, a farewell to our situation.

I called Max from work. When he answered the phone, he sounded distant. I asked him out once I made sure his schedule was clear for the night. He paused, as if debating it, before agreeing. That was all I needed to convince me that he and Lionel had an encounter.

Dinner and dancing was something I'd been dying to do with him since we met. Might as well go out with a bang, I figured. I sped home from work, determined to find something perfect to wear. I reached in the back of my closet and pulled out my spaghetti-strapped red dress, something nice to go with my skin tone. I found some matching sandals then leapt into the shower, so I'd be so fresh and so clean.

I showed up at Max's looking all sassy and elegant as usual. He was ready when I arrived and hurried out the door. I thought it was a little strange that he didn't show me in, but maybe he didn't trust us being alone anymore. I blew the matter off, as we had dinner reservations at Glaze. Max wore a black, long-sleeved shirt, with olive slacks and black shoes. His cologne smelled good as usual. I had to hand it to him; the boy was looking positively delicious. It was going to make it more difficult to have our little talk later in the night.

The drive was mostly silent, until we were on North La Cienega, heading toward Sunset. El Ami was on the right, along with its usual line in front. Max's attention shifted to it as we passed, and his gaze lingered.

"Would you prefer to go to El Ami, Max? We can if you want."

"No, I was just thinking about something. I've been there before anyway."

"Did you see any stars?"

Something was funny to him. His outburst was unexpected, but at least it broke the tension. "No," he answered, getting himself under control. "Just Smitty and my cousin, *the football player*."

"Your cousin plays ball?"

"No, I was joking. Long story."

When we arrived at Glaze, I embarrassed Max in front of the other patrons by running around and opening his door for him. Being silly eased the tension of a last meal and the long good-bye that was beginning.

We were seated inside shortly. After appetizers, I proposed ordering for one another. Max loosened up. That warm smile returned; that smile that I loved so much—and would miss.

Max ordered my entrée, the crawfish and shrimp étouffée with white rice. Max told me to go light with his, so I ordered the roasted salmon. It was Latin music night down at Sunset, so I would finally get to check out Max's moves on the dance floor. We women always watch a man's moves on the floor for obvious reasons. Sadly, I never got to the obvious reason with him, so that would be a moot point after tonight.

After we finished our meal, we sat around and engaged in small talk. We both seemed to be holding stuff back for later. Was he thinking the same thing? Our final night? After a few glasses of wine, the check, and tip, we hit the club.

I listened to Latin music sparingly, but that didn't stop me from dancing my ass off.

I recognized Shakira's sexy yodeling and a few others, like Elvis Crespo and Celia Cruz. The DJ spun meringue and salsa all night, as well as some of that Miami bootyshakin' from Pit Bull to literally shake things up. Max surprised me that night, adjusting with ease to whatever was playing. He seemed more comfortable than me. Of course, he wasn't the one getting married.

We held hands from time to time as we danced, but tried to keep the grinding to a minimum. Damn, it was hard not to do in this atmosphere of winding and twirling bodies riding the rhythm.

While we danced, I said, "I'm impressed. I didn't know you had it in you."

"What?"

"Your dancing, Max. You are good," I said just before he spun me around twice. Really good.

"Muchas gracias, Señora McDaniel. I love to dance. I just don't get much of a chance these days."

"And here I thought you were just a slow country boy."

"Not a lot slow about me. Now, are you gonna talk or dance?"

We left for Max's apartment around two o'clock in the morning, shutting the place down. I was worn out, so Max drove. The mood was still upbeat, until we walked into Max's apartment. The laughter ended as Max remembered why he'd kept me out.

His living room looked different. Things were missing or rearranged. Two pictures were still in their frames, but the glass wasn't there, and they were on the floor, propped against the wall. The coffee table was gone too. When he realized I'd noticed, his entire demeanor changed.

"What happened in here?"

"Why don't you ask your fiancé? He can fill you in."

"You weren't going to tell me about this?" I yelled.

"Nope. No biggie. We just had a difference of opinion. I can't blame him, though. You *are* his woman, right?" he asked with a sigh.

"Thanks. You make it sound like I'm a piece of property."

He punched the wall out of frustration, startling me. This was weighing on him as much, if not more.

"You know what I mean, Glover. Shit! I tried to do this tonight, pretending I'm okay, but I can't. You're about to get married and we're play-dating as if we're just friends. We both know it's more than that. A lot more."

He moved closer.

More than that.

A lot more.

My chest rose and fell, hinging on his very existence. With him alive, I was alive. The charge between us grew the closer he came. We were about to kiss. And then . . . after the kiss . . .

"We need to talk," I whispered, finding my voice before it utterly failed me. "Now."

It halted him. He said with a sorrowful look on his face, "You're right about that. I was going to bring it up earlier, but we were having such a good time. . . ."

"It's come to this?" I asked, already knowing the answer.

"Yep. I want you more than anything in this world, but not like this. This needs to be resolved one way or the other. Real talk."

"I had such a great time tonight. I didn't want it to end.

I . . . we can't see each other anymore, Max. I'm sorry." "Don't be. You made your choice. Things are back to the way they should be." He refused to look at me.

"Max. I—"

"I think you better leave. Now." Max rested his head on the wall, his eyes closed and fists clenched, shutting everything out—or keeping everything in, both equally painful. To try to stay right now would be sabotaging everything.

He deserved better. "Good-bye, Max."

I wept as I drove home, torn over whether I'd left the best man behind me for the right man in my life or vice versa. Max had breathed life into me like never before, but maybe his energy and passion belonged with someone worthy of him. Someone I clearly wasn't. My mascara ran down my face, its nasty taste on my lips. That night, I cried myself to sleep. Tears would tide me over, for I would wake to a brand new day.

36

Max

It tore apart my heart to deal with Glover like that, but it had to be this way. I went toward the door, but allowed it to slam shut. I slumped to the floor with my back against it, banging my head repeatedly.

After sitting there in silence, "manning up" to deal with my pain over losing yet another person that was supposed to be perfect for me, I picked myself up and went to my bedroom. I tried to fall asleep, but just tossed and turned. It was pointless. I gave up after half an hour, going to the kitchen to drown my sorrows. Maybe that would put me to sleep.

The refrigerator light formed a halo behind the six-pack of beer as if it were a sign. Not one to ignore signs, I carried the six-pack over to the couch. I normally would have placed the beer on my coffee table, but that was gone. I pulled one can free and left the rest on the floor on the side of the couch. Opening it, I noticed a small rip on the armrest; a reminder of my "disagreement" with Lionel. He'd won, and I'd blown my entire paycheck for the evening to end on this note. To think I'd intended on sleeping with Glover tonight as some sort of childish revenge against Lionel.

A last laugh on my part.

Yeah, that's it.

I let out a weak laugh of my own as I hit the TV remote. What was it about me that set me up for failure?

I sat on the couch, flipping channels between *SportsCenter* and *Anderson Cooper 360* while finishing off the sixpack. I had a good buzz going, but it didn't kill the hurt and confusion I felt. Maybe it was my buzz, maybe I knew what I was doing, but it was almost four o'clock in the morning when I walked over to my phone. I opened the drawer on the nightstand and looked inside. In the back corner, behind the West-tel phone book, were two discarded pieces of paper. I opened the yellow piece first. Scribbled on it was the number of the girl from El Ami, Diane, the one who left with Jay and her friend. I took a deep breath, stared at it. She certainly had my nose open that night, but there were too many lies wrapped around that. No more lies. On the white notepad paper was Velina's number. I honestly never planned on calling her, especially after meeting Glover, but I convinced my semi-drunk ass that she might be willing to take my mind off things with an impromptu foreign language lesson.

I walked back to the couch and took a seat. I hit the MUTE button on the TV. The phone rang twice before I considered hanging up. I realized that the booty call was shameless, as well as too late, for the best time for booty calls ended an hour ago.

"Hello?" said the man. A groggy man I had disturbed. Like I said, too late.

"Sorry. Wrong number."

"A'ight, dude." *Click.*

I hung up the phone and carried my pitiful ass to bed.

Four hours later, the small slits of sunlight coming through my blinds shook me from my coma. No matter how bad things were, I was still a morning person. My breath reeked of beer, my throat was dry, and I had a pounding headache to boot.

I never felt more alone.

I needed to get away.

I texted Jay to call me then waited. It didn't take long for my phone to ring.

"Hello?"

"Country, that you?"

"Cut that shit out." My head pounded when I raised my voice.

"A'ight. Whaddup?"

"I need a favor. Can you still hook me up on plane flights?"

"Yeah, cuz. I just need to make some calls. Gotta be sure she ain't went and got fired on me 'n shit. When you need this?"

"Today. I want to go back home for the weekend."

"F'real? Oh, shit. If I hook you up, you better bring me back some boudin or pecan candy."

Jay had a lady friend who worked for Continental Airlines. He always had someone on call for the hook-up, and loved to brag about it. Jay's bragging wasn't in vain this time. Two hours later, I sat in Jay's Beamer, still nursing my headache while rushing on our way to Terminal Six at LAX. My ticket was waiting for me at the airline counter. I called Samir earlier to let him know I was going out of town for a few days.

"That girl got you running out of town," Samir had remarked with a laugh.

I didn't reply.

"You know you coulda let me know about this earlier. I haven't been to Lake Charles since that last funeral. Coulda crushed some big, fine country girls. But I gotta work, though," Jay said.

"Sorry, cuz. I didn't know I was going 'til today. Anyway, Lake Charles ain't that country. You make it sound like people are walking around barefoot with tumbleweeds in their mouths."

"Whatever. I ain't worrying about no tumbleweeds. Bitches out there can walk around barefoot with my dick in their mouth, though."

When I didn't laugh or groan at his weak joke, Jay showed his human side.

"You okay, cuz?"

"Yeah," I mumbled, looking out the window at the traffic signs as we arrived. Jay drove into the departure lane and popped his trunk for me to get my duffel bag.

"Okay. How much do I owe you?"

"Don't worry about that, cuz. I took care of ya. Just don't forget to bring back that boudin. That's some good shit. I wish I could find some of the real stuff out here," he said, referring to the rice-filled sausage concoction I grew up on.

"Thanks, man. I owe you. I'll try to bring that boudin back, but you know how airport security trips over everything now."

"You know Pops gonna want you to come by for dinner when you get back. I'm sure he's gonna quiz you about what's going on back home."

I ditched my hangover during the flight from LAX to Bush Intercontinental. I had a short layover in Houston before taking a smaller plane on the connecting flight to Lake Charles. I took a cab from the airport to my mom's house, figuring I'd surprise her. I wasn't gone long, but there were already new restaurants along Highway 14 and on Prien Lake Road and Nelson Road, near the L'Auberge du Lac Casino. The area was in a state of flux after Hurricane Rita, between the infamous "blue roofs" still prevalent in the poorer neighborhoods years after the storm to the influx of gambling money from nearby Texas into the economy. With the money came the business boom, but also the loss of innocence that Lake Charles used to have. Things moved a lot faster in Lake Charles these days. Old ladies who used to be given proper respect were now victims of muggings and purse snatchings, all to feed the addictions of crackheads and other predators.

We turned off Highway 14 onto Oak Park Boulevard, where my momma's home was. We'd moved across Highway 14, the old dividing line, from the Terrace to Oak Park, when my father died years ago. At that time, the Terrace was a predominantly black middle-class neighborhood populated by those who worked across the lake in the chemical plants, including my dad.

My mom couldn't bear the memories of when my dad died in the explosion, so we left our house on Admiral Nimitz, and she'd been in her brick home in Oak Park ever since.

Oak Park was predominantly white at that time, but time seems to change all.

The blinds moved when the cab pulled into the driveway behind her Camry. Orelia always kept an eye open for strange cars in the neighborhood. As I paid the cabby, my mom ran out to greet me in her housecoat.

"Oh, my baby!" she squealed, almost lifting me off my feet, despite her small stature. I gave her a loving kiss on the cheek and returned the hug, savoring our reunion. A mother's love is something special.

While it was good to see my mom, I felt a little out of place being back. The area was changing, but so was I. It was like taking a fish out of the fish bowl, throwing him into the ocean, and then putting him back in the bowl. While in that ocean, it gave me a different perspective on many things; among them, friendship, family, and love. Now I was back where I started.

Orelia was disappointed when she saw only my duffel bag, and she was even more upset to find out I was only in town for the weekend.

"Baby, you sure you don't want to come home to stay?"

"I'm sure, Momma. I just needed a little break."

"You don't have somebody pregnant out there, huh?" What was this? Was my momma hanging out with Samir?

"Momma, you know better. Can't I just come down to visit?"

"Yes, but you didn't sound like you had any plans last time I talked to you. You hungry?"

"No, Momma. Just tired."

"Your room's the same. Go on back there and get some sleep then. We'll visit when you get up, baby."

I headed back to my old room, dragging my duffel bag behind me. On the hallway walls rested framed pictures of our family. I snarled at my kindergarten picture as I walked by. I had a big bush on my head and a tooth missing in the front. God, I hated that picture.

Before I'd made it completely to the rear, my momma yelled out, "Maxwell, are you going to see that Pitre girl while you here? I saw her in Prien Lake Mall last month. She said to tell you hi."

Instant migraine.

I clenched my duffel bag handle as if in a death grip. I wasn't expecting to get hit over the head with Denessa so fast, and it hurt like hell.

Denessa Pitre and I had been an item throughout high school and into part of my time at college. As with most things involving me, it didn't work out as planned. Her having a baby, courtesy of one of my boys, only five months after our break-up was another loud signal that things were over before I knew it. I never filled my momma in on the details. To her, I was just being a stubborn man who ran off a really good girl from the right family and right church. Despite Denessa's betrayal, Orelia was convinced we were meant to be, while I was left bitter about anything resembling a serious relationship, careful never to get caught up and burned again.

Until now.

Until Glover.

I dropped my bag on the floor and kicked off my shoes. I was about to crash, but decided to make a call to my apartment in L.A. to see if any messages were left.

None.

"Stupid, man. Stupid," I said as I threw myself onto the bed, just glad to be away for a while.

37

Glover

The wild ride I was on had come to an end. The game was over for me, no passing Go and no collecting $200. On the other hand, I didn't go straight to jail either. Enough with the Monopoly metaphors; the choice was made. I was going to be Mrs. Lionel Dunning, and everything would work out.

I cried myself to sleep after leaving Max's apartment, and woke up looking like shit on a very short stick. I showered, got myself right, and called my girls Saturday morning. I had an afternoon appointment scheduled at the bridal studio inside Barney's New York on Wilshire, where last minute fittings were to take place. Mona and Charmaine needed to be fitted also, Mona being my matron of honor and Charmaine being my main bridesmaid. Lionel's sister, Sarabeth, who was flying in from Europe, and his first cousin, Jazelle, were the other bridesmaids.

I surprised myself when I called Lionel, asking if he wanted to tag along; my way of telling him that my issues with Max were behind us. He was even more surprised by my request, but gladly agreed. I left the apartment, and along my route, stopped at the post office to put invitations in the mail before picking up Mona and Charmaine.

In Beverly Hills, we caught up with Lionel in front of the studio. He stood there, exuding his usual confidence, in one of his white linen shirts. It was as if we'd been reset to a more peaceful time, with a promise of better times ahead. I had gone through the motions before, but was determined to play a more active role from now on, affirming my decision as the right one.

The entire studio was ours during our appointment. Lionel's mother scheduled it, as everything else, in preparation for the event. The pampering and stuff made me uneasy, but Charmaine and Mona had no such problems.

A thin, middle-aged man named Carro greeted us at the door. He wore all black, was feminine in his mannerisms, and wore his thick black hair in a short ponytail. Carro hemmed and hawed around me while his fellow handlers served complimentary champagne to Mona and Charmaine. Lionel watched the whole scene with amusement. As my gown was finalized, samples of material rested on a small mahogany end table next to Charmaine, who sat in a highback chair.

"G-love, you sure about the dress?" Charmaine asked, holding a sample in one hand and an empty champagne flute in the other. "What about Nicole Miller or Carolina Herrera?"

"Charmaine, shush," I said as I gave her a disapproving glance. Their dresses were nice too, but I wasn't going to say it aloud. Carro heard Charmaine's remarks too. He stood motionless, with one eyebrow raised, before resuming his fussing over me. The last thing I needed was him getting ticked off and sticking me with a needle.

"I think Charmaine's enjoying the freebies a little too much," Mona said as she sauntered around the studio.

"Girl, you don't know what you're talking about. I've only had two of these teeny little glasses, for your information. You need to loosen up yourself," Charmaine said through squinty eyes. Then she stuck out her tongue at Ms. Mona.

Lionel tried not to snicker at the show. I suggested that the other handlers begin fitting Mona and Charmaine to keep them out of each other's hair. Now it was time for Mona's size four and Charmaine's size fourteen frames to be wrapped, taped, and measured like fashion mummies. I could only imagine what the wedding would be like with these two in it.

As I excused myself to go to the restroom, I quietly asked Mona if I could borrow her cell phone. Lionel was holding mine. She pointed to her purse, which was resting near the walkway. I walked past it on the way to the rest room, casually lifting her phone out.

I had to call Max to make sure he was okay and to let him know that I was happy. Even though our "relationship" had ended, I still cared about his well-being. Even in the midst of all this, it was hard not to think of him during the quiet seconds between the noisy minutes.

I entered the restroom and took a seat just inside the door. I dialed, letting the phone ring several times. I hung up just as the answering machine clicked on. No need to let my thoughts wander and ramble on there. I could wind up saying something inappropriate and further mess up Max's life—like how maybe I wished the final night I saw him had ended with us making love rather than arguing. He was too good a person for that.

I stayed in the restroom for a minute longer and splashed some water on my face. I'd begun to run on empty. My night before with Max and the lack of sleep was wearing me out. I needed some food for a quick burst of energy.

Upon my return, Carro had moved on to Mona and Charmaine. His fellow handlers scurried about as he barked out orders. While they watched Carro's antics, I slipped Mona's cell phone back into her purse and came over. I slowed by Mona.

"Had to call him, huh?" Mona cracked softly.

"Shhhhh," I responded. "It's all over. I was just checking on him. Real talk."

Her face twisted at my choice of slang. In reality, it was Max's. "If you say so, *Mrs. Dunning*."

"*Oh*. Mrs. Dunning. I like that. You say it so elegantly, Mona." I laughed.

"Would a diva do it any other way?" Mona replied, striking a pose with measuring tape dangling by her waist. A funny sight to behold, I think the free champagne had loosened her up too. Then we saw what the free bubbly could really do. Charmaine had begun singing to her handlers. Charmaine can't sing.

"We need to get that girl some food. Her ass is tipsy and about to fall over."

"And I ain't helping her up," I said.

38

Max

I didn't miss the heat and humidity of Louisiana. While only springtime, it was almost ninety degrees. Felt like I was walking around under somebody's armpit, but I was leaving for the cooler climate of Los Angeles tomorrow.

I spent the previous night just like old times, grubbing on okra and rice while catching up with my momma and visiting some of my people. I promised my momma that I would wash her car first thing after church. Since my car was thousands of miles away, Orelia allowed me to me roll in her Camry in exchange for cleaning it.

I had my momma's ride covered in suds at the car wash on Highway 14 when an old blue Buick slowly crept by the stall I occupied. The car, with its twenty-four-inch rims, was older than me, but the little baby gangsters inside were younger. The passenger had a mouth full of golds, but I couldn't tell if the driver shared his dental work. We exchanged nods before I resumed my scrubbing. No worries, no problems. I guess they were wondering who the "old guy" was.

Before returning to Los Angeles, I felt a deep-seated need to see my ex, Denessa. Maybe it was my momma's mention that set me on this course, but I think this was bound to happen from the moment my flight was booked. Maybe dealing with her betrayal could help me better understand myself. Maybe it was just a need for serious and legit closure. Or maybe I just never forgot about her and wanted to let her know. I'd know which as soon as I laid eyes upon her.

From what my momma knew, Denessa still stayed in the apartments off Fifth Avenue. My understanding was that she was no longer with my boy who fathered her baby, so I wouldn't be intruding on his turf by stopping by. Not that I was up for renewing old shit, but Denessa knew me in a way very few women did.

Maybe my time away had made me more critical, but her apartment complex seemed more run-down than I remembered. If I didn't recall them looking this way, I did recall the wild times we'd shared here, especially during finals, when I'd cram in more ways than one.

I didn't see Denessa's car, but got out to knock anyway. It had been a few years since seeing her, and she could've switched cars. A piece of folded paper rested between the doorknob and frame, along with a few colored envelopes, holding cards, no doubt. In spite of this, I knocked, to no response. I gave a final courtesy knock and waited.

"You a relative?" came from the unit down the hall.

"No, just passing by while I was in town," I answered, not feeling up for the questioning. I started to leave. Probably best she wasn't home anyway.

"Max? That's you?" the figure from down the hall asked, stepping out from the shadows of the doorway. A round, droopy-eyed brother covered in dirt and oil stepped into the light, jogging my memory.

"Monster?" I called out, recognizing my high school classmate from LaGrange. Monster, or Willie, his given name, was an all-star lineman who went to LSU on full scholarship. He was a sure shot at the NFL, until he blew out his knee leaping from a frat house window on a drunken dare. Now he was resigned to repairing cars at his cousin's shop on Mill Street.

"What up, dawg. You still stay out here?"

"Nah, dawg. Moved to Cali."

"Word? That's tight. You musta heard about Denessa, huh?" he said, motioning to the door on which I'd just knocked.

"No. What's up?" I asked, beginning to seriously consider the cards left in her door jamb.

"It was all over the news. Folks takin' it hard, dawg. She gone, dawg. Her, her little girl, and this dude from Texas that was hittin' that. They was movin' to Houston with cuz and he fell asleep behind the wheel 'n shit," he said, making an unnecessary sound effect. "Happened on I-10 just past Beaumont. Damn shame. Hey . . . y'all two used to kick it, huh?"

"Yeah," I said, reeling from the revelation. I had to get out of there before I lost it. Shit like this really showed me not to sweat the small stuff.

I went back to my momma's house and stayed there the rest of the day. Orelia was stunned when I told her about what happened to Denessa. She then called her town grapevine and confirmed it. She had seen something on the local news, but had missed the mention of Denessa's name. As distraught as she was, she was more concerned about my mental well-being. I won't lie; I was pretty beat up, but at least I was alive.

I gave my momma some money to put in on some flowers for Denessa's family. She was going to pick them up tomorrow to deliver them personally. When I found out the wake for Denessa would be tomorrow afternoon, I rescheduled my flight to later in the evening so I could pay my respects.

Monday morning, I got up early and headed to Goosport, on the north side of town, for a quick haircut from my old barber. Mr. Thomas' barbershop was off Opelousas Street, across from Immaculate Heart of Mary Church. When I arrived, he was outside doing some painting on the older building. He was happy to see me, but reminded me that he was closed on Mondays. My mind was so gone that it had slipped by me. After stowing his paint brushes, he opened to hook me up due to special circumstances.

While I got an edge and trim, I filled him in on how things were going with me in California.

"Don't worry, boy. I'ma send up some prayers for you. You gonna get that job you seek. You just gotta believe," he said as he edged me patiently with the straight razor. He followed it up with a smile and wink that seemed to indicate he was in on some higher-level stuff.

"Thank you, sir," I said. "I appreciate that."

"When are you going back?" he asked as he whipped the cover off me with his traditional snap. I was free to leave the chair and stepped down.

"Today. I have to go by a wake first."

"Family?"

"No, but someone I was close to once. Denessa Pitre."

"Yeah. I heard about that. A damn shame. Family lived off Shattuck Street. My condolences, son," he said, giving me a hug. "Just remember to put God first and to run, not walk, to those that He puts in our lives, for He knows why things happen, even when we don't understand."

I thanked him for both the cut on his off-day and the words of wisdom, giving him an extra tip before leaving out the door and down the steps.

There was a noticeable somberness in the car as my momma drove me to the airport. She knew I was in a fragile state after seeing Denessa's family and those closed caskets of her and the baby at Combre Funeral Home. I was selfish in my reasons for wanting to see Denessa, still clinging to resentments of the past. Obviously, she'd grown beyond crap such as me and my boy, and was moving to Houston to begin the next chapter of her life.

Then it was taken away in an instant.

Why?

I loosened my tie to help me breathe then turned the A/C vent on me as we drove up Common Street for the last flight of the night. I closed my eyes and took a deep breath.

"I wish you could stay longer, baby."

"There's nothing here for me, Momma." I regretted saying it like that, but she knew I wasn't referring to her.

Her last words were spoken to herself as well as to me. "I thought the two of you would get back together one day." She sighed.

I didn't respond.

Upon my return to Los Angeles, I was filled with restless energy. Unable to get Denessa out of my head, as well as Glover, I was consumed with rage and regret, feeling like a powerless little speck in light of events both past and present. Anything to take my mind off the grim shit would do, I thought.

It was after midnight, and the TV watched me as I darted back and forth, cleaning or putting away my things. I didn't have to be at Denny's until Tuesday evening, so I would have time to crash—or time to replay things over again.

Denessa.

Glover.

Both meant something. Hell, more than anything else in my life, at separate times. Now both were gone.

I was too young for this.

But that's just it. We have no control over when people come into or go out of our lives. We just have control over what we do while they're here.

I turned off the TV and put on my old Carl Thomas CD instead.

39

Glover

Monday was typically busy. The wedding preparation was in high gear and my bridal jitters were in full effect. Mona and Charmaine, the true friends that they were, made fun of me every chance they got. They looked forward to the wedding and reception at Catalina. Money was going to be in the air that day, and landing an available, financially stable suitor was a possibility for both of them.

I mailed invitations to my people back in Virginia, but I doubted they would show up, especially with the short notice. I didn't keep up with them once my grandmother passed away. When my mom died, a few cousins came down for the funeral, but that was it. Word has it that my mom was swept up in my dad's success and charisma and turned her back on most of the family, only to learn that he wasn't the good man he claimed to be. By that time, I was born and she'd burned her bridges with her people back home. That left just me and her.

I never really knew my dad's people and had no idea if he was even alive. Lionel's dad volunteered to walk me down the aisle, and I'd agreed to take him up on his offer.

Maybe that was another reason I didn't want a church wedding. It just didn't feel right with this situation. I mean . . . with my mom gone. The last time I had stepped foot in a church was for my mother's funeral, the day my best friend left me for good. It was an unresolved issue with me that I'd shared with no one.

Except for Max, the one person who was so considerate when speaking of her that day we first had lunch.

I considered spending the night at Lionel's after work, but only after stopping at my apartment to change. I'd resisted this long; maybe it was time to start moving a few things over there.

I had an unpleasant surprise when I jumped on I-10 after work. Some idiot in a stolen car had wiped out after a police chase, shutting down most of the westbound lanes. It wasn't until after eight o'clock that I came dragging in through my front door.

I was too exhausted to eat. After dropping my purse on the floor, I kicked off my shoes then dove onto my sofa. I arched back as I slipped off my bra and undid the button on my skirt. I let out a sigh of relief, as my slip had been rubbing my waist raw all day. The red skirt looked good on me, but it was getting a little snug and would have to go. Mona was smaller. Maybe she would have use for it after having it altered.

I leaned back once more, sliding off my pantyhose. The slip followed. I massaged the arches of my feet, applying pressure with my thumbs. Damn, it felt good. My dogs had been sore since the weekend. I did a lot of walking and standing Saturday during the fitting and stuff, but most of it was due to Friday night.

With a smile, my thoughts drifted to Max, and me trying to keep up with him on the dance floor. It was a wonderful feeling of freedom being there, just the music and us.

I chuckled, vowing to stow the memory away for safekeeping, before pulling myself up from the sofa. I poured myself a glass of white wine then sat back down. My last coherent thought was that I had to be at Lionel's, but a quick nap wasn't going to hurt anything.

I dreamed I was naked, soaring above the clouds. Below were lush green mountains, with birds chirping and waterfalls everywhere. The wind caressed my body as I did loopty-loops through the clouds without a care. This was fun. I'd never had a dream like this.

As soon as I got used to the flying experience, the weather suddenly changed. The white, fluffy clouds turned dark and stormy. Lightning flashed everywhere, frightening me. The thunder was deafening. Rain began hammering me to the point where I couldn't see. I suddenly fell from the sky, unable to scream.

As I came closer and closer to the ground, my heart threatened to burst from my chest. Clouds rushing past me, I flailed in vain, as I was still unable to scream or wake. I tried closing my eyes, but couldn't. My life was about to end and I couldn't do anything about it. When I had given up all hope, I was grabbed and pulled up to safety—

I woke in a panic, still on my sofa, and still in my shirt and skirt from work. I looked toward my blinds. Outside, I heard the rain crashing against the window. It was coming down sideways. I stared at the 12:15 on my clock at the same time a flash of lightning illuminated my apartment.

I had only meant to take a short nap before going to Lionel's. I knew I couldn't stay here. Thunderstorms spooked me, and my dream had me beyond rattled. I put my shoes back on, grabbed my purse, and ran out the door.

I hadn't realized how hard the rain was falling until I was outside running in it. My umbrella was in the car. I was drenched, but the awning over my parking spot gave me a break while I fumbled for my keys. Lionel was probably asleep, so I would just have to wake him up.

I drove my Civic west down San Vicente until I came to Hauser Boulevard. At the red light, the rain worsened. I focused on the wiper blades as they went back and forth. They were having trouble keeping up with the downpour, so I sped them up with a twist of the handle. The old truck in front of me waited for the light as well. When it turned, all I would have to do was make a right turn and head to Lionel's.

A left turn, however, would take me down Hauser to Venice Boulevard.

And to Max.

I was fighting this with all my heart.

Lightning danced across the sky, striking somewhere nearby. Then the traffic signal turned green.

Green.

Go.

It was time to make the right turn. I thought back to the dream that had left me so startled, as my wiper blades continued to move to and fro.

The truck ahead of me moved; then I drove off.

When I arrived, the rain wasn't coming down as hard, but it was still consistent. I decided to run for it rather than digging for my umbrella in the trunk. As I ran, I slipped in a puddle and almost busted my ass.

I'd regained my composure by the time I reached the door. I heard music playing. Knew the song, too. I grimaced over the thought of him entertaining company at this time of night. How embarrassing would that be? I almost didn't knock, but I had nothing to lose except my pride.

Pride only counts for so much. Sade put it best: Love is stronger than pride.

I knocked then waited. The music lowered, and then footsteps approached.

I was a pretty sick sight when the door opened, ruined bob and all. Max wore nothing but a blue towel. He paused, looked at me strangely.

"Are . . . are you okay?" he asked while watching the water puddle develop beneath me.

"Yeah. Just a little wet," I joked. "You have company?"

"No. No company."

Good.

"You smell good."

"Yeah, it's called soap. Look . . . Glover, I don't have time for this. I can't go through this again. Especially now."

I walked in, despite his objections, and pushed the door shut behind me. I stood before him and put my fingers to his lips.

"Shhh," I whispered. "Don't say a thing. I need you. Now."

I stepped out of my wet shoes and stood on one leg while I pulled Max against me. My other bare leg rubbed up against his. He began kissing my fingertips that were to his lips, then froze up and tried to back away. His towel had a slight rise to it.

He paused, closed his eyes, as if the sight of me would sway his thoughts. "Are you using me?" he asked.

"Maybe. I don't know. I was falling, and you caught me."

Max inhaled deeply, as if in a yoga class, taking a step back before he gave in and lunged. He was all over me, all into me, his kisses to my neck setting me afire wherever they landed. My head flew back as I sucked on my bottom lip in delight.

In the middle of his kisses, he whispered in my ear, "Why'd you come?"

The song Max was playing was Carl Thomas' "I Wish."

But, like the verse goes, I still belonged to someone else.

40

Max

"I'm here because I want you. I need you," Glover answered. The song playing said he wished he'd never met her at all, but I was glad I had.

My lips worked around her ear. Normally I might be able to fight it. Things were different, though. Just getting out of the shower, I'd been caught at one of the lowest points in my life. My trip to Lake Charles and learning about Denessa's passing had me reassessing things. I should be living every day like it was my last. Just like Denessa, Glover had been placed in my life for a reason. I could have made excuses about the jet lag and everything else, but they wouldn't hold up. I knew what I was doing, and so did Glover.

Our lips touched and we were back at that same point from a month ago, the point when her phone rang and we had stopped.

Glover moaned as I sucked on her tongue, tugging at it softly each time she offered it up. She ran her fingernails down my back and began tugging on my towel. It came off in her hand. With her other hand, she grabbed my dick, stroking it as she brought it against the warm area in the center of her skirt. I shuddered.

"I want it," she urged. "You gonna give it to me?"

Still embracing, we moved in synch, her following me with each backward step I took toward my bedroom. At my bed, I ran my hands from her shoulders down to the small of her back. I went past her skirt, reaching under to squeeze that bubble as I'd wanted to since the day I first saw it. Glover let out a moan as I gripped her ass cheeks with both hands, lifting her off her feet. She had nothing on underneath the skirt, heating me to no end. I yanked on the side of the skirt, sending the button flying and the zipper giving way. The skirt fell to the bedroom floor and she stepped out of it. The scent from her honey set my dick to throbbing uncontrollably.

"I was going to get rid of that skirt anyway," she joked.

She kissed across my chest and ran across my nipples before pushing me down onto the bed. I landed on a stack of clothes I hadn't put away yet, but quickly swatted them onto the floor. Glover stood there, her bare breasts visible through the damp white blouse, like some model who'd just stepped out of a waterfall. Her lovely golden legs rose up to that which the bottom of her blouse covered, teasing me, tempting me.

I was on my back with my hard-on saluting her. She crawled atop me, the light from my bathroom reflected off those crazy sexy eyes of hers. She smiled wickedly before taking me in her mouth with measured gulps, each one deeper and sloppier than the last.

"Shit. Fuck. D–damn," I muttered, pawing at the sheets as if on a runaway raft. As Glover brought me to that point, she eased off. She sat up, knowing how crazy she was making me, and began slowly unbuttoning her top. I relished the methodical striptease, waiting for the treat at the end as the blouse fell away, revealing those luscious breasts, her neatly trimmed bush and juicy mound. My mouth watered.

I sat up. While steadying her with my hand, I kissed her inner thighs, making them quiver. Kissed them tenderly while tasting the distinctive, salty flavor of sweat and passion mixed faintly with rainwater. The flavor of Glover. I immersed myself in it.

"Do—don't stop. You're making me so . . . so . . . hot," she gasped as I lapped hungrily at her melting center. As I indulged myself, she took my hands, placing them atop her breasts. She guided their squeezing and massaging, causing her to respond even more.

"Mmm. That's it. Eat it all up," she said as she worked her pussy against my mouth and tongue. Right there, if she could suffocate me beneath her desires, she would have. Her chanting grew louder the more she came. And the more she came, the more I took my fill.

Just then, a loud burst of thunder rolled outside, followed by an increase in the rain. Glover wrapped her fingers in mine and pushed me onto my back again.

"I want you," she confessed.

"I want you too."

She lowered herself onto me, my nose flaring as her essence overcame me. She let out an "Oh!" as I penetrated the welcoming warmth of her chasm. I was more than willing to oblige as she arched her beautiful body and began working atop me in a spasm of delight. The storm outside was nothing compared to the one raging inside the walls of my bedroom. Harder and faster we went, the springs in my mattress compressing and relenting.

Glover and I continued on until covered in each other's sweat. She climaxed several times as she rode. When I was close to coming, she would slow, to take me away from that cliff. She may have been making a mistake this night, but she was going to get everything out of it.

We eventually climaxed together as my toes curled and she collapsed beside me. Glover let out a low whimper, spent as she lay there convulsing and mumbling. Her eyes tightly closed, she clenched the nail of her pinkie finger in her teeth.

Once I was coherent, I turned over on my side and looked at Glover. The words just rolled from my mouth. I was still living in the moment and to hell with the consequences.

"Glover, I think I might be falling in love with you." It was a word I had intentionally avoided.

"Don't say that, Max," she replied with a smile, then left me in the bed to get some bottled water from my kitchen.

I caught my breath while Glover searched in my fridge. Stifled in my emotions by her response, I began to suspect I'd just been used.

She returned with the opened bottle of water in her hand. This was my first time to really take everything in. There was so much happiness in her smile at this point. I had gotten to know so much about Glover over the last month and a half, but tonight had brought me even further emotionally and physically with her. I had bared my soul tonight, and time would tell if she would do likewise, or if she even knew what was really there.

"Are you okay?" she asked playfully while climbing back into the bed.

"Yeah. Couldn't be better. Don't worry about what I said earlier. I just had to get that out. I'm not trippin'," I said, filled with false bravado. Glover reached out and handed the Dasani to me.

"Okay. You know what?"

"What?" I asked as I guzzled down the rest of the water.

"That was incredible," she said, her eyes widening for emphasis. "I mean it."

"Thanks."

"But . . ."

"But what?"

"It's not over."

Glover reached down between my legs and began stroking me with her hand. As the blood rushed once again, I rolled her onto her back.

41

Glover

"I feel like I need a cigarette," Max said as we cuddled, gazing into one another's eyes. It was four o'clock and I had to be to work in four hours. "Those things are bad for you."

"I'm joking. I don't smoke," he said before kissing me again. "What are you doing here?"

"I thought it was obvious," I answered, gesturing at our naked bodies with a smile.

"Cute. You know what I mean."

"I had a crazy dream and you were in it. I woke and was spooked. I just knew that I needed to see you. I didn't like the note things ended on last time."

"Neither did I," he said. "I see your ring is missing again. Forgot it?"

"No, not this time. I left it in my car when I was certain about what I was doing. I almost didn't come here. Real talk. I was trying to fight it with all my heart."

"I guess your heart gave up."

"No, maybe my heart won. For one night."

"One night?" Max sighed. "You're still going through with it, aren't you?"

"Yes," I replied softly, almost embarrassed. "Soon."

"I'll be checking my mailbox for the invite," he joked dryly.

"I saw your clothes on the bed. Were you going somewhere tonight?"

"Nah. Actually, I was just coming back. I went home for a few days. Had to clear my head. That didn't work out so well."

"It was hard on you too. I'm sorry."

"Sheesh. Enough with the apologies already," Max said as he tickled me. I felt electricity at his touch. "Instead of apologizing all the time and still doing things, you need to stay with me. Not that you asked for it, but in my opinion, you're making a mistake by going through with this."

"Something's different about you, Max."

"Yep. A lot can happen in a few days. My perspective's a little different now. It's still me, though. You never really told me much about Lionel. What does he do, anyway, besides providing you with obvious security?"

"He works downtown at B and G."

"Barnes and Greenwood? I thought he looked familiar when we *met*. I went over there the same day I met you. Maybe I saw him walking around or something."

"Oh yeah, when you met," I said, feeling sorry for the fight he'd been in because of me. I sat up in the bed, pulling the sheet up to my chest. "Max, I know you're tired of my apologies, but I am so sorry. Really. This is all my fault."

Max slid over and wrapped his warm arms around me. "Shhh," he said, shutting me up. "What's done is done. I'm as much to blame in this as anybody."

"Yeah. That smile is still the same," I said right before I kissed him. I pinned Max down onto the bed, climbing atop him as we continued to kiss. We wound up doing the do again. It was close to dawn, and I knew I needed to get home, but part of me refused to leave, for once I was outside this bubble, things would go back to the way they were.

That's life, I guess. The illusion has to give way to reality.

We never brought up Max's comment about falling in love with me. It was something I didn't forget, though.

After I borrowed his shower, Max was kind enough to let me borrow a pair of his warm-up bottoms. I could have used a safety pin to hold up my skirt, but some of my older neighbors would be gossiping.

We had a quick kiss as I rushed out the door to my car. My ring was sitting right by the gearshift, where I'd left it hours ago. I paused then closed my eyes as I placed the ring back on my finger.

I arrived home just as the sun rose in the sky. It was going to be another smoggy day in spite of the thunderstorms that had passed in the night. The damp ground was the only reminder of the storm—that and my sore body. Whew. I finally got to see him in action, and the pleasure was all mine.

I made it to work on time by the skin of my teeth. I was run down, but tried to play it off. I'd stopped at a Korean mini-mart on the way in and bought a can of Red Bull.

Mr. Marx had hired some more people, and things were at a bearable pace around the office. That was especially welcome on a day like today. The three chicas got to take a break together in the morning for the first time in weeks.

"G-love, are we doing anything this weekend? We haven't been out clubbing since that time at Drama." Charmaine smiled as she cut a sly look at Mona. After all this time, it was still a touchy subject with Mona.

"I can't. I have to go out to Catalina this weekend. The wedding's going to be here before I know it."

"Have you thought about the job here? Are you going to quit?" Mona asked. She was sitting back in one chair with her feet up in another.

"I'm still undecided, girl. There's so much I haven't had a chance to consider yet."

"You're going to have a bachelorette party, G-love? 'Cause I know some strippers who—"

"No, no. None of that," I blurted, cutting Charmaine off. After last night, I couldn't take any more excitement. "Y'all ain't getting me in trouble."

"Aw, c'mon," she pleaded. "You know Lionel's boys are gonna throw one for him. Hell, they're probably gonna truck in real live French whores for the event." Charmaine stood up and danced around the break room as if in a production of *Moulin Rouge*. We all burst out laughing.

"No, Charmaine. We already talked about that. Lionel's not going to have one either."

"I know I would want to go out with a bang—or two. We could've gone to Vegas," Mona said with a sigh, "but I guess you've made up your mind."

"Sorry. But you guys are right about one thing: the three of us need to do something together before I tie the knot."

"Um, G-love? I shouldn't bring this up, but you are about to be off the market and stuff. I was wondering about that fine-ass stud you were talking with in front of the office a while back. Since you don't really have a need for him, I was wondering . . . um . . . if you could hook your friend up. *Oh, the things I could do to him*."

Mona noticed me flinch in response to Charmaine's last comment and interjected, "Charmaine, please. Glover barely knows that guy. He was just checking on a job that day."

"Oh. Damn, G-love. You shoulda at least got the digits. I guess that's that." She shrugged.

"Sorry, girl." I gave Mona a thank-you look as I shrugged my shoulders at Charmaine. Mona was a master at reading people, and my body language had betrayed me. Luckily, our break time was over and we returned to our desks.

I was deep into my work when my phone rang an hour later.

"Ms. McDaniel. May I help you?"

"I'm calling about an interview." The joking voice on the other end of the phone perked me up instantly.

"Hey, you," I mumbled, curbing my excitement. No need for everyone in the office to know what I was talking about.

"Sorry to bother you, but I had to call. You think you're gonna be hungry Thursday night?"

"Thursday? I guess. Why?"

"No strings or anything. I wanted to know if you wanted some dirty South home cookin'."

"Are you cooking for me?" I whispered.

"Me? No! I'm having dinner at my Uncle Mo's . . . and I'm inviting you as a guest."

42

Max

After Glover left, I returned to the bedroom, where I stared up at the ceiling for about thirty minutes, reflecting on what had just happened. Glover was here. She really was here. And we'd knocked down some barriers while sidestepping others. While getting there was pleasurable, the end result was still frustrating. At least I'd offered her my opinion, finally getting that off my mind instead of being a pussy.

The sun was coming up and the rain had stopped. I needed to get some sleep, but I cleaned up and changed the sheets first. When I did sleep, I dreamed of making love to Glover over and over again. The damn girl had me feenin', and she was my drug of choice.

My dreams ended, giving way to total blackness. I had reached that point where everything shut down, giving my mind and body some needed downtime. Only the phone ringing brought me out of it just before noontime.

"Whaaaaaat?" I weakly groaned at the phone that wouldn't speak back to me unless I picked it up. Then I thought, *Maybe it's Glover.* Just enough to get my silly ass up.

"Hullo?" I answered just before the answering machine picked up.

"Hey, Country. Yo' ass made it back in one piece?"

"Yeah, cuz. Thanks. I forgot your boudin, though."

"How about the pecan candy?"

"Didn't get it either."

"Aw," he moaned. "That's fucked up, cuz. Let me guess, you ran into an old girlfriend and she fucked your memory away."

"No. An old girlfriend did die, though."

"Yeah, that's really funny," he snarked, not getting that I was serious. "You know you owe me double now."

"Yeah. I know, man."

"I told Pops you went to Lake Charles. Moms is cookin' Thursday, so you know the deal. Pops wants your momma to think he's taking care of you."

"I'll be there. Think they'd mind if I brought some company with me?" I asked, not knowing if she'd even agree; but I was living for the day now, and willing to take that risk. Besides, I had another motive for asking Glover to come along. Uncle Mo and them were the closest family I had out here. I wanted to see her through my family's eyes, as I was probably less than objective right about now. If the remote possibility existed of us somehow getting together, then Thursday night would give me a good indication about our future.

"Not that nigga Smitty, huh?"

"No, just a lady friend," I admitted.

"Oh shit! You got a woman, Country?"

"Naw, man. Just a friend."

Jay tried to get the details out of me, but there was nothing really to tell, and I was tired as hell. Besides, I could hear Jay's mouth now if he knew the details: *"Country, did you eat some of that girl's red gravy? 'Cause she got you trippin' and shit."*

I wasn't sure Glover would be interested until I called her.

When I picked up Glover Thursday night, I didn't know what she would be wearing. I played it safe and dressed up a little more than usual for dinner at Uncle Mo's. Instead of some dingy warm-ups, I wore a dark blue pin-striped Kenneth Cole dress shirt and my Lucky denims.

Good choice, considering how stunning Glover looked in her gray pantsuit. I dreaded having to keep my eyes on the road.

On the drive to Carson, I gave Glover some pointers on the Chavis family before we got there. The fewer surprises, the better, I figured. There was a spark in the air, different than our previous car rides together. We were no longer just friends, as evidenced by the way our hands kept wandering. It had to be awkward to be meeting my family in spite of her wedding day fast approaching, but Glover had indulged me anyway, leaving open the possibility that I wasn't totally crazy.

In spite of my warnings, I realized things were different when Aunt Lucy opened the door wearing makeup and one of her colorful shirts. Aunt Lucy was usually in the kitchen when company arrived, but not this time. Jay must have told them that I had company coming over, and she wanted to be the first to check out Glover. At the dinner table, the "good plates" were on display, and Uncle Mo, who was already seated, rocked one of his nicer golf shirts. Was that Old Spice I smelled too?

I pulled out Glover's seat for her before seating myself. I watched her eyes light up as the feast came out. Being free from ramen noodles again, I became pretty happy myself. Dinner consisted of smothered pork chops with rice and gravy, baked macaroni, green beans, cornbread, and rolls.

I pinched Glover's thigh under the table and she grabbed my hand before I could pull it back. Holding me captive, she gently caressed my fingers while Aunt Lucy explained how she moved heaven and earth for tonight's supper. This was the third time Glover had left her ring off; I contemplated it becoming a permanent condition.

Uncle Mo smiled approvingly as he fawned over my date. He'd cut a quick wink at me when he thought nobody was looking. I could attempt to reiterate later that we were just friends, but he probably wouldn't believe it. Based on our body language, I don't know if I'd believe it myself.

Uncle Mo looked impatiently toward the stairwell, ready to eat. "Glover, you'll have to excuse our boy, Junior. He should be down in a minute," he offered to her. Hey, what about me? Jay was keeping me from eating too.

"That's quite all right, Mr. Chavis. I'm happy to sit here and enjoy your company."

"Please, call me Maurice, girl," Uncle Mo said with a bashful grin, his old ass having flashbacks to his youth. If he didn't watch it, Aunt Lucy was going to clock him with one of her black cast-iron skillets.

Aunt Lucy joined in. "Glover, are your people from Louisiana too?"

Glover chuckled. "No, ma'am. Just Virginia," she replied softly. She had to be tired of people asking her the "Louisiana" question.

Finally, Jay jogged down the stairs. He wore red-and-black warm-ups with black Nikes. Something comfortable, like I would've done. I stood up to introduce Jay to Glover.

"Whaddup, cuz."

"Whaddup, Jay. This is my friend, Glover. Glover, this is my cousin, Jay."

Jay had a strange look on his face as he shook Glover's hand. His eyes squinted then suddenly widened. Glover's normal smile flipped into a scowl just as quick. Something was up.

Glover said, "Pleased to meet you . . ."

"Jay. Maurice Junior, but everyone calls me Jay," he shot off rapidly and with emphasis.

"I'm sorry. I almost had you confused with someone else. You ever been to Ohio?" she asked with a smirk.

"Nah. Just SoCal," Jay snorted before taking a seat on the side of Uncle Mo.

After that strange moment, we finally got to eat. Over dinner, I noticed Jay's gaze track from Glover to me and back again.

"What's going on?" I whispered to Glover as I wiped my mouth after savoring a piece of buttery cornbread.

"I'll fill you in when we leave," she said, cutting those dazzling eyes at Jay in a less than cordial way.

We were too full for dessert, but had four foil-covered plates for us as we prepared to leave. Aunt Lucy was talking it up with Glover as we started down the hallway. Jay shot away from the table, but started upstairs instead. He stopped halfway, where only his legs were visible.

"Ay, cuz. Let me holler at you real quick," came from the half of Jay I could see. I glanced at Glover. Aunt Lucy, and definitely Uncle Mo, would keep her entertained for a second.

I followed my cousin upstairs and into his room.

"What's up, Jay?"

Jay whipped around like he was wildin' out or something. "What the fuck are you doin' with that bitch?" he barked.

"Whoa. Slow your roll, cuz. What are you talking about?"

"That bitch down there!" He thrust his finger for emphasis. "Glover! Man, I thought I knew you better!"

"Again. I'm gonna ask you," I said, becoming heated at his tone. "What the fuck are you talking about?"

"Cuz, I fucked that ho. Met her at that club, Drama, a while back. Bitch is a straight-up freak. I can't believe you're bringing that up in my parents' house," Jay muttered, a disdainful gaze cast at me.

"Jay, you need to shut the fuck up right now because you don't know what the fuck you're talking about. And that *bitch* and *ho* shit ain't cool." A sick, angry feeling was gathering in the pit of my stomach.

"Cuz, I ran into her in the club before. Dropped her a line about being a TV producer 'n shit. Next thing I know, Bam! She up in the hotel sucking my dick, ass, and whatever. Straight hit it and quit it. I know you country and shit, but you can't be that stupid. That bitch playin' you."

I felt ill.

"You're crazy, man. Fuck you."

"You need to watch your mouth. That bitch got your nose all open. If you want to be parading around with a ho on your arm, then go ahead. Just don't bring her around here. She ain't that kind of material, cuz. How long you known her anyway?"

I ignored Jay and started out of his room. Answering that question would only further his argument. The mouth wouldn't let it end, though.

"Bitch was good, though. Rode me like a pro."

Game over.

I slugged Jay right in his mouth. Blood dripped through his fingers from his busted lip, staining his white T-shirt. As he lay there on the floor, I waited for him to get up. Dared him, with fists clenched. When he didn't comply, I turned around and headed out the door.

Jay blurted out through his covered mouth, "I hope you get what's coming to you, punk-ass nigga. She's gonna lie to cover her ass. Watch! See if I ever look out for you again!"

Shit. I'd scraped one of my knuckles on Jay's teeth.

43

Glover

I couldn't believe this shit. Max's cousin was the brother in the suit from Drama. Called himself Cary, Terry, or something like that. I wasn't positive, until his reaction to me confirmed it. A really small world, this town was. I think he squirmed enough at the dinner table. And living with his parents, too? Lawd, I hoped Max was nothing like his fake-ass cousin.

While I talked with Max's delightful aunt and uncle, Max had run upstairs. For a second, I thought I heard someone shouting. Max came back down, said a quick good-bye to his people, and then stormed out the door ahead of me. Something was up. He was to the front lawn before he noticed that I had four plates in my hands. Max caught himself and came back to take two of them from me. He then opened the car door for me. As I entered, I caught him flexing his right hand like it was hurt or something.

As we drove up the I-110 ramp to head north to my apartment, I was determined to find out what had him so riled up. Lord knows, Max wasn't going to willingly volunteer anything, having been the strong, silent type up to this point.

"Dinner was da bomb, Max. I'm going to have to jog eight miles to work this off—or maybe just have a repeat with you." He didn't respond, so I continued. "Your aunt and uncle were great company. You were too . . . up until we left."

"Oh. Sorry."

"What's wrong?"

"Nothing."

"Something's wrong. Mr. Sunshine is suddenly all cloudy and overcast. Is this about your cousin?"

"Yeah. I guess so. Kinda."

"Did he tell you about the club?"

"Yeah. He told me something."

"And?"

"And I punched him."

"Over that? I mean, he was an asshole, but maybe punching him was a little extreme."

"Naw, I don't think it was extreme at all. So the shit's true then?"

"Yes . . . I guess. I don't like your tone, Max. Wait. Wait. What did he say happened?"

"Some shit about you leaving Drama with him."

"What?" If I'd been driving, I would've slammed on the brakes. "That lying son of a bitch. Max, he tried to pick me up and was dismissed. He claimed he was a producer or something from Ohio. Even went by a different name."

"Oh."

"Is that all you can say? Oh? Your cousin said something else, huh?"

"Don't worry about it. It's nothing."

"Nothing? Max, you haven't looked at me since we left. What did he say?"

"I really don't want to talk about it. It's nothing."

"Max . . . did he say he fucked me?"

There was silence on his part. I had my answer. Now I was pissed.

I pushed further and asked, "That's what he said, huh? Shit. Ooooh! I hate motherfuckers like that!"

Max started to speak, but clammed up.

I swatted at Max out of frustration, my eyes watering up. "Answer me, dammit! Do you believe him then?"

Max blinked then turned slowly toward me. Looking at me, his silent rage was fading as mine was skyrocketing. "No," came softly from his lips, but it wasn't adamant. Lacked that resolve I would've expected out of Max.

And it hurt.

"Hmph. I guess blood is thicker than water," I tsked. "Well, fuck you and your lying-ass cousin."

"I said I didn't believe him."

"It wasn't what you said, but how you said it."

"How do you expect me to act, Glover? My cousin, who I've known my whole life, drops this shit on me and I wind up clocking him. You, who I've known a few months, are on the other side, screaming at me because I'm not jumping up and down. C'mon, let's look at our history here . . ."

It really hurt.

Max had lashed out unintentionally, but it still hurt. Tears streamed down my face. We merged onto I-10 west. I would be home soon.

"Can't say I blame you. Why should you think otherwise? I guess I have been acting like a ho since I met you. Why should you believe me when I say that what's going on with us is the first time I've done something like this?"

"Look, Glover. I didn't mean it like that. It came out wrong. I wasn't trying to hurt you. Jay can be full of shit, and I've seen him lie to women in clubs before. I'm just saying that—" He paused, ensuring his thoughts caught up to his mouth. "I've never had him knowingly lie to me. To others, yes, but not to me. And I definitely don't think you're a ho."

"Are you anything like him?"

"Like Jay? I don't think so, but he is my cousin, and I do love him. He's family. "

Family. I turned away, staring at my reflection in the window. "I don't need to be coming between you and anybody," I mumbled.

"I've got a lot of crazy shit going on in my head about now. I know I said no strings and stuff, but I would be lying to myself if I wasn't hoping that tonight would move us in another direction. I had no idea that *this* would be the direction." He sighed. And I knew it was coming. "You've got your thing with Lionel and I've got mine. I think it's time the games end."

We didn't speak the rest of the way home. Max did offer a kiss on the cheek before I exited his car. I told him that I didn't want to be walked to my door and to keep the food from his family. I started toward my apartment as he drove off, but turned around when he got down the street.

I decided I needed a walk, a chance for some fresh air. I reflected on Max's "no strings" comment, and about how I'd avoided the L word with him. Funny thing was that I was praying that tonight would move us in another direction as well, for as much as I put my head in the sand at every turn, I did love him.

44

Max

Confusion and pain ruled after our night ended. Jay had pushed my buttons, and I'd gone and lashed out at Glover.

Or *was* that how it went down? Was she playing me?

Tonight was the first time my unwavering belief in what I thought I knew was shaken. Glover had dictated the terms since the beginning. She pulled my application and called me, even though she was engaged. Then there was the other night, when she showed up at my doorstep. I could have stopped everything at any one of those spots, but I wasn't man enough. I liked the attention and her company. Hell, I liked her . . . and still do. *Love* was probably a more appropriate word, but I was too pissed to go there. To top everything off, I had come to blows with my cousin. That was some wrong shit.

Jay's venom-filled words were still smarting. I only paused to wonder what he would have to gain by lying to me about Glover. If I knew the answer to that question, I'd be a millionaire.

I ran into Smitty in the parking lot Friday. I was on my way to Denny's and hadn't seen him much since my fight with Lionel. Smitty's ride was working again, as his job was beginning to pay off. I could tell, as he'd added a bunch of new white dress shirts and a few more ties to his work wardrobe. We gave each other dap as we passed by.

"Maxwell, where ya at, boy?"

"Jus' chillin', Smit. How ya been?"

"Never better, man. Never better," he beamed with confidence. "At six months, I'll be up for a raise. Right now, I'm just saving to get another ride. Heard anything yet with the jobs?"

"Nope." I felt embarrassed at my failures just then. All of them. "I'll give it another week before I start looking further out."

"Yeah, it'll work out for ya, man. You haven't had any unexpected visitors lately?"

"Naw. That was the only time he came around. If he comes back, I'll tell him to leave another hundred-dollar bill for you. That whole chapter is closed, though—permanently."

"What? I know thangs ain't through between you and ol' girl. Wasn't your little crackerjack stereo blastin' the other night? Fine-ass Glover was there, huh? Tell the truth."

"Doesn't matter, man. Shit's in the rearview mirror, ya dig? I went home last weekend. Had to get away for a little while."

"Aw, dawg! You went to Louisiana and didn't think about ya boy? I coulda been the high yella hunter with my safari hat 'n shit, in the bush, stalkin' big game with my big dick."

"It came up suddenly, man," I said as I laughed at his silliness. "I'll think of you next time. Jay screamed at me about that too."

"Where's pretty boy been hiding?" I had to bring up Jay.

"At home, I guess. Saw him the other night. He's still the same." *A certified grade A asshole.*

"Bro, I'm off Wednesday. I've been working late and they don't want to pay me overtime. Wanna hit Venice?"

"That sounds good. You're still working on being the next Kobe?" I joked.

"Nah, dawg. Chris Paul, from your neck of the woods," he answered. "We little guys gotta stick together."

"*Whatever*, Smit."

"We're gonna do it up, Wednesday. Just you see. It'll be just like old times," he said in what almost sounded like a pep talk for my benefit.

"Yeah. Old times," I agreed, hoping my grimace wasn't evident. "Hey, I gotta run. I'll talk atcha later."

Yeah. Old times.

I was back to playing games. Idle while the world passed me by. One step forward, two steps back.

And off to Denny's I went.

45

Glover

I'd made the twenty-six mile trip from Long Beach to Catalina a few times before, but never in a helicopter. Every other time had been by boat, down there. Way down there. I cringed every time we dipped or turned.

As we drove down to the Port of Long Beach, past the surfers, Lionel had given me every chance to chicken out; but I was all woman—and a risk-taker, as evidenced by the way I'd been living recently.

As we drove into the Port parking lot, I did clench Lionel's free hand a little harder. He leaned over, giving me a kiss on the lips to calm my nerves. Behind my shades, I closed my eyes and let my fears subside. Like the morning fog, doubt had dissipated in more ways than one.

I wore a short-sleeved white linen dress with tan sandals and my little straw hat. The cool morning

breeze off the water made me wish I'd worn something warmer. The air swirling about the helicopter
wouldn't help.

Lionel wore a tight blue shirt with gray slacks.
His abs showed through the fabric, and the
weather appeared not to bother him. His faux
spectacles dangled on the end of his nose as we
strolled toward the heliport. Lionel had 20/20
vision, but liked to look distinguished from time
to time.

We had two fellow passengers this cool Saturday morning. One was an elderly, balding
white man with a camera around his neck. The
other was a middle-aged East Indian gentleman.
The cheery flight crew greeted us and gave their
safety speech. Lionel thought it cute how focused
I was on their every word.

"Babe, if it goes down, not much you can do,"
he teased before assuring me we'd be okay. Gee,
thanks.

They led us to the bright yellow bird in which
we were to ride. Lionel spoke with the pilot, telling him we'd need a taxi on the island. I still considered the boat trips to be more romantic, but
the aerial view of L.A. Harbor and the island was
breathtaking. Being near the clouds, it made me
think of my dream, where I was flying and Max
caught me as I fell.

Okay. Not what I should be thinking about.

The flight took about fifteen minutes, but seemed to last much longer. Lionel had his arms around me to keep me warm. When we landed on Catalina Island, our taxi was waiting to take us into town.

Our wedding was to take place at one of the inns on the island, with the actual ceremony taking place up the cliff overlooking Catalina Bay and the Pacific Ocean. A breathtaking view. I expected Lionel's mother, Adele, to make the trip with us, as she was the grand dame of such preparations. Just my luck, she was already there when we arrived. Lionel's father, Goodwin Dunning Jr., was also there. I guess Lionel spoke with him and he was there to keep Adele in check. Mr. Dunning was simply an older version of Lionel, except for the salt-and-pepper hair and the fact that he was a few inches shorter. Both of them gave me a hug and a kiss when we walked up to the outdoor staging area.

"Oh, Glover, you are looking so pretty this morning! Carro, the fitter, called me, you know. You are going to make such a lovely bride for my son. I was debating with Goodwin when you walked up. Do you think the orchestra should go here or over there?"

"I think it depends on the placement of the tables, Mrs. Du—Adele," I answered, catching myself. I still couldn't bring myself to call the roody-poo Mom.

"Well, we can decide that later. Have you heard from any of your people yet, Glover? I'm trying to get an informal head count for the caterer. It doesn't really matter. I'd rather err on the side of excess anyway."

"No, I haven't heard anything. There may be some friends from school, but I haven't heard from my relatives in Virginia."

Lionel's dad interjected, "Glover, I know it's short notice for them, so let me know if they need to be flown in. I'll take care of that, if you don't mind." Lionel's dad was helpful with no strings attached. I honestly felt like he had no problems with his son marrying a "commoner." His going out of the way to make me feel like family really touched me.

"Thank you, Mr. Dunning. I'll let you know," I said politely. I didn't expect any of my relatives to show, but I wasn't going to admit it in front of Adele.

"Hey, Glover! Come take a look!" Lionel hollered in my direction. He had walked away from us and stood admiring the view. I came over beside him. The haze had burned off, so we could see past the yachts in the bay and out into the never-ending blue.

"This is wonderful. It makes me think about our first time out here."

"Good. This time will be the best ever. See out there?" he asked, pointing to a position in the sky. "The doves will be flying out and turning around right there."

"I can't wait."

"Glover, I'm glad you made this choice. I love you."

I hesitated before saying, "I love you too, Lionel," crossing that threshold.

46

Max

I'd just hung up the phone when it rang. I had been checking on movie times. Hadn't seen anything since sneaking around with Glover, so this was going to be a solo run.

"May I speak with Maxwell Guillory?"

"Yes, this is he."

"Mr. Guillory, this is Amy Sorinson with Sandifer Industries human resources department. How are you today?" "Fine, fine," I answered as I ran around the apartment looking for a pen and paper.

"I'm calling to inform you that we received your job search information from the State of California. We're in partnership with the State. There were no current job matches available with the State, so they forwarded your information to us. Mr. Guillory, your employment application came with an impressive recommendation from your local Employment Development Department office. Okay?"

"Okay." Glover. It had to be. "Sandifer Industries is headquartered in Concord, but we also have offices in the Greater Los Angeles area. Would you be interested in interviewing for one of our openings, sir?"

"Yes, I would. Could you tell me more about the position?" I asked with paper in hand as I still fumbled around for a pen.

"Good. We have an opening for a human resources assistant in Concord as well as in Los Angeles. Sandifer Industries is involved in the field of medical equipment sales, and the interview would take place in Concord. Okay?"

"Excuse me if I sound dumb, but where is Concord? I'm not totally familiar with California." I'd found a pen and was scribbling madly.

"No, sir, you don't sound dumb at all. Concord is located in northern California, northeast of Berkeley and Oakland. Mr. Sandifer is a real hands-on employer, and he likes to meet potential employees personally. We will provide transportation, and all additional information will be forwarded to you in a packet via certified mail. The salary range will be included, and is open to discussion.

"We would like to schedule the interview as soon as possible, and would appreciate your calling us with the date you have selected. Of course, this is after you have had a chance to review the packet material. Okay?"

"Okay," I replied, now accustomed to her overuse of that word.

"And if you have a couple of minutes, I would like to confirm some personal information. Okay?"

We talked a little longer. Afterwards, I calmly turned off the phone and placed it on the counter.

Then I lost my damn mind.

After wearing myself out from kicking and flailing and fist-pumping like Tiger Woods on a Sunday, I sat down and caught my breath. I still couldn't digest it all, but if everything went as I hoped, I would be on my way to some stability and opportunity.

Finally.

I don't know whether Glover's recommendation had any bearing on the call, but I wanted to call and thank her anyway.

Who was I kidding? I just wanted to hear her voice one more time. I put the phone down. Getting out of town for the interview would do me good. If I distracted myself a few weeks longer, Glover would be happily married and completely out of reach.

47

Glover

Club-hopping before my wedding wasn't in
the cards, but Mona had to arrange something
for the chicas to do together. Wednesday evening, she let us accompany her to her strip aero-
bics class at S Factors. Personally, I think she
just wanted to show off how fit she was.

Mona stood one row in front of us, a figure of
grace and sensuality, while we struggled in back
just to stand on one leg without falling over. I
wasn't straining as much as Charmaine, but my
coordination left something to be desired. And
we hadn't gotten to the pole yet. Putting my best
foot forward, I paid close attention, as some of
these moves could come in handy on my honeymoon. By the time class was over, I'd learned
to do a mid-body spiral and one of the sexiest
Goddess poses you've ever seen. Mona awed us
with a perfect Ballerina, and Charmaine fell on

her head while trying to perform a Descending Angel. Lucky for Charmaine, there was nothing in there to damage.

Since we were near Santa Monica, Mona's turf, we followed her to the Jamba Juice on Santa Monica Boulevard. This Chicano dude who worked the blender struck up a conversation with the still-not-in-her-right-mind Charmaine. I swear if he could see the little birdies floating around her head, he would've passed.

While he worked on getting those digits, Mona and I took our Banana Berry and Aloha Pineapple to our table. Charmaine joined us shortly, her Mango Peach Topper in hand, whistling and waving her cell at us.

"Mona's not the only one with game. Free smoothie, plus I got the digits," Charmaine oozed as she pulled up a chair.

"Girl, leave me out of this. You know I don't run game on people, they just happen to gravitate in my direction. What's your new friend's name anyway?" Mona asked as she took out her compact mirror to look at her hair.

"Spill the beans, Ms. Fulda!" I egged Charmaine on.

"His name tag said *Rogelio*, but ya never know."

"Looks like it reads *minimum wage* to me," Mona cracked, her disregard apparent for any man without significant bank or significant status.

"Don't be so shallow," I urged Mona. "I'm just glad we got to do something together tonight."

"Even though I didn't come to watch Mona sliding on a pole," Charmaine shot.

"Hmm, what did you come here for tonight anyway?" Mona asked with one eyebrow raised. She chuckled then went back to fixing her hair.

"For your information, Ms. Stevens, I came here tonight to bond with my friends and to whip my fat ass into shape. Most importantly, I came to spend some time with my girl G-love before she gets hitched. Watch. She's gonna move to the 'burbs and never see us again."

"Aw, Charmaine. You know I'm not disappearing on y'all. I'll still be here and we'll be hangin' as always."

"Glover, I know you say that now, but seriously, do you really know what you want to do once you're married? You must have some plans or dreams other than staying at the office with us," Mona inquired.

"Don't laugh, y'all. I've always wanted to make gift baskets for people. I don't know how realistic it is, but it's always been a dream of mine."

The two of them just looked me, expressionless. I waited for one of them to either laugh or say something.

"And sell them at the swap meet? Eeeew," Mona complained.

"I think it's cool, G-love," Charmaine offered. "I'm still plodding through life in a daze. What about you, Mona? What do you want to do?"

"I don't know. I just don't know," she replied, playing with her straw. "As far as a career goes, I may return to college. Get my masters. I think I avoid moving up in salary intentionally. Deep down, I'm afraid of becoming like my dad. I'm not getting any younger, but to tell you the truth, I like my independence."

"So the diva likes to be a rebel," I said while sipping from my cup.

"It is the nature of a diva to be rebellious. I know these things."

"What *don't* you know, Mona?" Charmaine joined in. "You might as well write a diva tell-all book."

"Except no one would buy it," I cracked. That'll teach her for making fun of my gift basket idea.

Finishing her drink, Mona threw her straw at me. Times like this, I knew why I hung with my girls.

Mona, Charmaine—each chica crazy in her own special way.

I told myself things would be the same, but didn't really know the changes in store after marriage.

48

Max

"Good!" Smitty called, nailing the sweet jumper as he came off the pick I'd set for him.

We'd hit Venice early, determined to shake off the two-on-twos we'd lost previously. We had a short wait to get out on the court this time. The two dudes who beat us last time were there again. I think they remembered us by the way they started grinning when we walked up. This time, we played three-on-three, with us picking this big-ass "Q-dog," fresh out the weight pit, for our team. Brother-man was bigger than me and Smitty combined. Some rollerbladers in bikinis stopped to check out the game, so we didn't want to disappoint.

We played three games, with our rivals winning the first one. We took the next two convincingly once we got warmed up. Smitty kept nailing his shots in spite of the hands in his face. I think the bum had been getting in some practice on the sly. I wasn't a slouch either, playing much better this time. The game was stress relief to me as I took my aggression strong to the hole.

Slam!

We congratulated and high-fived each other on games well played, but our two rivals weren't smiling. They gave us the nod of respect, though. Our team even got a few cheers from the women by the fence. They could have been screaming over our teammate's horseshoe-branded muscles, as he flexed at them, but me and Smit knew what really made the women wet—our game.

Yeah, right.

I placed my towel over my head as we walked off the court, talking shit.

"Damn, dawg. We did that," Smitty boasted as he slapped me on the back.

"Hell yeah. Tired of being a victim, Smit. Nothing but wins from here on out."

"Sounds like you're still tryin' to get Glover out your system rather than winning a game of hoops."

"Too late. She's already out," I said, trying to convince myself. "And I got better news than that. Got a job interview next week. Up in Concord, dawg."

"For real? That's my boy!" Smitty cheered. "Looks like we're gonna be eatin' steak and skrimps soon. Your treat, of course."

"Wish me luck, man. I would be assisting with recruiting and hiring for this medical equipment company. I'll find out more when I go up there. I think Glover recommended me when she submitted my app to the State."

"I know she's *out of your system*, but you need to thank her. At least a handshake if you ain't gonna fuck her," he joked. "Seriously, though, y'all make a cute couple, and you normally don't hear that mushy kind of shit from me."

"I think the best way to thank her is to stay out of her life," I said as we continued walking.

"You know what's best for you, man. What you need is a good piece of ass that'll make you move on."

"If you're still trying to do Zena favors and hook me up with Niobi, you need to stop."

"Man, I apologized for that already. Besides, Niobi moved on after she saw you all googly-eyed with Glover at the barbecue. She hooked up with the brother that sold Zena her rims and shit."

"Good for her." I sighed. "What's up with you and Zena? Ain't seen her in a minute. Y'all still kickin' it?"

"Sometimes. We've always done our own thing, but things are coolin' off. She's been distant since I got my job. I kinda expected it. I think she liked it better when I was broke. There's also women at my job."

"Oh?" I reacted, knowing how Smitty was.

"Nah, nothing like that. Don't get me wrong, they're *foin* at West-tel, but I ain't about to get my ass fired. Zena liked it better when I was at Costco. Less women there."

"Sounds like she likes controlling you."

"She need to control all them damn lollipops she be suckin'. You hungry?"

"Hell yeah," I answered, looking at Jodi Maroni's up ahead.

"Good. Guess I can splurge on ya. Once."

I slapped him upside his head then took off running for some hotdogs.

49

Glover

I didn't realize how much junk I had until I tried packing it up. I sat in the middle of my apartment floor, wearing the same Hello Kitty sleep shirt I'd gone to bed in. Lionel would be by later to help move some things to his—um, our . . . the house.

I'd gone to bed early Friday, eyeballing the things I wanted to box up, and then putting everything into action at the crack of dawn. My lease expired at the end of the month, and my furniture was going to storage until we decided what to do with it after the honeymoon.

We were honeymooning at Victoria Falls in Zimbabwe. Lionel had fast-tracked my passport and was taking his queen back to the motherland, despite Adele's "suggestion." She'd tried to talk us into going to the island of Santorini in Greece, but we would have time to see it on a regular trip. To hell with her. It was my honeymoon.

I'd already filled a large green garbage bag with stuff I was throwing out. From all the junk I'd hoarded and accumulated, it was going to take several more bags. I was contemplating what to eat for breakfast when my phone rang.

Assuming it was Lionel, I reached over a stack of old magazines and located my phone.

"I thought your ass would be here by now. You know it's wrong to keep your bride-to-be waiting," I answered, lying on my back with my legs crossed.

"Hello?" Oops. The voice on the other end was confused, and it definitely wasn't Lionel.

I caught myself and said, "Yes?"

"Is that you Glover?" The voice was vaguely familiar.

While trying to place the voice, I answered, "Yes. May I ask who's calling?"

"It's your Uncle Robert."

That name brought back fond memories from years gone by. Robert was my mother's half-brother. I assumed he was still in Virginia. I'd met him once or twice while visiting my maw-maw as a little kid. He was mostly a loner. I think he was keeping up my grandmother's house since she passed away. I had sent an invitation addressed to him at that address.

"Hey! How are you?"

"I'm making it, niece. We're all doing fine out here. Look, we got your invitation, and I just had to call you. I called the RSVP number and spoke with this woman . . ."

"Adele?"

"Yeah, that's it! That's your mother-in-law, right? Nice woman. We talked for a good while. She speaks very highly of you. Anyway, she gave me your number so I could call you." Shit. She probably buttered up Uncle Robert, pumping him for the 411 on our family. Lionel's mom could be the charmer when she needed to be.

"I know we haven't been close, but I was so happy for you when the invitation came in the mail. Y'know, I'm married now myself."

"For real?"

"Yep. I slowed down long ago," he said. I never knew him to be fast. "Got a wife and two little kids now. Work up at the factory too."

"I'd love to see you again, and meet your family as well."

"Well, you'll get your wish. We're coming to your wedding, Glover. More of your people wanted to go out there to California, but don't have enough time to take off from work and stuff." Possibly true, but on the other hand, some wouldn't care for anything to do with my mom or her daughter.

"I'm sorry about that. That's all my fault, Uncle Robert. Look, I don't want to inconvenience you or put you guys out. I'll understand if you can't attend."

"No, don't be silly. I've got some money saved up, and my wife has always wanted to see the West Coast. We're coming to see our girl off properly . . . that is unless you don't want us there."

"No! No! Not at all. I want to see you, and I would be honored to have you at my wedding."

"Thank you, niece," he accepted. "Glover, you know your momma and me were never that close, God rest her soul. I just want you to know that I regret that to this day. You know how most of our family is, feelings easily hurt 'n stuff. Some of them were pretty spiteful when your daddy left you guys after your momma turned her back on them. Besides that, people get caught up doin' their own thangs, and it winds up being years before anybody speaks again. I'm probably the worst of them all. That why I personally want to let you know that I'm sorry and that maybe we can make a change starting now."

"Yeah. Maybe we can, Uncle Rob," I replied in agreement as a lump formed in the back of my throat.

"You're going to make a lovely bride. Girl, last time I saw you, you were the spitting image of your momma. Except for them eyes," he mumbled. "Those eyes you got from your dad. Worthless scoundrel. Sorry about that."

It was a time to heal. My Uncle Robert had taught me that. Maybe this wedding could be the start. "Uncle Rob?" I said.

"Yeah, Glover?"

"Um, I know it's late and all, and I'll understand if you say no, but I was wondering, would you walk me down the aisle?"

"Of course, niece," he replied.

From a better place, my mom was smiling.

50

Max

"Excuse me," I said as I moved aside for the people who knew where they were going and how to get there. Having adjusted to Los Angeles, I was reduced to tourist status here. Nevertheless, I adjusted my tie and moved with the flow.

My airline tickets, along with instructions to Sandifer Industries, had arrived just as Amy Sorinson had promised. Upon arriving at Oakland International, I'd changed into my interview suit and taken the BART, after learning what it was. I'd travelled north to Oakland City Center station, where I had two hours before my interview in Concord. Per the mini-map in my briefcase, it would only take thirty minutes to get there. Having a little time, I skipped the first train and went exploring.

Goosebumps popped up on my arms and neck as I walked through the crowd, imagining it was my daily routine. The thrill of a new challenge and a new place gave me a nervous feeling, but a good nervous feeling. I inhaled deeply, envisioning success on this trip. I'd imagined something similar when I stood in the CBD of downtown L.A., but the feeling was stronger this time. I felt sure that I belonged.

Right here.

Right now.

I wanted to stretch my arms out and proclaim, "Hate it or love it, the underdog's on top," but decided against it. There'd be plenty of time for the haters.

The spirit uplifted me from Oakland to Concord. From the BART train to the taxicab that took me through the main gate of Sandifer Industries, it was with me. I admired the precise, manicured landscaping on the grounds as my cabby droned on with the history of Concord, California and Sandifer. The only thing that stuck was him saying that Concord used to be called All Saints by the Spanish.

We entered a large circular drive and came around the Sandifer logo in front of the headquarters' main entrance. The building was only five stories tall, but the shiny metal-and-glass facade stretched on forever, curving like a rippling wave. I gave the cabby a generous tip, hoping I would recoup it with my first paycheck.

A security guard guided me to the front desk, where I was presented with my visitor's badge. I was early for my interview, so asked for the restroom.

Inside the restroom, I opened my briefcase and reapplied cologne, did the breath and underarm checks, and eyed myself in the mirror. While I checked my nose for stray boogers, a bearded, middle-aged white guy in a Hawaiian shirt and shorts exited a stall and washed his hands. Nothing I could say.

"That bad?" he asked with a laugh.

"No, just freshening up. Been flying 'n stuff."

I adjusted my suit a final time in the elevator on the way up to the fifth floor, becoming conscious of every little wrinkle and line. The pinging sound indicated I'd arrived, just before the doors parted. Waiting for me was the same guy from the bathroom.

"Small world, huh?" he teased.

"I—"

"Just breathe. I'm Brad, by the way," he said, patting me on my shoulder. I assumed he was HR, or simply helping out, as he escorted me down the hall. We talked some small talk, with him offering to get me some water, which I declined. At the end of the long corridor, we stopped at a large corner office. On its massive door was a plaque, which I scanned as I went by: BRADLEY SANDIFER III.

An HR rep was in the interview, but my guide was not that person. This was the president of the company who was walking with me. I'm glad I didn't do or say anything too stupid.

The interview was conducted by both of them, with Brad doing most of the talking. The HR rep sat and took notes, only joining in from time to time. I felt pretty comfortable, hoping it was reflected in my answers without my seeming cocky. Brad was an energetic fellow, straight out of an infomercial at times, explaining their business and products at a frantic pace. The only uncomfortable moment was when my cell phone began ringing. Being on vibrate may have been better, as it played the opening verse to Li'l Wayne's new song. I quickly turned off my phone, apologizing profusely. By the time the interview was over, I had forgotten all about it.

With no further questions, Brad gave me a brief tour of Sandifer Industries headquarters. I was given the impression that I had this, pending my physical and drug test. I wasn't sweating that, as I never touched drugs. Salary still had to be discussed and agreed upon, and Brad was unsure if the opening would be in the Bay Area or L.A., but I wasn't picky.

A change of scenery would do me good, as a certain someone still lurked in my mind, in spite of the craziness with Jay. I still wrestled with the issue of who was telling the truth, but it didn't matter now. Glover was jumping the broom this weekend, if I remembered correctly.

As I headed out the front lobby, I asked the receptionist if she could call a cab for me. My flight back to L.A. left in a few hours, so I called home to check my messages while I waited. My answering machine told me I had two messages. The first message began playing when I remembered my missed call during the interview. I was looking down at the displayed number I didn't recognize when I heard the message:

"Max, this is your Aunt Lucy, baby. I need you to call us as soon as possible. Something's happened to your cousin. Junior's been shot." Aunt Lucy's voice was shaken.

I was in shock, felt the weakness in my knees as I hung up.

"Could you call the cab company and tell them to hurry up?" I asked of the receptionist. Not bothering with the second message at home, I hung up and called my Uncle Mo's number.

Something told me to stop, though. I hung up again and checked the missed call one more time.

The area code was 310.

I pushed the button to call it back. The phone rang a few times, and then someone answered.

"UCLA Medical Center," they said.

51

Glover

My recent nights were spent at Lionel's. I was on leave from my job, finalizng the wedding plans and going over last minute details. I apologized to Lionel's father for my Uncle Rob replacing him in the wedding. An apology really wasn't needed, but I felt obliged, as Goodwin had been kind to me throughout. Uncle Rob had his measurements taken at a tux shop in Virginia and called them in to me. He and his family would be here Friday, so I offered up my apartment, as there were still a few weeks on the lease. I would just hold off on moving my furniture.

It felt good knowing I'd have family at my wedding. Deep down, something still didn't feel totally right, but there was no turning back.

A lot of my belongings were moved or packed up now. I was going to miss my place. Once cozy and cluttered, it now felt vanilla and soulless. A lot of my personality had gone into it in the five years I'd lived there. From the odd picture frames to the little green ceramic frogs in my bathroom, this place had been me.

Most of my stuff didn't fit with the theme of my future home. I entertained the thought of setting up a little private room to myself over there, a place to which I could escape and retain a piece of me. *Maybe do my gift bags in there*, I thought with a laugh. I dismissed it all, though, as being childish and immature.

Fuck it. Lionel would just have to put up with my little frogs in the bathroom. It still wasn't perfect, but it would do.

My last piece of unfinished business needed to be taken care of. Something I could only do alone and in the privacy of my apartment. I picked up the phone several times before putting it back down on the stand and walking away. I even let out a shriek of frustration as I kicked one of my throw pillows across the floor, terrified of somebody answering and my cool melting.

Yep, I was one trifling sister right about now.

After pulling out enough of my hair, I went for it. I left my eyes closed as it rang. My wish that the answering machine would pick up was granted. I kept my eyes closed, letting my thoughts flow—the last thoughts of Glover McDaniel before she would be swallowed up by the House of Dunning, never to be seen nor heard from again.

"Max, it's me. You probably didn't expect to hear from me again and probably don't want to hear from me."

Eyes still shut, I bit my lip before continuing.

"Don't worry. This is the last time. I'm through fucking up your life."

I exhaled deeply.

"There's just stuff I need to get off my chest, and I don't trust myself talking directly to you. As strong as I believe myself to be, I guess deep down I'm a scared little girl. More like a coward, the more I think about it. I've done some awful shit since I first met you. I've schemed and given in to temptation. I've done some wrong things to both you and my fiancé."

A nervous giggle escaped as I bared my soul more to a lifeless machine than I could to a real person.

"Max, for that shit that went down with your cousin, I don't blame you for believing him, even if you say you don't. As misguided as your loyalty may be to him, it is loyalty that you have. That's probably one of the things I like about you. Loyalty is something that . . . that I've been lacking. And I'm trying to make up for that these days."

I paused, debating whether to continue. I hoped I'd run out of time and the phone would just hang up on me. It didn't, so I kept going. Virtual confession.

"We've never said the words, but Lionel knows or suspects what was going on with us. I don't have to tell you that, though, and I'm sorry for things going down like that. I'll have to live with what I've done and with what I'm about to say . . ."

My heart screamed out for the first time since my mother had passed away. Tears wanted to burst forth, but I wouldn't let them. Held them back out of fear.

"I love you, Max."

Four simple words that had weighed a ton until I'd set them free.

"Heh," I chuckled. "I think I realized it when we first had lunch at the diner. Oh God, I can't believe I admitted this." I began choking up. My words slowed. My throat constricted.

"I love you enough that I want nothing but happiness for you with whoever is lucky enough to be all yours. I wish that were me, but unfortunately, it can't be. Max, I will never speak these words to you again—or even admit saying them.

"It was incredible knowing you for this brief time, so I thank you for that. Don't think about calling me back. I won't be here. And I'm sorry for . . . for all of this. Good-bye, Max."

My eyes hurt from being clenched shut for so long. After hanging up, I still refused to cry. I was Glover, my mom's tough little girl.

I unplugged the phone permanently from the wall and left.

52

Max

I treaded through the isolation of the ICU, nothing more than the hum of respirators for company. I hated it. Some warmth and hope would have been welcome in its place. Aunt Lucy's wailing shattered the cold serenity. I followed the sound, rushing headlong around the corner to see Aunt Lucy going ballistic in Uncle Mo's arms. He held her tight, rocking back and forth to soothe her. They stood in the hallway outside a room, positioned as if defending it from unseen forces that threatened their son. I slowed as I came upon them, waiting for the right moment when they'd see me. The look of relief on their faces told me the most important thing: Jay was alive.

Aunt Lucy's eyes were painfully swollen, with dried salt from her tears on her cheeks. In spite of him being the rock of the family, Uncle Mo's eyes were red too, his voice straining as he greeted me. We all embraced in silence then said a prayer.

Aunt Lucy had done her best to fill me in when I called the hospital earlier. Jay had been shot last night. He took two in the back after work. He was on the mall parking lot with some woman when someone came up from behind and shot him. The guy was still on the loose after leaving Jay bleeding on the ground with two nine-millimeter slugs in him. Talk was that it was gang-related, even though Jay wasn't a gang member. It was touch and go most of the night, but they got Jay stabilized just before dawn.

Aunt Lucy had left a message on my answering machine this morning, but I had already left for the airport. Uncle Mo found my cell number, and they called it when they didn't hear back from me.

"Maxwell, your cousin done it this time. Messin' with them girls finally caught up with him. I told him time and time again, but his ass wouldn't listen," Uncle Mo said as he cleared his throat.

"I'm sorry I couldn't be here sooner. Is . . . is he gonna be all right, Uncle Maurice?"

Aunt Lucy composed herself and answered, "Junior had his spleen taken out. He . . . he can't feel his legs, Max." She broke down once again.

"The doctor just told us about his legs when you got here. My boy might not walk again. If I catch the punk that did this, I'ma kill his ass." Uncle Mo's voice broke off as he covered his face with his hands to hide how he was losing it too.

Uncle Mo's primal howl rocked me to my core. One of them I could handle, but not both. My control started to slip as I tried to tend to them.

A petite nurse came out from the nurses' station to render assistance, seating my aunt. She told Aunt Lucy that God would take care of everything, as she rubbed her back.

A doctor and another nurse emerged from Jay's room. He was stable and conscious, but in a great deal of discomfort. One of the slugs was still in him, and it wouldn't be known if the paralysis was permanent until the swelling had gone down.

"Are you his cousin?" the doctor asked.

"Yeah," I replied.

The doctor told me that Jay was asking for me, but to make my visit short. I was surprised by his request, especially after our last encounter. I don't think my aunt and uncle knew anything about that. I gave them a smile to reassure them, then wiped my face and went in.

Jay's eyes flickered as I approached. His face, laced with tubes in his nose, looked dry and pale.

Aunt Lucy had placed a set of Rosary beads in his hand. My gaze trailed down to his legs out of instinct. I was hoping to see a twitch or something.

"Whaddup, cuz?" Jay asked, his crackly voice trailing off at the end. His lips barely moved when he spoke.

"Hey. Don't talk too much, man."

"Moms okay?"

"Yeah. She's in the hall with Uncle Mo."

"How do I look?"

"Like shit."

"Still hatin' with yo' country ass," he joked, fighting off a cough.

"Who did this, cuz?"

"Remember dudes in my store that day?" he asked, referring to the gangbangers I'd seen once. "Talkin' smack is one thing, but I . . . never . . . thought . . ."

"You told the police?"

"Nah. Way . . . too much . . . trouble." He coughed. "Ol' girl this was about knows where I live. Don't need Moms and Pops catching anything. Besides, they didn't touch my face."

"Look, I'm going let you get some rest, cuz."

"Sit, man. For a sec."

I debated ignoring him, but complied. I took a seat in the chair and scooted closer.

"Remember when I dropped out of school?"

"Yeah."

"That was over a girl, man. Can . . . you . . . believe? I was wildin' out when I got to UCLA. Met shorty my second year." He smiled, medication having him here and somewhere else simultaneously.

"Man, we can talk about that later. You just get some rest."

"Shut up. If I don't talk about it now, I never will."

Not one to question what my cousin needed at this moment, I did as he said. I listened.

Jay went on to tell me about this girl with whom he'd fallen madly in love. No one off campus knew about it, including his parents. They dated for two semesters and were inseparable. Jay gave up his playing for her and was about to propose. He'd even bought a ring and planned on moving out of Uncle Mo's. Jay had the ring with him and dropped by her dormitory to surprise her.

"She surprised me," he mumbled. "All three of them did. Fuckin' dudes from the football team were runnin' a train on her. Whole dorm knew. Then . . . motherfuckers beat my ass for interrupting them. She wasn't sorry. Shit . . . hurt."

"Damn, man," I gasped, realizing so much about him now. My cousin sought payback on some level for the humiliation he'd suffered, taking it out on every other woman he'd been involved with from that point on. I put my hand on his shoulder, glad I'd taken a different path after Denessa's betrayal with my friend back in Louisiana.

The nurse came in to check on Jay, and I got up to leave. I was pulling on the door handle when he spoke again.

"I'm sorry, cuz." Not being sure of what I heard, I stopped and listened.

"Jay?" I called out while the nurse checked his monitoring equipment. His pain meds were kickng in, and I wasn't certain he was still awake.

"I'm sorry, cuz," he repeated, more like a groan than a statement. "I lied, man."

"About what?"

"Your girl. I made that shit up."

I stood in stunned silence, unable to move.

Jay continued, still conscious. "I met . . . her ass in the club, but she wouldn't give me any play. Pride was hurt. Maybe I was jealous when I saw her with you. Dunno."

"Dammit, Jay!" I yelled. I caught myself when I looked at the monitor Jay was hooked up to. The nurse was startled by my outburst, but went back to pretending to ignore our conversation.

"Guess I was dumping a lot of my baggage on you when I made up that . . . shit about her. Good punch, Country," he wheezed.

I was fuming still, but it was under control, due to the circumstances. "Don't worry about it, cuz. You just concentrate on getting better. That's all over with now anyway."

"Why you fuckin' with me, nigga? You in love with that woman. Could tell from the look on your face that night. That's why I was so mad. Knew . . . that . . . look. It was the same one I had . . . before . . . You wouldn't have hit me like you did if you weren't."

"She's getting married, Jay. It's over."

"No shit? Damn," he said as his voice tapered off all wispy-like. Jay's eyes shut. The nurse didn't like something she was seeing with his readings.

"Sir, you have to leave now," she insisted.

53

Glover

Early Friday morning, Lionel drove me to LAX. Uncle Robert and his family were in from Virginia. Lionel had rented a minivan for Uncle Rob and them to use during their stay. He figured they would like the extra space and might want to do some sightseeing while in California. Uncle Rob's wife wasn't going to let him get out of here without hitting the tourist stops.

I saw them as they waited for us in passenger pickup. My uncle was, with the exception of his beer gut, just as I remembered him. I spotted him right away, due to the Hampton University T-shirt he sported. I remembered that he used to do maintenance work there and still had mad love for the school. His wife, Tasha, stood at his side, her braids sticking out from her denim baseball cap. She talked to him while holding the children's hands. She and the kids wore T-shirts and shorts, but the shirts were obviously purchased here. The women, Tasha and her daughter, Tandy, wore Lakers T-shirts, but the little boy, Randy, wore a red Clippers tee. Yikes. He was only three, so I could excuse it. Either he liked the colors, or they'd run out of his size in Lakers gear.

Listening to my uncle and his family during the ride to my apartment brought so many memories rushing back from my trips to Virginia. This was my first time meeting Tasha, but she felt like family right off. She was funny as hell, with a real down-to-earth manner about her. She and Charmaine would make for an interesting wedding.

We planned on letting the family unwind first at my apartment, since the dinner/rehearsal was later that evening, but they were ready to go. Uncle Rob and them wanted to eat at Roscoe's, so we headed there after unloading their luggage at my place.

I had more to take care of before the rehearsal, so we left the van with them for the rest of the day. I had a map of the area, with some directions to different attractions programmed into the GPS for them, but Tasha was one step ahead of me. She had a highlighted map with every place she wanted to see. We took some pictures with them for Tasha's photo album then left in my Civic.

"That was so sweet of you to rent the van for them," I said to Lionel with an appreciative smile as we drove off. I leaned over and gave him a kiss as he pretended to blush.

"Nothing to it, baby. I'm glad some of your family could make it. After all, they're going to be my family, too, in a couple of days."

"Yep, one big, happy family," I said, tongue-in-cheek, knowing the two worlds would never cross, except in a Hollywood production.

The rehearsal dinner took place at Lionel's parents' home that night. My uncle and his family followed Lionel and me over there. I watched the reaction of Uncle Rob and them in the rearview mirror as we drove through the gate. I smiled, as I had the same reaction my first time.

Iris escorted us to the enormous glass-walled room in the rear. She didn't exit back up the hallway this time. Instead, she disappeared amongst the extra servants that were on hand for the night. The other members of the wedding party were already in attendance: Lionel's sister, Sarabeth; his cousins, Jacob and Jazelle; his co-worker, Derek; Leu, his friend from Stanford; and Esai, this Dominican brother who was Lionel's childhood friend. Of course, my girls Mona and Charmaine were in the house, lighting it up with their presence.

It was different seeing the large space filled with people, tables, and food. Even with everything in here, there was still enough room to hold the wedding in this place. Once she had everyone's attention, Adele coordinated a brief run-through/rehearsal of what was to be expected on the island. The wedding party would take the boat out to Catalina tomorrow for a walk-through at the inn, and then spend the night there. The guests and other family would be ferried in for the ceremony on Sunday.

Following the dinner, the obligatory mingling took place. Chatter, emotion, and piano melodies overflowed throughout the Dunning home. Lionel introduced me to his buddies, but I left them shortly so they could play catch-up and indulge in male bonding. Adele had a group in her clutches, standing at its center on one end of the room. Goodwin, ever the smart one, had stepped out to smoke one of his Cuban cigars. Uncle Rob and Tasha were still seated, as the kids wanted more to eat, so I decided to hang out with them later. I went by the glass wall, trying to peer out into the night, when I was tapped on the shoulder. My friends had located me.

"I done died and gone to heaven, y'all. You think your mother-in-law would give us a tour of the rest of the place?" Charmaine asked.

"Probably not. She's busy right now doing her thang before her audience."

"She's right, Glover. This is sweet. My father's place down the street is nothing to sneeze at, but the square footage here is colossal," Mona chimed in, lifting her glass up in an imaginary toast to the residence itself. "Enough about the house. How are you managing tonight?"

"I'm doing all right," I answered as we lightly touched fists. "Don't know how I'd be if you two weren't here."

"We got your back as always, G-love," Charmaine assured me.

"I know. Part of me still wants to run out of here, y'know. I guess it's time for the jitters."

"You wouldn't be human if you didn't get the jitters. Now, someone like me couldn't be caught having jitters."

"Brrrrrrrrr, Mona the ice queen," Charmaine teased while looking cross-eyed at her.

"Keep up that shit and your eyes are going to stick just like that," Mona replied as she playfully shoved Charmaine. "Seriously, though, you are going to make a beautiful bride and an incredible wife, and we are both sooo happy for you."

"Thanks, you two. For everything."

As I smiled, I looked out the glass and into the darkness, broken up by tiny little dots of city lights. I picked one spot of light and focused on it. I closed my eyes and let my mind take me there.

54

Max

It was Friday evening before it set in that I'd been wearing the same clothes since Wednesday. A simple whiff under my arms was all it took as I unlocked my apartment door. I'd stayed at the hospital with Uncle Mo and Aunt Lucy until they chased me out of there. A shower and some sleep were what my exhausted body and mind needed. Jay wasn't out of the woods completely, but was much better than when he'd been carted into the joint. With no feeling in his legs still, we were praying for a change. I wasn't sure if I could look at him straight again after his admission, but that didn't matter just then. Jay's health was more important than any hurt or anger that lingered in my heart.

I'd called Samir from the hospital, filling him in on the news, both good and bad, that had come up all in one day. He told me to take off

whatever time I needed and to let him know how
Jay was progressing. He'd offered to check with
his former friends from the hood about the guy
who did this, but I declined. Jay just wanted to
put this behind him. As far as my interview, he
congratulated me on that, joking about training
me too well. Samir was always more optimistic
about my future than I was. It was time I shared
that optimism and generated a healthy dose of it
myself.

After prying my clothes off me, I immersed
myself in some soap and water. The hot shower
helped release the knotted muscles in my back,
reminding me that sleeping in hospital chairs
was something I didn't want to master. As the
steam filled the bathroom, it was time to get
some sleep before I wound up making a bed of
the bathtub. I staggered out of the shower, tow-
eled off, and carried my weary body to the bed.

I was asleep before my head hit the pillow.
Clothes would have to wait.

Instead of the peaceful embrace I expected,
my mind wouldn't shut off. It raced; it darted; it
erupted, attempting to process everything from
its whirlwind tour of interviews, gunshots, rev-
elations, and betrayals. As I tossed and turned,
images of Oakland, Concord, Los Angeles, and
Lake Charles blended together in peculiar pat-

terns. Jay stood over me, screaming in pain one moment and laughing the next. Suddenly, I was in the hospital bed. Instead of Jay, I was the one paralyzed, unable to move or do anything about what I was witnessing.

Lionel and Glover were at the foot of the bed, a minister standing before them as they kissed. I tried to get out of the bed to stop them, but crashed onto the hard floor. My legs wouldn't work. I cursed at them to stop, but Lionel kept kissing her, only stopping to look down at me and smile. Glover looked my way too, but wouldn't say anything. Just a sorrowful gaze in my direction before resuming her business with Lionel. I tried to drag myself toward them but couldn't. The world slowed with every crawl I tried to make with my arms.

Then I felt a sharp pain. Somebody's foot stomped on my hand. My eyes traveled up to see the foot's owner.

I looked up to see Mr. Thomas, my barber from Lake Charles. Although yelling at me, I couldn't understand a word he said at first. His words became clearer the more I concentrated. "Didn't I say to run, not walk?" he asked, referring to our conversation about Denessa back in his shop.

Denessa, my ex. Betrayal. Now gone.

Glover had been put in my life now, but I had neither run nor walked to her. I'd gone away . . . thanks to Jay.

And myself.

Lionel and Glover were still kissing passionately. I'd forgotten the pain from Mr. Thomas stepping on my hand. As I concentrated on Glover, she began to flicker and fade. In and out, like a snowy image on an old black and white TV, or that creepy girl from *The Ring*.

I looked at Mr. Thomas again and he nodded at me. Understanding what he meant, I reached up to grasp the bed railing. He disappeared as soon as I touched the bare metal. I began to pull myself up. I still couldn't feel my legs, almost slipping to the floor again, but something changed. I was standing now.

I began to move, step by step, as feeling returned to my legs. Glover was still fading in and out, but now her image was a lot blurrier. It got worse the more my slow movements toward them increased. As I finally began to run, it was as if they were further away, always the same distance apart from me, no matter how hard I tried. I now couldn't make out Glover's image at all as she continued to kiss him.

Finally, I made progress. As I got closer, I prepared to leap at them.

Then I did it, launched myself in the air, sailing toward them like some shit from *The Matrix*, when suddenly, Glover's image cleared up; but it wasn't her anymore. Lionel was still there, but he was kissing this new person now.

The phone awakened me in mid-leap. I don't know how I heard it. I lay there naked, across the bed, blinking my eyes. Such an odd dream.

The phone rang a few more times before I got my bearings and sat up. I didn't know how long I had been asleep.

"Hello?"

"Max, you okay, baby?"

"Um, yeah. I'm fine, Momma. Just getting some sleep," I said between yawns. "Been at the hospital since Wednesday. Jay's doing better, though."

"Your Uncle Maurice told me. He called me from the hospital a little while ago. That was nice of you to stay and look after your cousin. I raised you right. He said how tired you were, so I wanted to make sure you made it back okay."

"Yeah, I made it, Momma. Thanks for checking on me."

"I'm your momma, boy. I'm supposed to do that."

I threw on a pair of boxers, trying to write off my nightmare as a product of a sleep-deprived mind. The answering machine showed two messages on it. I decided to check them before falling back asleep. The first message was from Aunt Lucy. She must have called me twice, as I had heard the first one while in Concord. The second message was left on Wednesday also. I was rubbing my eyes when I heard Glover's voice: "Max, it's me."

Twenty minutes later, I was speeding my Corolla down San Vicente to Glover's apartment. I tried calling her home number before running out of my apartment, but it had been disconnected, with no new number. I cursed at myself for not having memorized her cell number, deleting it from my phone after the dinner at Uncle Mo's. Even if I had it, she probably wasn't answering.

Glover's car was gone from her parking lot, but that didn't stop me from pounding on her door until my knuckles hurt. She was out there somewhere. I just didn't know if I was going to have enough time to do or say anything to her.

55

Glover

The hum of the motor and the subtle rocking of the boat didn't help my hangover. I sat motionless, with my legs up on the bench and my back resting against Lionel's shoulder. Those of us in the wedding party were going over to the inn on the island. Adele had gone over via helicopter at the crack of dawn. I didn't know where she found the energy. That was one thing I could admire about her; that and the fact that she gave birth to such a fine man as Lionel.

Uncle Rob was seated down the bench from me. He found out the boat ride was going to take over an hour, and was in dreamland five minutes into the trip. At least there were no bugs around this morning to collect in his open mouth. Charmaine was playing on the upper decks with Uncle Rob and Tasha's kids. She was going to make a good mother one day. Free to explore, Tasha was out by the railing taking pictures of the channel and the shore. Earlier, she'd taken a bad picture of me, over my objections. She was family, so I excused it—as long as it didn't wind up on MySpace. Besides, I could always get her to delete the photo later in exchange for some more Roscoe's or Harold & Belle's.

"I'm having trouble keeping my hands off you, baby," Lionel said in my ear as he rested his head against mine.

I adjusted my hat and playfully replied, "Baby, this pre-wedding abstinence must be kicking your ass, huh?"

"Yep. Bad idea. I don't care if Jay-Z and Beyoncé did this before theirs. I'm ready to break you in half."

Tasha woke up Uncle Rob prior to docking, and then the kids jumped in his lap. Mona came over from where she'd been hiding and stood over us.

"Your big day is almost here, Ms. McDaniel. Yours too, Mr. Dunning," Mona said with her attention focused on him. "Treat my girl right. Okay?" she demanded, her eyes refusing to blink.

"Of course, Mona. Would you think otherwise?" Lionel asked, returning the same stare.

The strange little interchange between Mona and Lionel was interrupted by the boat's docking announcement. Once ashore, we spilled out into the island's town of Avalon. Our bags and accessories were being delivered straight to the inn, and Uncle Rob went with them. He had to have a last minute adjustment made on his tux, as the sleeves were too short. "Girl, this is Saks Fifth Avenue. I may never wear this stuff again, so I want to be looking right," he'd commented before leaving us.

Lionel and Leu mumbled golf lingo to themselves as they discussed the courses on the island they wanted to hit. We had time for sightseeing before the walk-through at the inn, so I excused Lionel to give the links a look-see with Leu. Esai left with the two of them. Derek, Lionel's coworker, decided to shop for souvenirs for his wife. Lionel's best man, Jacob, who appeared to be smitten with Mona, lingered for a while before following the other three to the golf course. Jazelle, Jacob's twin sister, was sleepy from her Aunt Adele's party the night before, so she gave me a hug and kiss on the cheek before excusing herself for a catnap.

That left me with Mona, Charmaine, Tasha and the kids, and Lionel's sister. I never really got to know Sarabeth during my relationship with Lionel. She'd spent most of her time abroad, flying in for holidays. Just as Lionel shared his dad's complexion, Sarabeth shared her complexion with her mom. She was an exotic beauty with an almond complexion and deep, penetrating eyes. She wore her black hair long and straight, just like her build.

Sarabeth was not one of many words, except with those people she was close to. I felt I would never be in that category, so I didn't let it get to me. My thoughts about her mom, the matriarch of the family, didn't help the situation, though.

As our group walked along, I tried to break the ice with my future sister-in-law.

"What have you been doing in Europe, Sarabeth?" I asked harmlessly.

"A little of this, a little of that. You know, one can never be too rooted in any one place or thing. So much class and culture out there," she answered, the silent insinuation about her current surroundings heard loud and clear.

"I wouldn't know. Never been there."

"*Oh*? That's right. I had forgotten. Lionel told me that before. You work at the *unemployment* office, right?"

"Employment Development Department is the actual name of the place."

"Riiight," the bitch said with a dismissive grin. Like mother, like daughter, except the mother knew restraint. "So, are you quitting there before or after you go to Greece?"

"I don't know if I am quitting. And it's Africa we're going to, not Greece."

"Yes. Silly me. Lionel told me about that change of plans. My mother was quite upset."

"Lionel tells you a lot, huh?"

Sarabeth stopped in mid-step. "Glover, my brother tells me everything, even while an ocean away." Her body language, as well as her eyes, reaffirmed that remark. I knew what she meant. And I knew where I stood.

Sarabeth took that moment to dismiss herself under the pretext of wanting to be fresh for the walk-through. She gave a parting smile to all of us, then headed through the crowd to the inn.

"Bitch act like she got a worm up her ass," came from someone's mouth. I immediately looked to Charmaine, who was dumbfounded. She hadn't said it. Someone else had stolen her thunder. It was Tasha. She fit in with Mona, Charmaine, and me to a tee. The three of us erupted in laughter as we welcomed her to the three chicas plus one.

Our walk-through took place on time up the canyon from the inn. The orchestra was there a day early, assisting the grounds crew with assembly of their stand. The doves were already on the island as well. It looked like it wanted to rain, but we were lucky so far. The chance of rain was less for the wedding day.

Lionel stood in the front by the cliff overlooking the bay, while the coordinator called out instructions. Lionel's dad walked his mother up first. They took their places in the first row of chairs. Next came Jacob, walking up the main aisle holding Mona's hand. Charmaine and I both giggled, as we knew Jacob was going to either have a heart attack or bust a nut from being so close to Mona. Charmaine went next with Esai. It was only rehearsal, but Charmaine worked it down the aisle. I was glad music wasn't playing. Leu was preparing to walk next, and took Sarabeth's hand. She glared at me for a brief second before they began their walk. The coordinator ran around positioning people on their marks and pausing the mock procession.

As Derek and Jazelle got into position to begin their walk, I lined up nervously alongside Uncle Rob. My stomach was doing backflips. Uncle Rob saw my change and calmly held my hand.

"Thank you, niece."

"For what?"

"For allowing me and my family into your life." Uncle Rob nodded toward the family. Tasha, Tandy, and Randy, seated in one of the back rows near us, were waving up a storm.

I smiled at Uncle Rob and said, "I owe you." My stomach had calmed, as it was our turn to walk up.

56

Max

"You did what?" Smitty stared at me as if I were insane. He tried turning the volume down to the song "Diamonds in that Pussy" using the remote. When it didn't work, he popped the back off and rolled the batteries with his thumb, but still got nothing. Frustrated, he dropped the remote and ran over to the stereo, all the while cursing to himself, to do it the old fashioned way, by hand. He'd just listened to me baring my soul and had taken everything in stride until now. Even during my talk of Jay's shooting, he'd stayed calm.

"So, it's midnight and you're in your drawers, bangin' on Glover's door 'n shit? Oh, that's priceless!" he howled. "You know I could go on, right?"

"Stop playin', man. Are you gonna help me find her?"

"Yeah." He sighed. "I'm down. But what if ol' girl already jumped that twenty-four karat broom?"

"She hasn't. At least I don't think so. It's supposed to be this weekend, either today or tomorrow. I gotta find her, man."

"Know where the wedding's at?"

"No, but it's out here. Somewhere."

"Man, this ain't no Louisiana. Thanks for narrowing the search."

"Smit, I don't have time for this. I tried my computer, but don't know where to look."

"Just fuckin' with ya. Let me get some breakfast in me and I'll help."

I needed a plan for finding a wedding that may or may not have been taking place in southern California. While Smitty ate a bowl of microwave grits, I started going through the Yellow Pages. It was nearly impossible to reach anybody on the weekend, as most of the offices that did the scheduling were probably closed. I couldn't let that stop me, though. I snagged a notepad with the West-tel logo on it and began scribbling.

I split up places to check out: churches, chapels, halls, hotels, and ballrooms. Smitty finished his grits and sat down across the unsteady glass table from me. Being as he was more familiar with the area, he would be able to eliminate a lot of these places at a glance. A woman would have been a bigger help, but I wasn't about to bother Aunt Lucy with this. I didn't know Lionel's last name, and if the wedding was at somebody's house, I was fucked. I slid my list over to Smitty.

"Uh-uh. Too small."

"No way. Wrong part of town for them."

"Too white."

"Too brown."

"Too broke."

"I dunno."

"I dunno."

"Is there something you do know?" I asked, tired and frustrated.

"I know she had to tell you something about the wedding while you were tappin' that ass. Why don't you think instead of gettin' all on my case?"

"Sorry. Honestly, I didn't want to hear anything about the wedding, so we never brought it up much. Wait. It's outdoors. I remember her mentioning the weather."

"Outdoors? You're fucked then. It might be along the coast or something, but I'm lost on that kind of stuff. You really need a woman, or someone with connections. Or both."

"I wish I knew someone. The only people who fit that description wouldn't help me do this. Fuck!" I got up from the table and paced.

"Max, his people got money, right? Maybe there's something about it on TV."

"It's worth a shot." I turned on Smitty's TV and put it on one of the local channels. The news wasn't on; only a commercial for an attorney, promising money for injuries. I watched as he bragged about their computerized databases and legal library that guaranteed top dollar for their clients. Wait. I knew about this guy. I froze in mid-thought and ran to the phone.

I broke every speed limit posted as we sped to Samir's house. On the way there, I'd called Samir, and he told his wife. Yvette wasn't going to be happy. He was right about that, but she did agree to help me. Samir stayed home with the kids while Yvette left with us. I had a sinking feeling as I looked at my watch. Half the day was gone.

"You know I could lose my job for this," Yvette told me as she unlocked the door to her office, that of the attorney I'd just seen on TV. I couldn't say anything, so I just nodded.

Yvette turned off the security alarm and turned on the lights. She logged on to her terminal and then began her search. Smitty pulled up a chair, but I couldn't sit. I told her about the wedding being outdoors, and she began her search in the Malibu area, using all their resources; but she found nothing. Private weddings could be off the radar when people wanted them to be just that, private.

"Do you know the groom's last name?" Yvette asked.

Groom. The word made me wince. Brought me back to my bizarre dream.

"No. His first name's Lionel."

"That won't help. How about where he works, what he does?"

"He works for Barnes and Greenwood."

"*Oh*? Good company," Yvette remarked. "I know they must have a website."

Within mere seconds, Yvette brought up the B&G Web site on the monitor. In eloquent style, their top performers were displayed along with their names. Lionel's face jumped right out at me. Smitty noticed it too.

"That's him. That's the fool," Smitty snarled as he pointed. I think he wanted to fight again.

"Lionel *Dunning*," Yvette read aloud, emphasizing his last name. "I'll bet his dad is Goodwin Dunning, the retired lawyer."

Two spaces below Lionel's photo was another vaguely familiar face—a pretty young thing with a smile to match and a nice tan. Yvette was saying something, but I tuned it out as I stared intently at the girl's photo. How did I know her?

Combing my memory, I went back to my dream, where I couldn't walk. It was her. She was the woman kissing Lionel in the dream when the phone woke me up.

But why her?

I was missing something and it unsettled me.

"Yvette, what floor is B and G on?"

"Let's see. The—"

"Fortieth floor," I said, completing Yvette's answer for her. "I'll be damned."

In my old psych classes, I learned that the subconscious was a mother, full of all kinds of things if one dug hard enough. I always thought Lionel looked familiar. Now the light bulb had finally come on.

"What?" Smitty asked.

"Yvette, you said his dad's a lawyer?"

"I said I think so. His dad could be a different Dunning."

"You've done such a big favor for me already, but I need one more. Would it be out of the ordinary for a law firm to consult with a retired attorney, or to try to reach him for an emergency?"

"You mean try to track him down? Find out where he's at? Specifically, where the wedding is that he's at? You've got some balls, Max."

"That's why I'm in this situation now. I just found my balls. Yvette, please."

"You must really want to get me fired. You know how odd it would be to call a retired attorney on a weekend? Especially when he's at a wedding?" she replied with a scowl. Then her features softened. "I'll see what I can do."

57

Glover

"You are so beautiful, girl. I'm about to cry," Charmaine said as she fiddled with my train. She'd done more than enough crying for everyone. As she worked with my dress, Mona worked on my nails, finishing them right on time. I wasn't one to be pampered, poked, and prodded, but this was the biggest day of my life.

That said, I was only feeling it eighty-five percent.

Charmaine, Mona, and I stayed up most of the night, holed up in my suite, drinking and reminiscing over old times. Someone would say something, and the next thing you know, we were all crying. Tasha popped in to join us after the kids and Uncle Rob went to sleep. Even Sarabeth and Jazelle were civil and passed by to enjoy a drink or two. Maybe it was a drink or three, but I was sloppy drunk and in no shape to count. It took a lot of willpower to watch my mouth and keep Charmaine and Tasha quiet in Sarabeth's presence. It also took a lot of willpower not to think about Max, but the festivities were a good distraction.

When Charmaine was done, she turned me toward the mirror. My eyes watered as I thought of my mom looking down on me. She should have had a wedding like this, to someone worthy of her. I was draped in a satiny-white silk wedding gown with spaghetti straps. The gown was drop-waisted, with embroidered pearls in the bodice. My train, which Charmaine was still handling, was cathedral style. Charmaine was already dressed, but Mona was waiting to finish with my hair and makeup. Ms. Stevens wanted everything in place on her when she stepped out of the suite.

There was a quick, light tap on the door. Someone used to having doors opened for them. Should have known it was my soon-to-be mother-in-law.

"I just wanted to check on the bride," Adele gushed as Mona let her in. Darting in my direction, she tossed quick smiles to my friends. "Oh, you are a living doll!"

"Thanks, Mom," I offered, straining to jump past that eighty-five percent. Might as well get used to it.

"Lionel is a nervous wreck, my dear. I just left his suite and told him I would check on you."

"I'm here," I said with a weak giggle. "It looks like everything's on schedule."

"I suppose so. The guests are arriving like clockwork. I'm glad I reserved some of the regular boat runs exclusively for our use. If somebody is planning on taking a trip over here from the mainland, they're going to have a bit of a wait on their hands.

"Hmm, did you know that your makeup is uneven, dear?"

"That's because it's not finished. Mona was working on it when you came in." Adele wanted her own people to do my makeup, but I pulled the plug on that. I needed someone I trusted by my side the entire time. Besides, I'd conceded too much to her already.

"I should have known. Glover, I know we rub one another wrong sometimes, but I'm wondering if we can put that all behind us from today on and start anew."

Adele didn't wait for an answer, simply excusing herself to attend to other matters.

"Well, that was noble of her," Charmaine cracked.

With Adele out of the way, Mona and Charmaine completed their assignments flawlessly.

All that was left was my veil. Charmaine went looking for a pin, while Mona excused herself to get dressed. I heard the orchestra warming up outside.

Soon.

I was to be escorted up to the cliff at the appropriate time, which was quickly approaching. Alone for once, I had time to reflect on everything in its entirety. I took a seat and took a deep breath.

The door to the suite opened again. This time it was Tasha, wearing a navy blue dress with a matching hat. So much for time to myself.

"Girl, it is sooo nice out there! I saw them bringing the doves out in their cages, but I'm already out of space on my camera. Robert said to tell you he loves you and to break a leg. And look atcha. Ain't you lookin' too good."

"Thanks, Tasha. You are a trip, girlfriend. I'm glad we met. Uncle Rob is blessed to have you."

"Thanks, niece. Um, Glover?"

"Huh?"

"I have to tell you something. Robert told me not to, but I can't let it go. I get these feelings from time to time. My momma used to call it the gift. Robert told me to leave that foolishness alone because he didn't want anything ruining your happiness; but you ain't all that happy, are you?"

"What makes you think that?" I asked, trying to conceal how emotional she'd just made me. I don't know if I believed her about her gift, but maybe my body language had betrayed me.

"I dunno. Just the feeling I get. I got a bad feeling about this wedding. I mean, it could be nothin', but I could not let it go unsaid."

"I'm going to be okay, Tasha, but thanks."

She paused, eyeing me with more than idle curiosity. I gave her a long hug then let her rejoin the other guests. Charmaine and Mona returned shortly afterward.

After pinning my veil in place, we were ready to roll after a last minute check. I may have played it off to Tasha, but she was right. I kept myself immersed in the wedding so much that I managed to keep my heart at bay. Now everything was coming to a head. I'd only wanted something out of life that was real for me, and it was crystal clear that this wedding wasn't it. I loved Max, and suddenly didn't think I could go through with this.

With each step closer to that door, my convictions burned brighter. I cleared my throat to finally speak up for myself, to stop being afraid, when there was another knock at the door.

We all thought it was the coordinator telling us it was time to begin. No one came in. Mona sighed then went to get the door. It was a delivery boy from town with a package for me. I guessed someone couldn't wait until the reception. I signed for it and began to open the box.

"Want me to take it?" Mona asked. "We can open it later."

"No, I got time," I replied, grateful for the delay. Maybe whoever sent it could get their money back.

It was a black rose with a note, a bad joke that was probably from one of our co-workers. I showed the rose to Charmaine and Mona then read the card aloud: "Dear Glover, on this most special of days, hope you enjoy my gift, you bitch. You don't deserve him. He's mine and always will be. Misha."

Misha.

Misha?

Lionel's perky little co-worker?

"Oh shit," Charmaine whispered, finally breaking the silence.

I'll be damned. I was stressing over this whole sordid triangle when it seemed like Lionel had his own going on.

A geometry of lies amongst us all.

Almost on cue, Lionel burst into the suite. While his English-style tux looked good, the man wearing it looked very ill. Misha had probably sent him a little gift too. His mouth dropped as soon as his eyes fixed on the note I held.

I let the card drop onto the floor.

"Could you ladies leave us alone for a minute?" Lionel asked, motioning Charmaine and Mona with his hand. They looked to me first.

"No, they can stay, Lionel. We might as well get it all out."

"Is that from Misha?" he asked, pointing at the tiny card.

"I think you know already."

"Baby, she sent me a crazy note too. I just got it. I . . . I think she's infatuated with me." Always Mr. Smooth, he was. Even now.

"Go on." I took off my veil and folded my arms.

There was a commotion in the hall. Someone knocked on the door.

"Wait!" Lionel shouted. The knocking ceased. He renewed his focus on me. "Misha's been acting strange lately. I think she mistook my friendship for something else."

"Friendship?"

"Yes. That's all that it was," he swore. Charmaine smacked her lips, to which Lionel glared at her.

"You don't need to be here," he said to my friend as if threatening her. Charmaine, not appreciating his posture, looked ready to throw down.

"Lionel, don't bullshit me," I said, getting back to the matter at hand. "I should have seen the signs. The way she ran out of your office the day I was there. The way she—"

"Stop. I don't want to hear any more of this wild speculation. This is my wedding day! And this is not the place to speak about Misha and her delusions or . . . or these lies."

"Delusions and lies. C'mon, you can do better than that," I taunted. "I guess I was too busy with my own issues to notice what should've been so obvious. It should make me feel better about what I did, but it doesn't. Well, you're free to enjoy your little protégé because I'm out."

"No! No!" he yelled. "Baby, it was never like that. You have to believe me. Look, the wedding's ready to start. Everyone's waiting on us. If you just let us talk this over and get these two out of here . . ."

"These two? My girls? That's what they are now that they're inconvenient to the game you're trying to run?"

"Trying to run game? What are you talking about, Glover?"

"Real talk. There will be no wedding, Lionel. Do you understand? I had reached that decision even before this shit arrived," I said, flipping over the box that contained Misha's gift. Mona's and Charmaine's mouths dropped open in unison.

Lionel chuckled. "Run game. Now, *real talk*? What's gotten into you with all this hood slang, Glover? That little boy you were playing around with, huh? I forgave you for that lapse, so there will be a wedding. And you know why? Because I love you, and that bitch Misha is a liar!"

"No, she's not."

"What?"

Mona stepped forward and repeated herself. "Misha's not a liar."

Things took a strange turn. Charmaine began rubbing her head, and Lionel flew around in a rage. A deathly silent pause filled the room as everyone digested what Mona had so crisply stated. What did she know about this? And why hadn't she shared it with me?

Lionel, ever the sharp one, regained his bearings and resumed damage control. "Glover, don't listen to her, baby. Let's discuss this alone."

"Shut up, Lionel," I said, grasping a table lamp near me. My fiancé froze. I turned back toward Mona.

"And how do you know this?" I asked of my friend. Instead of the sadness I'd felt in my heart, enough rage and pain for two was welling up to quickly replace it. But to whom should I direct it? Lionel tried to interrupt again, but the whispered reply that escaped Mona's lips was loud enough to answer my questions.

"Because I've been sleeping with him too." Tears trickled down her face. Amazingly, they didn't freeze. The icy façade was melting. "I—I'm sorry, Glover. It wasn't supposed to happen. You're like a sister to me. I never wanted to hurt you. Never. You have to believe me."

A double betrayal. Lionel seemed helpless as he turned toward Mona and then back to me. He repeated the same fruitless motion several times, finally at a loss for words.

"I ended it when I realized you two were serious about getting married. Lionel will tell you," Mona offered weakly as her closing argument. I wouldn't have surprised me if she'd been the one who told Lionel about Max in the first place.

Damn. I'd been so fucking clueless.

I ran across the room and grabbed Mona by her hair. Nobody was quick enough to stop me. My fist rained down on her face until one eye was swollen shut. She tried to resist, but it was futile. I was about to kick her a few times when I awakened from my momentary revenge fantasy.

"G-love? Are you okay?" Charmaine asked, bringing me back to reality.

"Yeah, Charmaine. Never better," I replied.

"You mean you're okay with all this . . . this shit? *With what Mona did, too?*"

Mona's hands were on her hips, her head hanging low in shame. Lionel was beside himself.

"Fuck it. Fuck them all," I answered Charmaine.

"Nah! Nah! That ain't right!" Charmaine belted out. She took off her pump and swung it at Mona, whacking her in the head with the heel.

Thwack!

Mona shrieked and fell to the floor, holding her forehead. "Now it's right," Charmaine added. She and I stepped over Mona, leaving only Lionel barring our exit.

"Thanks for the memories, Mr. Dunning," I offered. He said nothing. "Are you going to move? Mona there probably needs some TLC or something. Besides, she's probably more to your family's liking anyway."

I watched his brow furrow and face contort as those familiar gears turned. He looked like he wanted to conduct a business transaction of some sort—maybe concoct some story to save face or try to talk me out of this still. But this was irreparable; and in the end, he gave up, quietly stepping aside. I didn't know what Lionel would tell his mother, but I was sure it would be creative, for Mr. Dunning was certainly a creative person.

With Charmaine's help, I pushed my way through the chattering and confused crowd of wedding guests and out the inn. I would explain everything to Uncle Rob and make it up to my other guests later. What I really needed right now was space. I gave my uncomfortable pumps to one of the inn staff who looked to be about my size, and left barefooted. Charmaine stayed behind to keep people from following me. I just needed to be free to breathe for the first time in a long time.

I ripped my train off after tripping over it on the way down the hill. Once in town, a tourist couple took a picture of me shooting the bird as I stormed by. Near the boat landing, I found an empty gazebo, where I parked my ass. Out of public view, I let out a good cry. As strong as I pretended to be, I just wanted to be held. So many things I took for granted were utterly wrong. I punished myself, trying to think about how or when things began with Mona and Lionel.

Oh, my girl.

No.

She was my sister. As much as we'd been through, knowing there'd be no new memories or fun times beyond today hurt like hell.

"You tryin' to hide from me?" Charmaine asked, coming upon my brief sanctuary. She'd changed into a pair of shorts and a T-shirt. She dropped a red duffel bag by my feet.

"You know, I used to tease Lionel about what a perfect couple he and Mona would make."

"Don't beat yourself up, G-love."

"Charmaine, you have any confessions you'd like to make? I don't think I can take any more surprises."

"Nope. Never fucked Lionel, and damn sure never fucked Mona. No surprises from me, except maybe that algebra test I cheated on in high school," she joked. "I told your aunt and uncle about what went down. Uncle Robert went looking for Lionel, but Tasha stopped him.

"You plan on staying in that gown? There are some clothes in the bag."

"Thanks . . . sister."

"You're welcome . . . Glover."

I began unzipping the bag.

Charmaine put her hand on mine. "Oh, I ran into a couple of people that were looking for you. I told them that I didn't know if you felt like talking."

"What did they say?" I asked, trying to imagine who from the wedding party wanted to incur my wrath right about now.

"They wouldn't go away. I'll tell them to come over. Be right back."

She didn't even give me a chance to say no, which pissed me off to no end. Charmaine cheerfully strolled up the street and disappeared around the corner. I took the towel from the bag and began wiping off my makeup. I looked at the beige streaks left on the towel as I lowered it from my face. The things women do to look good for men. Yuck.

"You missed a spot," he said as my eyes came up from the towel, the sunlight obscuring my view. I could make out the smile first, and my heart skipped a beat. "Scared ya, huh?"

"What are you doing here? How did you get here?"

"Long story. I could write a book about it. Real talk," he joked. "You're a hard one to find."

"I wasn't supposed to be found. I thought you knew that."

"I'm hard-headed. You look good."

"You're full of shit."

"I love you."

"I love you too. Real talk." I stood up in my ruined wedding gown and walked out of the gazebo into Max's outstretched arms.

As we kissed, I saw Max's little friend, Smitty, standing amidst the crowd with Charmaine. Both of them were applauding.

58

Wallace "Smitty" Lewis

"Know what you orderin', man?" I asked my boy. He kept grabbing green bean fries from the appetizer plate, so I could tell he was starvin' like Marvin. We'd met up at the TGI Friday's in West Covina by his crib.

"Probably the New York strip," Max answered while crunching on another fry.

"Know what Glover's orderin'?"

"Of course, man. She is my wife." Dude was so proud. Did you know that we wound up gettin' tore up at a bar back in Catalina that day? Some good memories from a pretty fucked-up time as far as my boy was concerned. Still got a group photo of us that I keep in a frame atop the TV.

Not too long after that, my boy got hired by that company in Concord. Took him four months to transfer back down here, but those two got married within a year. Loved the wedding. I was my boy's best man 'n shit. Glover's people came down from Virginia, and Max's crazy folk came from Louisiana. Never seen people drink and eat so much in my life. Max's mom and his Aunt Lucy did all the cookin'. Still got shit in my fridge to this day.

"What about you? Are you ordering for your girl, or are you going to wait until she gets here?"

"You know she's in traffic. And I don't know what the fuck she wants besides this dick later tonight."

"You never change, Smit."

"You know, dawg," I said, grinning.

Glover entered the restaurant, and Max waved her over. She'd finished her mission in the parking lot.

"Hey, Smit," she said, giving me a kiss on the cheek. Think she had a crush on me from back in the day, but I let her settle for Max. She handed Elijah over to his daddy. She'd been in the parking lot changing my godson's diaper.

Elijah Guillory.

His middle name's Lionel, by the way.

Just fuckin' with ya. It's what I do.

"Where's your girl, Smitty?" Glover asked as she sat next to my boy.

"She comin'. How's the new house?"

"Love it. We just painted Elijah's room," Glover answered. Max was playing with his son and making those "daddy faces." Loud-ass kid, but it's all good. Got his dad's smile and his mom's eyes.

"Actually, that would be me," Max interrupted. "You slept while I painted."

"After nine months, I think I deserve a nap every now and then."

"You're right, baby." They leaned over Elijah and kissed one another.

"All right. Stop that. Max ate all the appetizer, and I'm ready to order my ribs and skrimps. I'ma wave the waiter over."

I could afford a decent dinner these days. Even splurged on tonight's meal, my treat. I was still at West-tel, but I was promoted into sales. Something about my being a good bullshitter. Go figure.

"You're serious?" Glover asked. "You're not going to wait for your girlfriend to get here? That is so rude."

"Uh, she just got here," I said, shutting her down. My baby had arrived.

"Sorry I'm late," she offered to the table.

"That's okay, baby. We were waiting for you so we could order. Glover wanted to order right away, but I made her wait for you. She can be so rude." Glover rolled her eyes while Max laughed. I stood up, gave my baby one of my patented mackalicious kisses, then pulled the seat out for her.

"Hey, Max! Hey, Elijah!" she offered the men. "Hey, G-love!" she offered to her best friend.

"What's up, Charmaine?" Glover asked. She hadn't seen her in a few weeks. Charmaine left her job, just like Glover, but went to work at the law firm with Samir's wife, Yvette. After taking time off to tend to Elijah, Glover's started her own business making gift baskets. I sometimes use them to close my deals.

"Besides missing my little Smit? Not a lot," Charmaine answered. Oh. Knew I forgot something. Charmaine and me wound up hooking up that night back in Catalina. I'm supposed to be the crazy one, but she puts me to shame sometimes. Guess that's why I'm feelin' her—and probably why we moved in together.

But don't get it twisted. If she finds a rich motherfucker and wants to run off with him, I'ma tell her to do it and split the money with me.

My name is Smitty.

And I'm still the shit.

About the Author

Eric Pete is an Essence bestselling novelist whose previous books include:

Real for Me,
Someone's in the Kitchen,
Gets No Love,
Don't Get It Twisted,
Lady Sings the Cruels,
Blow Your Mind,
Sticks and Stones.

He has also contributed short stories for the following anthologies:

After Hours,
Twilight Moods,
On the Line.

He currently lives in Texas, where he is working on his next novel. His Web site:

www.ericpete.com.